Praise for *The Ex-Girlfriend Murder Club*

"Unexpected, fast-paced, and hilarious, *The Ex-Girlfriend Murder Club* was an absolute delight. Chao's lovable characters and clever writing will draw you in immediately. Come for the murder, stay for the heartwarming testament to the power of female friendship."

—Jilly Gagnon, author of *All Dressed Up*

"A wildly funny, clever, and heartfelt debut. The hijinks will have readers laughing out loud, and the many twists and turns will keep them on the edge of their seats. But it's the friendships that blossom between three wronged women that give *The Ex-Girlfriend Murder Club* its beating heart. In this story, revenge is best served by a trio of unlikely friends—with lots of laughs on the side."

**—Laurie Elizabeth Flynn,
USA TODAY bestselling author of
Till Death Do Us Part and
*The Girls Are All So Nice Here***

"*The Ex-Girlfriend Murder Club* has it all: wacky shenanigans, heartfelt vulnerability, and a cleverly plotted murder. Throw in the most ride-or-die friendship ever and you get a book I could NOT put down. Such a fun read!"

**—Mia P. Manansala, author of the bestselling
*Tita Rosie's Kitchen Mystery series***

Also by Gloria Chao

Ex Marks the Spot
When You Wish Upon a Lantern
Rent a Boyfriend
Our Wayward Fate
American Panda

And look for the next Hu Done It mystery, coming soon!

THE EX-GIRLFRIEND MURDER CLUB

GLORIA CHAO

ISBN-13: 978-0-7783-8721-3

The Ex-Girlfriend Murder Club

Recycling programs
for this product may
not exist in your area.

Mira
22 Adelaide St. West, 41st Floor
Toronto, Ontario M5H 4E3, Canada
MIRABooks.com

Printed in U.S.A.

For Anthony, for every night you read a new chapter and asked me for the next one. And for your reaction on the plane when you finished it.

And for anyone who's ever needed a reminder that even the worst storms can lead to a rainbow.

Through the Looking Glass

Three Weeks into the Future

Harsh fluorescent lighting, a two-way mirror, an incessantly ticking clock. There was no way out, figuratively or literally. My current situation couldn't be worse if it had been planned by my mortal enemy. How did I end up here? I swear I made good decisions at every step, but now I was in doo-doo so deep I needed a grave-digging machine—both to dig myself out of said trouble and maybe to cover up the dead body. Except it was too late for the latter. If only I could redo the last twenty minutes of my life—or, hell, while we were at it, how about the last three weeks? Three months?

Or was it all inevitable? Predetermined by laws, forces, and the universe.

Kathryn's Fifth Law of Luck, now proven: Everything that can go wrong will go wrong. And no one's coming to save you.

CHAPTER 1

Hypothesis: Bad luck in motion stays in motion, even if another force acts upon it. Otherwise known as Kathryn's First Law of Luck. Unlike Newton, I was using my first name because Hu's First Law of Luck was the start of an Abbott and Costello bit. I can already imagine it:

"Hu's First Law."

"Whose?"

"Exactly, Hu's."

I didn't laugh at the jokes playing out in my head because of said Law and the fact that at only ten thirty in the morning, I was in the work bathroom for an unusual reason for the second time today. Trip number one had been two hours ago, when I'd spilled coffee on my favorite button-down shirt, which was pink, professional, and made my small boobs look bigger than they were. I didn't even drink coffee normally—I was a tea gal through and through—but after lying awake last night worrying about today's experiment, I needed an extra-large jolt of caffeine. Unfortunately, most of it ended up on my shirt, not in my stomach.

As for bathroom trip number two, well, I wish it had been a number two—that would have been cleaner, less smelly, and more pleasant. Instead, I'd just had another run-in with the lab tech who's had it out for me since the first day of my Harvard chemistry postdoc, when he introduced himself and I misheard *Johannes* as *Your Highness*. Of course, when I called him that, he told everyone I made fun of his name, then stopped aiding me in the lab. It didn't help that my attempt to apologize was a joke about name confusion that did not land. "*Hu* is sorry," I'd tried to say, to which Johannes had said, "You! You should be sorry!" It also didn't help that I have poor social skills and am maximally awkward when I'm uncomfortable. Needless to say, I've been the lab pariah since.

Johannes and I have had many incidents in the three months I've been here, and this particular time, he deposited a pile of dirty beakers in front of me, claiming I wasn't following proper autoclave protocol and was thus banned—from using the autoclave or beakers, I wasn't sure. In the process of shaming me, he spilled some of the beta-mercaptoethanol I'd just retrieved, which of course he then reprimanded *me* for, since I hadn't brought it to the fume hood as I was supposed to. The stench of rotten eggs quickly permeated the air, and I frantically cleaned it up, then ran here to the bathroom to dry heave into the sink and also to escape the flaming daggers my lab mates were throwing at me. I was not doing my already abysmal popularity any favors; in a small shared space, bad smells travel even faster than the latest gossip, especially smells as revolting as beta-mercaptoethanol.

Today was so not my day. To be fair, most days did not feel like the universe was on my side, but this was worse than usual.

After I opened a bathroom window for some fresh air, I retrieved my phone to text my boyfriend.

Terrible day with alkynes of bad luck.

Then I sent a close-up photo of my shirt's coffee stain.

As three dots popped up on my screen, I smiled, already feeling better. And a second later, I burst into laughter at his response.

Oh no! How can I help get rid of the unsaturated hydrocarbons containing a triple bond?

Tucker Jones wasn't a science nerd like me, but he always looked up what he needed to—in this case, *alkyne*—so he could understand my jokes and make some of his own. Then he added:

The stain looks like a fried egg, with the blobby shape and darker center. How perfect is that?

I looked down at the stain again. It did look like a fried egg. Which was perfect, as Tucker said. Because frying an egg was how I fell in love with chemistry when I was younger. I started learning to cook as a way to bond with my parents—whose main way of showing love was making Taiwanese dishes for me—and none of it made sense until I learned the science behind it. Frying an egg was simply changing the egg's molecular structure irreversibly with heat energy.

How was Tucker so good at turning bad situations around? Hoping he could find a way to turn bathroom trip number two around, I responded:

That's especially fitting because eggs seem to be a theme today; I spilled beta-mercaptoethanol and now the lab smells like rotten eggs and everyone's mad at me.

His reply came immediately:

Sorry, babe

If it makes you feel better, it wouldn't bother me in the least if I were there

I chuckled. Tucker was born without a sense of smell. Congenital anosmia.

I wish I could see you today, I texted back. With my postdoc and him working in private equity, we both had long, inflexible work hours that made it difficult for us to find time to spend together. Because of that, we decided early on in our relationship to carve out Wednesday nights and Sundays for each other. That way, I knew how to arrange my schedule without having to check in with him, making it easier for me to plan longer experiments where I had to stay late at the lab, like tonight.

He replied quickly with:

I wish I could see you too, but I get it, work comes first

I hope your day gets better and you manage to reduce disulfide bonds without it being too smelly

Also, your brain is really hot ☺

Okay, Tucker may not know much about chemistry beyond Google definitions of *alkyne* and *beta-mercaptoethanol*, but he was an expert at *our* chemistry. In about three minutes, Tucker had lifted my spirits and made it so that I now smiled when I looked at my fried-egg stain. Even if my hypothesis was true and bad luck stayed in motion, it didn't matter because I had Tucker's shoulder to lean on.

When I returned to the lab, everyone was still glaring at me.

"Sorry," I tried to call out, but it was barely audible. I cleared my throat and tried again. "I'm really sorry about the smell. I'll keep a better *ion* the beta-mercaptoethanol from now on, I promise."

Not a single person laughed. Johannes rolled his eyes at me from where he was unboxing a new shipment of pipette tips.

Against my better judgment, I tried again. "No *reaction?*"

"Please stop," begged my coworker Don. And he was even a dad.

Never, I thought but didn't say. I couldn't help wondering if they would have laughed if the joke had come from someone other than me.

Out of ideas, I sat back down and tried to work up the nerve to retrieve the beta-mercaptoethanol again so I could run my experiment.

An hour and a half later, I'd done every non-beta-mercaptoethanol item on my list and even not on my list, like reorganizing the glassware and testing the pens in my bag.

"I heard you all could use a pick-me-up!" called out a deep, familiar, and may I add, very sexy voice from the doorway.

I popped up from my seat so quickly I almost bumped my head on the cabinet above. When I turned, there he was, my knight in shining suit. My heart fluttered, and only in small part because of how hot he looked. The bigger part was what was underneath that suit, and no, my mind wasn't in the gutter—I meant his heart. Because that giant heart of his had made him not only show up at lunchtime to cheer me up, but he was also carrying a giant Dunkin' Donuts box.

He winked at me, and I wanted to run across the room and throw myself into his arms.

"Kat wanted to apologize to everyone for the accident with some donuts!"

The entire lab cheered. Well, the entire lab except for Johannes, who yelled, "No food in the lab!"

Everyone stood and rushed out, with Johannes grabbing

the box to bring to the break room. A flurry of *thank-you*s was thrown in Tucker's and my direction. And finally, we were alone.

I ran at him, and he was ready for me, scooping me up and twirling me in a circle.

"Hi," I said, my grin so wide the edges of my face hurt.

He booped my nose with his. "Hi."

When he set me down, I squeezed him as hard as I could.

"Whoa, okay, killer!" he said with a chuckle. "I don't need the Heimlich right now."

"Wrong direction—Heimlich is from behind so you can activate the diaphragm muscle to expel any foreign objects in the trachea."

A crooked smile appeared on his face, and with two fingers, he tapped my forehead twice—the gesture he always made to tell me how much he loved my brain.

"Is your day better?" he asked.

"It is now," I said genuinely. "I can't believe you're here."

"Well, you said you wanted to see me. And I thought maybe I could help with some damage control at the same time."

I gazed at him fondly. "Thanks for buttering them up for me."

"Ooh, um, Thanksgiving origin? Cooking a turkey?" he asked, and I laughed.

He knows I love to look up the origins of sayings. Before him, I never shared these tidbits with anyone—I'd learned the hard way in high school that most people weren't interested in the weird stuff I liked—but on our third date, I'd accidentally blurted out to Tucker that "no dice" came from when gambling was illegal, and if authorities couldn't find any dice, they couldn't charge you with a crime. When I told him that some people went as far as to eat dice to vanish the evidence, he'd laughed and asked me what other expressions had unexpected origins.

"Buttering someone up comes from a religious act in India where they throw butter balls at statues of gods to seek favor," I told him.

"I knew you'd have that one in the bag."

I grinned—that one we've discussed before. In the 1910s, when the San Francisco Giants were in New York, they used to carry a ball bag off the field when the team was in the lead, hoping that the game was "in the bag" and couldn't be lost.

Tucker took my hand in his. "I know you're busy and have to work late tonight, but I figured you'd have to eat lunch?"

I nodded eagerly.

"Let's go out. You need some fresh air. How about a fried egg? I'm suddenly in the mood for one, with a side of Kat."

I laughed as he lifted our conjoined hands to twirl me in a circle.

How did he always know what I needed?

• • • •

Maybe I was wrong about bad luck staying in motion. Because after Tucker left, I was floating on cloud nine (the highest type of cloud on the international cloud atlas). Thanks to a lunch full of laughter, kisses, and runny egg yolks, I returned to the lab with enough confidence to retrieve the beta-mercaptoethanol again.

No spills this time, thank god. Partly because Johannes was uncharacteristically leaving me alone, maybe because of the donuts.

Once my experiment was underway and I had a minute to relax, I retreated to the break room.

The Dunkin' box was still there, but only jelly was left now. No matter, it was still a donut, fried and covered in powdered sugar. And it had been brought here with love.

I bit into it.

Pssht! A giant glob of bright red jelly squirted out and landed exactly on top of the coffee fried egg.

Kathryn's Second Law of Luck: Lightning does strike in the same place twice.

And maybe my first Law of Luck wasn't so off either. Because five hours later, the bad luck had not only continued in motion but had snowballed. My experiment did not yield the results I was expecting, just like all the other experiments I'd run in my three months here. I was back to square one, a failure. (Origin: when BBC Radio used to cover soccer games in the '30s, the pitch was divided into imaginary squares, with square one being the goalmouth and "back to square one" being said by the commentators when the ball went out of play.)

Feeling wounded inside and out—the latter because my coffee-and-jelly stain had set and darkened—all I wanted to do was lay my head down on the bench. But then I remembered that I'd spilled beta-mercaptoethanol there earlier today.

Right now, I needed a pick-me-up more than anything. As a personal rule, I kept my phone on silent and tucked away while in the lab, but this was an exception.

I ungloved and took my phone out to text Tucker, but there were already texts from him waiting for me.

Hope your day got better

Sending a hug

Let me know if there's anything else I can do for you

How did he not only know what I needed but also before I even knew?

That was when I realized: Why was I still staying late? No progress was being made, and I didn't have it in me to keep going.

I needed to see Tucker. Maybe we could order in hot wings and have some messy but fiery kisses. Maybe he could rip my stained shirt off and throw it on the bedroom floor to be forgotten. It was Friday, not our usual date-night Wednesday or Sunday, but he hadn't mentioned any plans earlier.

Thumbs flying, I texted back:

> There IS something you can do. A real hug. And a hug
> without "u" is deadly, so I'll be there soon!

I wasn't sure if he knew Hg was the chemical symbol for mercury, but whatever. Screw today's failed experiment, screw Johannes, and screw the fact that I'd been so embarrassed by the second stain I hadn't even finished my donut. I had someone in my life who turned an ugly stain into an inside joke and showed up at the lab with bribe donuts for my coworkers. And I was on my way to see him.

A slight bounce appeared in my step as I exited the building.

On the familiar drive to his place, I tried to channel Tucker's superpower that allowed him to find the fried egg in my stain. I needed to find the fried egg in my failed experiments.

And then it hit me. I *did* prove a hypothesis today—my bad luck hypothesis. It wasn't going to help my career, but it did make me giggle as I tapped my fingers on the steering wheel to the Taylor Swift song playing in the background. I couldn't wait to tell that to Tuck. I could almost hear his deep, resounding guffaw filling the space and my heart. And we'd have a new inside joke after this: finding the fried egg.

I parked across the street from Tucker's luxurious condo building, not having access to the garage. The anticipation bubbled up inside me like carbon dioxide tickling my throat. I punched in the code for the building, then took the stairs two at a time up to the third floor, not wanting to wait for the elevator.

My fist froze an inch away from knocking.

There was a sign on the door.

Come in, my love!

My heart was beating so hard I could hear it in my ears. We'd just told each other *I love you* a few weeks ago, and it had felt so early—only three months into our relationship—but nothing about Tucker has felt normal. Everything with him has been out of this world, extraordinary, epic.

I turned the unlocked doorknob and had to stifle a gasp, actually covering my mouth with my hand when I saw the rose petals and lit candles lining the floor.

My day was about to turn around. Completely. Screw Kathryn's First Law. This wasn't just any force trying to disrupt the bad luck, this was a dinosaur-ending asteroid. This was Tucker freaking Jones, the best boyfriend in the world and the best person at turning bad situations around.

And this wasn't an everyday pick-me-up. This was an extraordinary, epic one my mind hadn't wrapped itself around yet.

Was this really happening? If movies, social media, and books have taught me anything, the answer was a hearty, romantic, resounding *Yes!*

This was wild. Ridiculous. Yet it also made so much sense.

Just last week, Tuck had asked me about my taste in rings. But it had been while we were watching a rom-com and discussing the lead's princess-cut engagement ring, so I hadn't thought much of it at the time. But now that I was thinking about it, he had chosen the movie. Had it been an incredibly clever way to ask my preferences without arousing suspicion? And a week before that, he'd asked me where to get his watch battery changed—had he been asking me for a jeweler recommendation?

Was this too fast, after only three months? But that was my brain talking. Repeating what society had deemed normal by arbitrary standards. And weren't societal timelines based on an average? This relationship was not average. And my bottom line was: it didn't *feel* fast. I wanted to see more of him, live together, not keep our worlds so separate.

My life was about to change. I was about to experience one

of the biggest romantic moments of my life. And I was wearing a coffee-and-jelly shirt.

I silently snuck up the stairs to the master bathroom, hoping Tucker wouldn't hear me from the kitchen or wherever he was, likely finalizing the setup. Thank goodness he hadn't heard me come in. One of the many benefits of his having a massive condo with two floors.

Unfortunately, I didn't keep any clothes here. Tuck was a bit of a neat freak, and everything in his condo had a place. Even everything on his person had a place; he wore these special expensive high-end underwear that had a separate pouch for each part. Seriously. The first time I took them off, he stopped kissing me to tell me about them. If it had been anyone else, it would have been weird, but with him, it was adorable how passionate he was.

Normally I appreciated his need for order—his condo was always spotless, a rare trait for a bachelor—but it meant I didn't have anything to change into. My best plan was to clean my current shirt or find a scarf or pin or even a pretty handkerchief, though Tucker wasn't a handkerchief kind of guy.

The rose petals led my way. Had he done this in the fifteen minutes I'd been driving? The petals did look haphazard and not all the candles were lit—a rushed job. I should have just waited to see him on Sunday as planned, not make him hurry to get everything ready now. Then I would have been wearing something cuter, too. But this was real life, not a social media post.

I had to stifle another gasp as I entered the bedroom and spotted the rose petals in the shape of a heart on the bed. Ducking into the bathroom and closing the door behind me, I tried to work fast. First, I used water to smooth the baby hairs sticking up near my part. Then I brushed my teeth quickly with some toothpaste on my finger. And finally, the stain. Why hadn't I cared more when I was at the lab? I could have whipped up a solvent to get rid of it (which actually would have been fun if I hadn't been in such a sour mood), but it hadn't seemed important at the time.

I had just taken off my shirt and started scrubbing when…

Footsteps. Coming upstairs.

I held my breath. I hadn't thought all this through, which was unusual for me, but everything about today was unusual. I'd messed up, though. I was supposed to come in the front door, gasp, and let Tucker see my reaction to all the effort he'd put in, not already be upstairs having seen the setup without him.

I'd have to find a way to distract him, then sneak out. Maybe I could text him? Say I needed him to come down because the building code wasn't working? Or, wait, he didn't know I had the code. I knew it simply from watching the pattern of his fingers punching it in all the times we came home together from dinner, the movies, the grocery store. Maybe I could just tell him I was waiting for him out front, then when he came downstairs, I'd text that someone had let me in and I'd taken the stairs up.

I threw my shirt back on. But before I could fasten a single button let alone take out my phone, from the other side of the door, Tucker began speaking. I jumped, startled, wondering if he knew I was in here. But as I pressed my ear to the door, I realized that wasn't it.

"I fell in love with you the day I met you."

He was practicing his proposal. So cute. I couldn't interrupt. And besides, how many people were lucky enough to hear their proposal twice? A huge smile spread over my face as I leaned my upper body against the door, my ear flattened against it.

"I can't imagine my life without you. I've waited long enough, and I think it's time."

I was going to be Mrs. Kathryn Hu soon. Not Mrs. Kathryn Jones; as an academic with a completed dissertation and a published paper, I didn't want to change my name. But the Mrs. would be new. And, surprisingly, welcome.

"You are the love of my life."

I was aching to repeat those words back to him. But I'd have the chance soon. And now I could prepare what else I was going to say. I could tell him how he'd changed me. How I didn't even know what love was until I met him. How I couldn't imagine my world without him. That he was the only good thing in my life.

I spread my hand on the door, fingers splayed, as if the gesture could reach through the wood and touch his heart, let him know I was here, my own heart already bursting.

There was a pause. He must be gathering himself, taking a moment to appreciate the weight of the words he was about to say. An inhale, a smile, a beat before the final most important question.

I removed my hand and tried to press my ear even harder into the door. Then, dizzy with giddiness, I held my breath.

"So with that..."

Here it was. Now I was dizzy from a lack of O$_2$.

"Will you—"

Maybe it was the lack of oxygen, but I suddenly couldn't wait any longer. This was out of character for me, but I was a changed woman thanks to Tucker. On impulse, I burst through the door, blurting, "Yes! I'll marry you!"

At the same time, Tucker finished his sentence: "—marry me, Olivia Valentina McCarthy?"

My mind blanked. My heart stopped beating. The world stopped spinning.

And then when everything started up again, I realized I was standing there, shirt still open, pink bra fully on display, and my arms spread open like freaking Maria from the beginning of *The Sound of Music*.

Despite being nearly topless, I couldn't move.

I wasn't just witnessing him practicing. I was witnessing the actual goddamn proposal. Because as my eyes swept past him toward the rose-heart bed, there she was.

Olivia Valentina McCarthy.

The other woman.

No, I was the other woman.

Kathryn's Third Law of Luck: When it rains, it fucking pours shit and beta-mercaptoethanol straight into the fan.

CHAPTER 2

Olivia Valentina McCarthy was staring at me with her mouth wide open. Her beautiful, perfectly glossed mouth.

She'd been ready. She had known today was going to be special. Her stunning gold dress with a thigh-high slit hugged her as if it was custom-made for her lean, model-like frame. Her bronze skin glowed, her hair looked recently blown out, and her makeup was flawless—enhancing, but minimal and natural. She embodied everything I was not.

Little had she known that my no-good, terrible, bad-luck day was so epically bad that it would shit on her world, too. Explosive diarrhea right into the fan.

"What the fuck!" I yelled at Tucker, who was staring at my left breast.

That was when I realized that when I'd burst into the room, my boob had popped out and my left nipple was now on display. I hurried to cover myself up, only to button my shirt wrong.

If the earth was ever going to open up and swallow someone, now would be the time, please. But my Laws of Luck forbade it.

Was this all a bad dream? This wasn't happening. It couldn't be. This was Tucker, who held my hand when I had to put down

Cinnabun, the best Mini Lop to have ever lopped. Tucker, who hated spiders as much as I did but took care of them in my shithole apartment because I couldn't go near them without hyperventilating. Tucker, who, despite not knowing how to cook, tried to make my mother's scallion pancakes for me and almost burned down the kitchen.

"Kat, what are you doing here?" he asked as beautiful goddess Olivia Valentina McCarthy just stared, completely frozen in shock.

Tucker, who was a colossal jackass with the gall to ask what *I* was doing here.

I thought I knew everything about the man standing in front of me, but it turned out I didn't know any of the important parts.

"How long— Why— How could—" My insides were dying as abruptly as my words.

Suddenly, Olivia unfroze and ran down the stairs and out the door.

"Liv, wait!" Tucker ran after her.

He had a cute nickname for her, too. I'd always been Kathryn until Tucker insisted on shortening it. Though more often than not, he called me *babe*, which I used to love but now saw for what it was—a way to keep from accidentally calling me the wrong name.

The weight of his lies coming to light held me fastened to my spot, unable to move. Part of me wanted to run after the two of them and hear their conversation, another wanted to throw everything in sight at Tucker, and a third wanted to turn his condo upside down looking for all the clues I'd foolishly missed before today.

His need for order, being particular—that wasn't a personality trait. It was a way to explain why I couldn't leave any of my stuff around for Olivia to find.

Everything about him looked different in this new light. His avoidance of social media in general and phone and internet when we were together wasn't about his desire to embrace life or be "totally in the moment" with me.

He was a fucking cheater.

I only got the tiniest sliver of satisfaction from this coming back to bite him in the ass—maybe he could have avoided this blowup if he'd just checked his phone like a normal person and saw my text saying I was coming over.

The front door opened and closed again. I had no idea what to expect. Olivia coming to ask me questions? Tucker to throw me out? Both of them to throw me out? I wanted to run into the bathroom and lock the door behind me for the rest of time, but I couldn't make my feet move before the footsteps arrived.

"Kat." It was Tucker. His face was flushed red, his forehead covered in sweat. "I'm so sorry. About how this all happened."

Are you sorry about how it happened or for what you did?

"I thought you were going to propose to me."

Of all the things to come out of my mouth, why that? It was the least of my worries, but there were so many questions I didn't know where to start. So instead, like always, I tore open my chest and showed him my bleeding heart. Why did he still hold that power over me?

His eyes lit up. "Really?"

And before I could react, he knelt on one knee and pulled a velvet ring box from his pocket.

Was this the universe laughing at me? Giving me what I'd asked for but in the most opposite, shit-covered way? As if Thunderbolt had popped out of the pen and granted it for me? *You didn't specify in your wish that you wanted your proposal to be completely yours, and not to be happening because his first proposal to his actual love failed.*

The solitary princess-cut ring in his hand was not mine. What an ironic choice for the stone—I felt like the furthest thing possible from a princess right now. And how ironic that Olivia and I had the same ring preference.

"I fell in love with you the day I met you," he began.

Even the proposal was not mine. And in that moment, I realized just how generic his proposal to Olivia was, having been so bland and devoid of details that I'd mistaken it to be about me.

"I can't imagine my life without you. I've waited long enough, and I think it's time."

The boy in front of me was not mine.

"You are the love of my life. So with that...will you marry me, Kathryn Yushan Hu?"

How much I had wanted to hear those words just ten minutes ago when my world was still right-side up. Or I guess my world had been upside down then. I was finally seeing clearly now, which only made me question every decision I'd ever made and how I could have been so utterly wrong about Tucker Jones.

I felt a smile creep onto my face. Tucker's spirits seemed to lift, like he'd found a way out of this mess.

I grabbed the ring, shoved it into my back pocket, and snatched the ring box to chuck at him. And I ran. Down, down the stairs, following the rose petals to my freedom.

Tucker Jones was dead to me.

CHAPTER 3

I had so many questions. Too many. But I ignored Tucker as he followed me to my car and yelled lies about how it had always been me, how it was real, how he cared for me.

How could he even say those things? What was wrong with him? What *wasn't* wrong with him?

As I started the engine, Tucker jumped in front of my car, his arms outstretched, palms forward in the universal *stop!* gesture. I thought he was going to beg me to stay, apologize, tell me he loved me, but no.

"What about our romantic trip next weekend?"

The trip I'd planned and paid for by eating so much thirty-five-cent ramen I was scared to take my blood pressure now.

I rolled my window down so he wouldn't miss a single word. "Have a romantic trip by yourself, jackass! We're so fucking through!"

Then I held the horn down for so long that Tucker had no choice but to move aside. I tore out of there without looking back.

When I arrived home, I was worried his car would be outside my apartment building, but it wasn't. I looked over my shoulder, wondering if he'd pull up, but no dice or cards or roulette wheel. Just pain and anger and regret in my stomach, swallowed down but coming back up as I realized that he'd most likely gone after Olivia.

All I wanted to do was curl up in bed and cry. But at the same time, I didn't want to go inside my empty apartment, which had felt even emptier since Cinnabun passed. Cinny helped me through five years of my PhD but only made it one month into our move to Boston. I missed her so much I still couldn't bring myself to get rid of her cage.

As I entered my apartment, I realized just how alone I felt. I was in a new city I barely knew, my lab mates hated me, and my very limited free time had always been spent with Tucker. He had been the person I turned to for everything—for comfort, for safety, for fun. Now that I was suddenly without him, I realized just how dependent I'd been.

It was like the ground had been yanked out from under me. I was free-falling. No net, no end in sight. My heart was broken into so many pieces I'd never be able to put it back together without instructions. And previously, I would have thought Tucker to be the one who had those instructions. Who knew my heart and me best, and loved me for it. How could I have been so wrong? How could he have done this to me?

I wanted to cry, but I also wanted human contact. Someone to reaffirm that Tucker was the worst, that it wasn't my fault, that maybe I'd even be okay somehow, eventually.

The first person who popped into my head was Melissa, my closest friend from college. But she had since moved to London for work, and it was currently the middle of the night for her. Sure, she'd see any texts I sent when she woke up, but that wasn't the same. Besides, our messages had been growing sparser and sparser every year, and I felt weird reaching out, even about something this huge. Becoming an adult was the worst. I was never good at making friends on account of being the shy, quiet, weird one in the corner, and I didn't know when I was younger that even the few friendships I had managed to make would fade over time. Or that making friends would become *even harder* with age. Maybe that was why Tucker's attention and charm had dazzled me so much.

Without allowing myself a moment to think—because if I did, I'd 100 percent realize how bad of an idea it was—I called my parents.

My mother picked up on the fourth ring. "Wei? Yushan? Is you?"

"Yeah. Hi, Ma." As I paced back and forth, I clenched my hands into fists so they'd stop shaking.

"You eating your vitamins? Swinging your arms? You get that article I send you about how swinging your arms three thousand times a day leads to good health?"

Always such great priorities with her. "Yes, yes," I said so we could move on.

"You think more about becoming a dermatologist? I tell you, dermatologist is the best job. So much money, you a doctor, so respectable, but so easy—just popping pimples and cutting out skin cancer. With a flexible schedule, is perfect for having kids. It is great you at Harvard—better than Brown where Wei-Ling's daughter works—but don't you remember? I been telling you since you were three: research is for people who cannot get into medical school, and you not even apply yet!"

We haven't spoken in months, and this was what she was bursting to tell me for the hundredth time?

"Also, more urgent, you get my package? I send you step stool! Because you single. No man to reach things high up for you."

First, that was sexist, and second, I was so tired of this. My mom was constantly sending me items she thought I desperately needed because I was single. A key chain jar opener because I was too weak to open jars on my own (again, so offensive), a key chain alarm to pull if I was ever in danger (useful and a good idea, but still annoying that she bought it just because I was single, as if that was my only defining feature), and most recently, the step stool. I once argued that now that I had these things, I didn't need a man anymore, and my mom had blown a gasket, sputtering unintelligibly into the phone. I couldn't take much more of this, partly because my key chain was getting really heavy. I'd take the items off, but she checked in at random intervals, making me send photos to prove I'd kept them on. It was easier to lug around all that crap than lie to her.

"Ma, can we—" I started, but I was interrupted by a click and then my father's voice.

"Eigh, Yushan, that you?"

My parents were the only people I knew who still had a landline.

"Hi, Ba. Look, I wanted to call because…" *I'm hurting and I want to be comforted.* "My boyfriend and I broke up and—"

"Aiyah, you have boyfriend?" my mother exclaimed. "No, no, you should be focusing on your career! As a dermatologist."

"Or in business. You think more about business school?" my father asked. "But your ma is right. Breakup is good."

"Especially if he is not Taiwanese," my mother said. "Why you never let me set you up but you go out with this random boy? You need to settle down—you getting old. More important, your eggs going to start expiring soon. By your age, I already have you."

I wanted to talk about anything else, but I also couldn't help saying, "Which is it? I need to focus on my career or I need to find a man and settle down?"

"Bai tuo, Yushan." I could almost see my mother slapping the air with an open palm. "It couldn't be easier. Become a dermatologist while I find you a husband."

I couldn't do this right now. "I have to go, okay?" .

"Okay. You better off without that boy," my father said.

"I send you the phone number of Zhuang Ayi's son. I not

meet him yet, but I know Zhuang Ayi for thirty years and she is good, so he must be good. *And,* his family has money and he is a doctor, so he will be the best husband."

When I hung up, I felt worse than before. Even after twenty-seven years, nothing had changed. No matter how hard I tried, my parents and I always talked past each other. Sometimes I blamed my lack of social skills, dearth of friends, and even my mistaking *Johannes* for *Your Highness* on them. I knew that wasn't completely fair, but also, if I hadn't been so sheltered, if I hadn't grown up in such a traditional Asian household, if I had parents who understood American culture and could have taught me to be normal, maybe I would have turned out better. Maybe I wouldn't be in this mess and I would've seen Tucker's red flags from miles away.

Red is lucky color, I heard my mom say in my head.

I shouldn't have called.

I was about to throw my phone onto the couch when I spotted the string of texts that had come in while I was talking to my parents.

Kat, baby, I love you

I meant every word of the proposal

The one to you, of course, not the other one

Is it a yes? Can you think about it?

Please come back

Is this about Olivia?

Because I can explain

It's always been you, babe

Don't you know? I'm only myself with you

Olivia is a complicated situation. It's hard to explain. I'm
stuck between a rock and a hard place, with the diamond
being the rock and you being the hard place because,
you know ☺

I swear Olivia doesn't mean anything to me

Can we meet? It's easier to explain in person. Please,
Kat, just hear me out. And could you bring the ring?
I desperately need it

Was he serious?

I grabbed a throw pillow and screamed into it. I couldn't
decide if the emotion filling me was sadness, rage, or an
uncontainable amount of both. I simultaneously wanted to
drown in my tears and also burn his condo down.

With a sigh, I plopped onto the sofa, only to be poked in the
butt. For one blissful second, I didn't remember what it was,
but once I reached my fingers into my pocket to retrieve the
engagement ring, anger spread through every cell of my body.

Why did I take this? I didn't want it. What I wanted was to
chuck it across the room or, even better, throw it to the bottom of the ocean, old-Rose-from-*Titanic*-style.

Then I realized it hadn't been mine to take. It wasn't mine
in so many senses (I hadn't said yes; Tucker bought the ring),
but the most important one: it hadn't been meant for me. It
was Olivia's to steal, pawn, throw to the bottom of the ocean.

Olivia. Olivia Valentina McCarthy. How could I compete
with a girl like that?

I couldn't stop thinking about her now. Even though I
didn't want to—I'd only find more ways to feel bad about
myself—I couldn't help it. It was like my thumbs suddenly
took on a life of their own.

It took me a while to find her because we didn't have any friends in common. Had Tucker made sure of that? But I eventually found an image of her that led me to her work, which led me to her social media.

Olivia Valentina McCarthy was twenty-seven, like me, and that was where our similarities ended. According to her bio, she was a criminal defense lawyer at a fancy Boston law firm with a million surnames in the firm name—meaning it was legit. Her photos painted a life of adventure: snorkeling, skydiving, hiking among jungles and ruins and mountains. But surprisingly, Tucker wasn't in any of them. He had been there—or at least someone had taken those stunning supposed candids of her—but never an appearance other than an arm or leg. Olivia mentioned a loving boyfriend in her captions, but not by name. What lie had he told her in order to stay out of the photos? Given that he'd taken pictures for her to post, he couldn't have fed her the same BS he'd fed me about wanting to "live in the moment."

I scrolled angrily, my right thumbnail clicking a steady beat on the screen.

Swimming with dolphins. So cliché.

The Eiffel Tower inside a hand heart—oh my god, hers and Tucker's. I recognized the small, light brown freckle on his left index finger.

For some reason, I sat up straighter. I didn't need proof of his cheating or whatever—I'd witnessed the fucking proposal—but seeing his hand in Olivia's photo still sent a shock through my system. Maybe I'd been hoping he wasn't the one jet-setting with her. Because he'd never gone anywhere with me. Our trip this weekend had been my idea (and treat), and it would've been our first time away. Why her and not me?

What was I doing? None of that mattered. It was over. There was no hope for Tucker and me. No reason to compare relationships.

Yet all I could think about was how I knew him well enough to know his index finger freckle, yet I didn't know any of these extremely huge, elephant-sized secrets. How many of his work trips and long days at the office were actually spent with her? How was I not even suspicious before today?

My scrolling grew angrier and more frantic.

And then it happened.

I *liked one of her photos.*

From *over a year ago.*

I didn't know which was worse, that she would know I was snooping on her account or that they'd been together for at least a year.

I quickly unliked it, hoping that would undo the damage, but it was too late. A DM popped up. From her.

I have questions

I didn't know if I had the stomach for this—especially after smelling beta-mercaptoethanol all day—but I didn't have a choice, did I? I had to do this.

My hands shook as I typed.

Let's meet.

• • • •

I didn't know what I expected, but it wasn't this.

Olivia and I met at Bubblicious, one of my favorite boba shops fifteen minutes away—her suggestion. I briefly wondered if we'd ever crossed paths here before, and whether Tucker actually disliked boba or if he was just scared of coming here with me since Olivia was also a fan. Did Tucker tell her he hated boba, too?

Olivia had changed out of her dress and into an oversize

lavender sweatshirt and navy leggings, still looking as beautiful as ever.

"Hi," she said solemnly when I arrived. And then she stood and came toward me. I cowered, worried she was going to hit me, but she enveloped me in a hug.

I stiffened, caught off guard for the millionth time today. My reluctance was only partly because of who the hug was from and more because I didn't like physical contact. My parents were not huggers and showed affection by cooking for me and sacrificing to give me opportunities. I hadn't been comfortable with touching for most of my life.

Until Tucker.

Which made me want to recoil all over again, his betrayal taking back the changes I'd made with him, because it had all been a lie anyway.

But as Olivia held me close and I inhaled the spicy floral scent of her perfume—how could Tucker want me when he had her?—I realized that she was the only person who knew how I felt. But just as I was ready to melt into the hug and maybe even cry on her shoulder, Olivia pulled back.

"Sorry. I didn't mean to make you uncomfortable. I just… well, I needed it and thought you might, too."

If I were someone else—like Olivia—I would have reached out and initiated a second hug, but I was me. So I just gave her a tiny smile and sat down.

"Do you want to order?" she asked.

"I already did," I said, a little embarrassed. I was such a regular I had my order saved in my phone and only needed to press one button on my way here.

"Kathryn!" the barista called out, and I got up to retrieve my honey jasmine green tea, cold, with boba.

It was awkward as I sat back down, and neither of us commented on how we both loved boba and this place…and the same guy. At least her order was different from mine—something brown, maybe a classic milk tea or a brown sugar boba.

"So—" we said at the same time, then stopped.

"Sorry."

"You go."

"No, you go."

Silence. I already felt awkward in normal social situations, so I was completely out of my depth here. I waited, hoping she'd take the lead.

She forced a small smile. "I'm Olivia, as you already know. Um. And you're Kathryn? Or Kat?"

Tucker was the only one who called me Kat. I liked it. But it also reminded me of him.

I just nodded. "Hu."

"Who what?"

"Hu, my last name." My god, I did it to myself.

"Oh! Sorry. Of course. Nice to meet you, Kathryn Hu."

Silence again. Was it my turn to say something now? Where did I even start?

I had so many questions, but all I could think about was how she had been with Tucker longer and it was her proposal that had been interrupted. Given how I was feeling...well, I couldn't even imagine her situation.

So I pushed aside all the other questions and asked, "Are you okay?"

Her eyebrows shot up in surprise. "Oh! Um, thanks for asking. I'm..." She paused. "Well, I'm not engaged, that's for sure!"

A loud laugh burst from my lips. I hadn't been expecting her to say that.

"How about you? Are you okay?" she asked hesitantly.

I nodded, but I didn't feel it in the least.

Another beat of silence.

"Were you..." she started, but trailed off. "I mean, not that it matters, but..." She couldn't seem to get the questions out.

"Let's just rip the Band-Aid off," I suggested. I refrained from telling her the history behind that phrase, that it was actually better to remove a Band-Aid gradually, but because nurses at hospitals didn't have time for that, they lied to patients and the myth spread.

"Rip the Band-Aid off," Olivia repeated, nodding slowly. "Okay. Let's do it."

"How long?" I asked, trying to keep my questions short and punchy so we could get into a rhythm. "Three months," I answered for myself.

"Two years."

Holy shit. But I kept my thoughts to myself. I had to. No reaction. I was an inert gas.

"Family introductions?" she asked.

I shook my head as she nodded. Obviously I never introduced him to my parents, and he had told me his parents lived in Canada so I couldn't meet them yet—but was that true? I felt like the fool that I was.

"Just him meeting mine," she added before mumbling, "Which now makes sense." Then she asked, "Serious?"

"It was for me," I said honestly, hating myself for it being true. "And I thought for him as well."

She sighed. "Clearly for me, too."

I hesitated, then reminded myself—Band-Aid. "What did he say earlier, after?"

"That you were his cousin who had come to help him set up the proposal, and you spilled wine on your shirt—"

"It's donut jelly."

She rolled her eyes. "Of course *everything* he said was a lie. Anyway, he said you were trying to clean it and—"

"And what, I suddenly decided I wanted to marry my cousin with such passion I had to burst out of the bathroom half-naked?"

She laughed. "Basically, yeah. Then he backtracked and

said you were a friend who was in love with him, but he didn't have feelings for you."

"Pathetic."

She nodded. Then she asked, "What did he say to you after?"

"He proposed to me. With what I assume is your ring."

"WHAT?"

Everyone in the café looked over.

"What?" she repeated, quieter this time. "For real?"

I nodded, then pulled the ring from my pocket where it was burning a hole. She stood and took a step back as if I'd taken Tucker himself out.

"Why do you have it?" she asked, staring at the ring in horror. "You didn't—"

I shook my head. "Of course not. I don't even really know why..." I was suddenly embarrassed. Then I realized I had no reason to lie to her. "I thought about pawning it."

She barely seemed to hear my words as her horror turned to anger and she sat back down. "He's dead," she said, her eyes ablaze. "He needs to pay for what he did."

I shared the same fire but didn't feel like I had any power. "Well, we took away what we could—us."

She blew out a breath. "It doesn't feel like enough."

"I know." But what else was there to do? "Maybe we can also sign him up for Jehovah's Witness home visits," I joked.

She laughed, then jumped on board. "Timeshare presentations and free cruise mailings."

I smiled. This made me feel better than anything else had all night. "Newsletters for weird stuff."

She nodded. "Horse dildos."

"What?" I couldn't help laughing. "That's so specific."

"Weren't you referencing *Dish Served Hot*?"

"Uh, no. What's that?"

"It's a podcast. I can't believe you haven't heard of it—I

could've sworn that's what you were quoting. It's hilarious! It's about revenge stories. All kinds. Fired employees, cheating exes, horrible siblings."

"Dish served *hot*?" I asked. "Revenge is supposed to be more satisfying when delayed, hence the original phrase, which originated in the seventeenth century from *Don Quixote* and was later made popular by *Star Trek*." I just couldn't help myself.

But luckily, Olivia smiled and continued our conversation like she didn't think I was a weirdo.

"I don't know if I agree. Revenge seems better hot, when the fire's burning. Wouldn't you rather do something to Tucker now than in a month?"

"I guess so," I said slowly. "Which is maybe why I took the ring." It was still sitting on the table, shiny and innocent-looking but secretly harboring the rage of two scorned women.

I pushed it toward her. "Here. It's not mine."

"It's not mine either," she said, her face disgusted as she pushed it back toward me.

"More yours than mine."

It was the strangest game of hot potato in the world, us shoving this two-carat princess-cut diamond ring back and forth. At the same time, we both must have wondered what we were doing because we stopped, the ring settling equidistant between us.

"What are we supposed to do now?" she asked, her voice small.

I didn't have an answer.

Her eyes were glued to the ring as she said, "I thought he was it. I thought tonight was going to be the first night of the rest of my life."

I knew exactly what she meant. But not to the same extent, so I kept my mouth shut.

She sighed. "I wish I could just...get away from all this, you know?"

I nodded. "Next weekend was supposed to be my first vacation, well, ever." My parents did not believe in taking time off despite their long, grueling hours working as an accountant (my father) and nurse (my mother).

"Why can't you go?"

"I was going with Tucker. I even paid for the damn thing, and it's nonrefundable."

"Where's the trip to?"

"York Beach," I said, feeling slightly ashamed after seeing Tucker and Olivia's world-gallivanting photos. Even after my ramen diet, I was only able to afford the Airbnb because September was offseason.

"Fun! Bring one of your girlfriends. Girls' weekend."

"I just moved here. I don't have anyone I can ask." Maybe Johannes would like to go with me, ha.

I felt like Olivia had X-ray vision and was staring straight into all the most embarrassing parts of me. Guess it made sense—she'd already seen my left boob.

Suddenly, she said, "I'll go."

Was she serious? She looked serious.

"It'll be a great story," she said. "And it'll be fun. If you'll have me."

I didn't care about the story—who would I tell?—but I did like the idea of getting away, not losing the money I'd painstakingly saved, and not being alone. Maybe I also had an unhealthy desire to know more about Olivia and Tucker. Or maybe I had a healthy desire to spend more time with the one person who understood exactly what I was going through.

Without hesitation, I said, "Let's do it."

CHAPTER 4

I finally understood Dickens. Because it was both the most awkward of times and the most cathartic of times in the car with Olivia on the way to York Beach. I was embarrassed by my used Honda with the hand-crank windows, but she didn't comment on it. I briefly wondered what she drove, then remembered the sleek silver Lexus from her social media photos. Was it better or worse that she didn't say anything?

At first, we avoided the topic of Tucker like the plague (obvious origin of expression). We made small talk about our jobs, our families, our hobbies—of which I didn't have much to contribute. My family was too hard to explain, and I didn't have any hobbies. One of many reasons I hated small talk.

I listened politely, nodding as Olivia told me about her parents as well as her younger sister with whom she was very close.

"I always wanted a twin," Olivia was saying, "and I'm pretty sure I willed Celeste into existence by begging repeatedly for my parents to have another kid."

I smiled. I would have loved a sibling. A built-in friend, and also someone I could commiserate with about my parents.

Then, another reason I hated small talk surfaced: I always managed to put my foot in my mouth (origin is weirdly related to foot-and-mouth disease, which makes no sense).

"What's your sign?" Olivia asked.

Images of street signs popped into my head. Then sign language. Neither of those could be what she was referring to, so I didn't respond.

A few seconds later, I realized she meant my Zodiac sign. I'd heard of Gemini and Leo, but that was where my knowledge ended. I didn't know any other signs let alone what mine was. I knew my Chinese Zodiac animal, but it would only make me look weirder if I told her I was a rabbit.

"I don't know," I said, feeling insecure.

But instead of making fun of me, Olivia simply asked, "When's your birthday?"

"March thirty-first."

"Aries. Passionate and fiercely loyal. And you likely dive headfirst into challenging situations and make sure you come out on top."

I laughed. "I've only figured out the diving-in part, not the coming-out-on-top part." And even the diving-in part was questionable.

She laughed with me. "I hear that. I'm a Sagittarius. But I didn't feel like one until Tucker. He pushed me to chase adventure."

A heaviness fell over the car. We'd only managed to avoid talking about Tucker for ten minutes. He loomed too large in our lives, and now in this car.

After five painfully long minutes of silence, I ripped off the second Band-Aid—the one that was needed because the wound was so big.

"Did he give you a reason for why he avoids social media?"

She turned to me, confused, but she answered anyway. "He said he was private for the sake of his career—not wanting to jeopardize anything with his high-profile clients."

"In private equity?" I asked, looking for confirmation.

She nodded. So at least that had been consistent. But his reason for avoiding social media had not been, likely because she was active and I wasn't.

Thinking back to Bubblicious, I asked, "Did he tell you he hates boba?"

"You know, he used to like it, but then one day a few months ago, he suddenly told me it 'tastes like slimy boogers'—oh."

That asshole. It was what I'd suspected—Tucker knew there was a chance we'd all cross paths at Bubblicious and did what was necessary to avoid it once he and I started dating.

The lies were unending.

Olivia changed the subject. And since the second Band-Aid was already off, plague be damned, she asked, "How did you and Tucker meet?"

I swallowed the lump in my throat. "In the grocery store, over the last sriracha bottle." I forced myself to refrain from explaining how Huy Fong sriracha is dependent on the harvest of one specific jalapeño pepper from Mexico and is thus prone to shortages after a season of bad weather. "We both also had three other hot sauces in our baskets," I told her.

At the time, I had thought it was romantic—I'd been looking for spice and fire and found Tucker. Now it sounded ridiculous.

"I hate spicy food," she said quietly, almost to herself. I could hear her wondering if that was why he'd cheated, to fill some ridiculous hole—mostly because I was wondering it myself. Which was so messed up. He was an asshole. There was no other explanation, and I needed to stop looking for one.

"Does that have something to do with his anosmia?" she asked.

I nodded. Lacking a sense of smell affects taste as well, but as Tucker had told me on our second date at my favorite Szechuan restaurant, "I can feel spicy food." After I explained that the heat from spicy food wasn't a taste but a response to pain, he told me for the first time that my brain was hot.

I wasn't sure I wanted to know the answer, but I also didn't want to keep thinking about my first dates with Tucker, so I asked Olivia, "How about you?"

"We met on a bus. He was on a work trip and I was on my way to visit Celeste at RISD—she's a very talented sculptor, just started a job in San Francisco after graduating a few months ago. Anyway, it felt like something out of a movie. There was only one seat open, right beside me. I was thinking to myself that if another person got on, they better not be a creep, and then..." Her words had started off robotic, but now they were filling with nostalgia. "I might have fallen in love with him the second he appeared through the door. That messy, tousled-just-so hair, the crisp suit..."

We both sighed. As much as I hated Tucker, I couldn't deny the fact that he was a total babe. This whole time, he had seemed too good to be true, and I should have listened to my gut. I needed a new set of hypotheses, an extension of Murphy's Law.

"So he sat next to me," she continued, "and I was so nervous! I kept staring out the window, pretending I didn't notice him."

Even though I knew where this was going, my breathing sped up. I was half invested as a listener and also half sick as Tucker's other ex.

"I eventually glanced over, and he was looking at me. Instead of being embarrassed about being caught, he just smiled. A gorgeous, gigantic smile, as if I'd made his day just by looking back at him."

I knew that feeling. Was that his secret weapon? His ability to make a woman feel like she was the most important, most beautiful person to have ever graced this Earth? Did he actually believe it in the moment or should he be making millions in Hollywood?

"I said hi, and for the first time in my life, I couldn't find any other words. But he carried the conversation, and before I knew it, I was comfortable, like I'd known him my whole life. We talked about traveling, all the places I wanted to see, and how I'd never been out of the East Coast."

I couldn't help picturing all the photos of her and Tucker in exotic locations. Then I told myself to stop. Green had never been my color.

"And then…" She stuck a painted fingernail between her glossed lips and chewed, and I cringed at the thought of the lavender polish cracking. I looked away, but only for a second because the next thing she said was "Then the bus crashed."

"What?"

She nodded, not meeting my eye. "It was…awful. The worst. I can't even…"

"You don't have to talk about it," I quickly said.

She nodded again, jumping past that part. "We were okay—some minor injuries, nothing serious—but we were so shaken. Once we…climbed out, with him helping me…" She took a breath. Her eyes grew glassy. "He looked at me and said, 'It's time to live. No more waiting. It's in your name.'"

She laughed, startling me.

"It sounds so ridiculous now!" she exclaimed. "So cheesy! *It's in your name.* But my god was it romantic then. I kissed him on the spot. And then over the next two years, he held up his promise. I became Liv, both in name and person. We checked off almost every item on my bucket list."

"What's left?" I asked.

"Barcelona. I thought maybe we'd go for our next anniversary…"

Her face dragged down, the weight of what happened this week flooding back.

It was my turn to say something. I knew it was. But what the hell did one say in a situation like this?

"I'm sorry." It was all I could think of.

"Why did he have to be like that? So...him. It would've been easier if he'd been an asshole through and through, you know?"

I nodded, completely understanding. That was partly why I couldn't stop thinking about him and asking more questions even though I'd been telling myself that Tucker Jones was dead to me.

"I don't know who I am anymore," I admitted to Olivia. "I liked who I was with him, who I'd become. Which makes it all the more confusing now."

A heavy silence fell over the car. Nothing but the hum of the engine and the wind whipping past. Until Olivia said, "You know what Celeste would do if she were here?"

Of course I didn't. But I shook my head like a normal person and refrained from pointing out the logical flaw in her question.

"She'd make us belt our hearts out. Feel the pain, then get rid of it."

I never—and I mean, *never*—sang in front of other people. But Olivia wasn't just any other person.

"Taylor Swift?" I found myself asking.

Her grin was ear to ear. "You read my mind."

• • • •

Forty minutes later, we arrived at the Airbnb with lighter chests, smiles on our faces, and hoarse throats.

I pulled up the parking brake, then looked over at Olivia, who sat there, facing forward, completely still. I waited, not sure if she needed a second.

Suddenly, she screamed, "Fuck him!"

I froze, feeling awkward turtle through and through.

"Come on," she said, gesturing with her hand. "You'll feel better."

"Fuckhim," I said, quickly and quietly.

She laughed. "Seriously, Kat? Let him have it!"

"Fuck him," I blurted, only a little louder.

"Fuck Tucker Jones!" Olivia shouted.

And finally, I let go, joining Olivia in yelling louder and louder until we were both howling at the top of our lungs.

Soon, we were howling with laughter.

It's him, hi, he's the problem, it's him.

I paused. In a previous life, I would have never said that joke to anyone besides Tucker. But fuck him, fuck this.

I said it out loud to Olivia. We *had* just been listening to that song, after all. What was the worst that could happen?

She howled louder. And for the first time in the past week, my heart filled slightly.

Wiping the tears from her eyes, Olivia opened the car door. "C'mon. Let's get settled and see if we can find some tea and honey. Unfortunately, there probably won't be slimy boogers, but we'll make do."

I repeated her words from earlier. "You read my mind."

For a split second, I couldn't help thinking about how our similarities were weird reminders that Tucker had chosen both of us. But really, at the end of the day, what human didn't like Taylor Swift, car karaoke, or tea with honey and preferably boba? They were simple coincidences with great likelihood, nothing statistically significant in proving any hypotheses about Tucker.

Or maybe they were the start of a friendship. A really weird, meet-ugly kind of friendship, but friendship nonetheless.

Together, we retrieved our luggage from the trunk.

As we rolled up to the front door, Olivia said, "How about we make a pact? No more thinking about him all weekend."

"Agreed," I said enthusiastically. We shook on it.

I punched the security code into the keypad above the handle, then pushed the front door open.

To reveal Tucker. Tucker mothereffing Jones.

How was he even here, inside? And then I remembered. I had forwarded him the Airbnb info before everything blew up, so he had the address and entry code.

Olivia and I dropped our bags at the same time that Tucker's jaw dropped open.

"Why are you here?" Tucker asked, beating me to the punch. "And together! That's fucked up, isn't it?"

Too. Many. Things.

First, how dare he. Second, why was *he* surprised that I would be at the Airbnb I paid for?

Have a romantic trip by yourself, jackass! That was what I'd said when he'd asked me about this trip. He hadn't taken that literally, had he?

"Tuuucker," a sultry voice called from farther inside the house. "Don't you want to come unwrap your present?"

Of course he ignored the *by yourself* part.

The voice grew closer. "Surprise! I already unwrapped it for you!"

A petite woman wearing a lacy black teddy complete with garters and stilettos popped into the hallway.

She screamed when she saw us, though she made no move to cover herself—which, she didn't need to. Even I couldn't stop admiring her in a wish–that–were–me way. Or maybe it was just the confidence she wore, which also was not me.

Olivia turned to Tucker, eyes hot enough to burn down the entire house.

I had so much anger in my stomach I was either about to

spew fire or throw up. "Seriously?" I blurted, not sure if I was talking to Tucker or the universe.

Tucker looked from the woman to Olivia to me. His eyes weren't focused on any of us as he yelled, "I don't know her!"

"Who are you talking to?" I asked. Was he really still trying to cover his ass and make it work with all three of us? He couldn't pick one even now, with his carefully curated world falling apart?

"Who are you?" the woman asked, her eyes ping-ponging from Olivia to me.

"Elle—" Tucker started to say, but I cut him off.

"We're Tucker's girlfriends—*ex*-girlfriends."

Somehow, Tucker seemed surprised at the word *ex*. Like, really?

The woman whirled around and shot daggers at Tucker with her eyes. Meanwhile, Olivia was shooting bullets with hers.

"I can explain," Tucker said, still not speaking directly to any of us. And his voice was strangely calm.

Suddenly, he turned and bolted. Sprinted like his liar, liar, pants were on fire.

We chased, hurling a cacophony of insults after him, our words jumbling together. Olivia's and Elle's were much more colorful than mine. Even in insulting him I couldn't measure up.

Out the front door and down the driveway we pursued. Unfortunately, Elle was almost naked and in stilettos, and Olivia and I couldn't physically keep up. Even though we were fueled by rage, Tucker was running for his life.

Olivia went the farthest, following him into the street. Elle and I walked to where she'd stopped, and there we stood side by side, watching our shared man sprint away from us with the speed of Tom Cruise in *Mission: Impossible*—except instead of saving the world, Tucker was trying to save his own ass.

Elle spat on the street in his direction. Then she turned to Olivia and me. "C'mon, ladies. We need to go blow off some steam."

She started walking, but Olivia said, "Um, don't you need to put on some clothes?"

Elle shrugged, but Olivia pushed. "I don't think they'll let you in wherever we're going. Unless we go to, like, a strip joint."

Elle's face lit up, but Olivia was already shaking her head. Elle rolled her eyes. "No fun. Fine."

Olivia and I shared a wide-eyed look, but neither of us said anything as Elle turned around and marched back toward the house.

I'd underestimated Kathryn's Third Law of Luck—apparently, the shit and beta-mercaptoethanol were still raining down.

CHAPTER 5

Elle reemerged in a crop top and pleather leggings. She'd kept the stilettos.

"I know just the place for us," she said with such certainty I wondered if it was actually a strip club despite Olivia's protest. "And we're walking, for the fresh air."

She led the way, her hips swaying with that intoxicating confidence. I worried she might sprain an ankle, but since walking had been her idea, I didn't say anything. I couldn't help glancing at her feet every few steps, though.

We made quick introductions—her full name was Elle Henderson and I managed to say my last name without any confusion this time, hooray—and then Olivia ripped off yet another Band-Aid.

"How'd you meet?"

Elle shrugged. "Nothing to write home about. Tinder."

Olivia's mouth dropped open. "He's on Tinder?"

I had to admit that surprised me, too. Before, it had felt plausible that Tucker had maybe fallen in love with two people—which didn't make it okay, not in any sense—but it was certainly different from him chasing after whoever was willing.

"It wasn't serious," Elle said. "We were just having fun. A

lot of it, but, you know, just fun. I never would have if I'd known about you two, though. Or even just one of you."

"God, does he suck," Olivia said. "How many girls do you think there were?"

I hadn't thought about that, but now that she'd said it, I realized the number could be anything and I'd believe it.

"How did he have time for that?" I blurted. I really didn't understand. Sure, we only spent Sundays and Wednesday evenings together, but he was also supposedly holding down a very busy high-paying job that covered his fancy condo and BMW and name-brand suits and expensive pouch underwear. All while having at least three girlfriends. I didn't know what part of that was more ridiculous—the *at least* or the *three*.

I guess Elle never called him her boyfriend. But they were seeing each other regularly, so whatever it was, it wasn't a one-night stand.

Olivia and I told our no-longer-meet-cutes to Elle, and just as I was finishing up and marveling at how quickly I could tell a story that once felt so epic, Elle exclaimed, "We're here!" as she gestured to the old-school arcade in front of us—as in pay with quarters for games like Skee-Ball and air hockey. There was also a bar in the back that looked like it hadn't changed in the last three decades. Several middle school kids were running around waving tickets, a group of teenagers was playing multifighter games, and a lone older guy sat at the bar sipping a beer.

"Which one are we here for?" I asked, gesturing to the arcade, then the bar.

"Both," Elle said, putting her arms around Olivia and me like a Mama Bear protecting her cubs. "Arcade first."

Elle steered us to the air hockey table, handed Olivia and me the paddles, then popped two quarters in.

Olivia served, her plastic paddle making a loud *crack* against the puck. The sound made me want to cringe, but there wasn't any time. I swept my own paddle over the table, feeling slightly weightless because of the air rising from the vents. When it crashed against the puck, tiny vibrations fired up my arm. The sound was satisfying when it came from me. And the feeling of smashing something—pure catharsis.

Olivia and I sped up our play, whipping that poor plastic puck back and forth faster and faster with increasing force.

Soon, we were whooping and laughing and hitting with such gusto that the puck was flying off the table.

The three of us rotated turns, playing and screaming until our arms grew sore and our throats raw. Then we whacked the shit out of some moles.

As we took seats at the bar opposite the lone guy still drinking, we were sweating and smiling.

"You were right," I told Elle. "Definitely needed to blow off some steam."

Elle waggled an eyebrow. "That's not the only way to blow off steam. Best way to get over someone is to get under someone else. You know, get back on that horse! A new, hotter horse."

Olivia frowned. "I'm not ready for that."

"Of course not," I said supportively. "You were almost just engaged."

"Wait—" Elle gaped at us.

Olivia and I both nodded.

"He *proposed*?"

"To *both* of us," I said. "The same night. With the same ring. Though I was the afterthought."

"WHAT?" Elle looked at me, then Olivia, in disbelief. "No shit!"

"Shit," Olivia said, her face dark. Then she nudged me. "I should have brought the ring to throw into the ocean."

Back at Bubblicious, I had left the ring on the table and she'd grabbed it at the last moment as I hoped she would. It didn't feel right for me to keep it, but I didn't want to leave it at the café either. "What'd you do with it?" I asked.

Olivia couldn't meet my eye. "Nothing. It's in my jewelry box."

Elle tapped the table urgently. "You should return it to him."

"I don't know," Olivia started, but Elle finished, "Covered in poop."

Olivia chuckled. "You know, Kat and I were just talking about *Dish Served Hot* the other day."

"I love that podcast!" Elle exclaimed, and that somehow made sense even though I'd just met her.

Suddenly, she jumped off her bar stool. "I know what we're doing next." She looked around, but there weren't any employees in sight. She started to go behind the bar, but the old guy drinking a beer came over.

"What can I getcha?"

"Oh! Sorry, I didn't know—is that allowed?" Elle gestured to his beer.

He laughed. "I own this place—who's stopping me?"

Elle contemplated this as she said, "Oh. Nice. Lucky you."

She sat back down and ordered a round of shots. Once they were in front of us, she grabbed her phone. With a click of a button, a song began playing.

I didn't recognize it, but Olivia freaked out, waving a hand toward the phone. "Play the horse dildo episode! That's the one I was telling Kat about!"

Elle scrolled for a second, then pressed a button and put her phone down.

"Welcome welcome, ladies," Elle said as the same song began to play, "to the *Dish Served Hot* slash Tucker Jones Can Go Fuck Himself drinking game!"

Olivia and I cheered.

Elle beamed. "For every revenge prank we hear that we want to do to Tucker, you take a shot."

Olivia laughed. "I love it! So much!"

I felt a smile grow on my face. "Okay. I'm in."

We couldn't stop giggling as the podcast began, and we weren't even drunk yet.

Fifteen minutes in, I had taken only one shot (Tucker receiving horse dildo newsletters was A-OK by me). Olivia and Elle, on the other hand, had taken a shot at every possible opportunity and were now sinking fast.

As the podcast discussed doing unspeakable things to sugar, a light bulb seemed to go off in Olivia's head. With her face flushed, she reached over and paused the episode. "Hey, why don't we do this?"

"Do what?" I asked, not sure she was with it enough to know what she was talking about.

Olivia waved her hands urgently. "The stuff from the podcast! Get revenge!"

"I thought you meant we should go on the podcast," Elle said.

Olivia's eyes brightened. "Why not both? Revenge first, then podcast to talk about it. Anonymously, of course."

"Oh, anonymously?" Elle said. "Okay, I guess I won't write my name on his carpet in poop."

Olivia laughed but I was thinking about how I didn't want to touch poop, even if it was for revenge.

"I can get into his place, but not the building," Olivia offered. "Damn it, I should've paid more attention whenever we entered."

"I can get us into the building," I found myself saying. "But I don't want to do anything too big." *Or mean*, I thought but didn't say. The non-newsletter pranks from the podcast seemed extreme to me. "Maybe we can just scare him a little," I suggested. "We can even use chemistry. Like, if we poke holes in his plastic bottles, the surface tension will hold the liquid in until he opens it, then it'll leak. And we can dangle a Mentos in the neck of a Coke bottle with string, and when he opens it, the Mentos falls in and the whole thing erupts."

"I've always wanted to know," Olivia said, "why does that happen?"

"The rough surface on the Mentos promotes carbon dioxide formation."

"Are you a scientist?" Elle asked.

I nodded. "Chemist."

"That's awesome," Elle said, and she seemed to mean it. Or maybe that was the alcohol talking. "You're like Bill Nye the Science Guy, except you're Kathryn Hu the Science Guru."

"Do you think Bill's last name is actually Nye," Olivia pondered, "and that's why he got the job? Or did he change it, shorten it, whatever, so it rhymed?"

"Actually, funny story," I said. "Bill Nye was a writer and actor on a sketch comedy show. He got his nickname after he corrected the host on the pronunciation of the word *gigawatt* and the host responded, 'Who do you think you are— Bill Nye the Science Guy?'" The alcohol had loosened my tongue; that wasn't a fact I'd normally share.

Elle gestured in my direction. "Well, we know who the smart one of the group is."

I shook my head. "Just knowing random facts doesn't make me smart."

Elle smirked. "Exactly what the smart one would say. Actually, scratch that. If it were a movie, the smart one would be talking about their Harvard degrees and whatnot."

I definitely was not going to mention where I was currently a postdoc. Instead, I argued, "Olivia's the successful lawyer."

"I'm sorry to say that my law degree is not going to help us come up with any revenge pranks."

Elle whistled. "Damn, ladies! I'm bringing down the group average."

Then she stopped talking. It was awkward for a second, during which it felt like Olivia and I couldn't follow up. We glanced at each other.

Elle started laughing. "We've all had the same penis inside us, and you two can't ask me what I do for work?"

I was thankful no one except the checked-out bar owner was around to hear that, but then I realized, why should I care? I wasn't the one who'd cheated.

Elle suddenly smacked the bar with an open palm. "Oh my god, I just realized something. We're the perfect trio: chemist, lawyer, writer. The three of us could get into some real she-nanigans. And we're about to, apparently."

"You're a writer?" I asked.

Elle nodded.

"If you write crime or mystery or vengeful cheating stories," Olivia said, "then that'd really be perfect."

Elle raised a mischievous eyebrow. "Not yet, but that doesn't mean I can't. Switching from romance to romantic thriller isn't such a big jump, now, is it? I can already see the movie montage introducing each of us by expertise." She waved a hand in the air, trying to make us picture it. "Kathryn Hu. Smart, science-y— she whips her glasses off—sexy. The one who knows how to mix shit together to make other shit." Another wave. "Olivia McCarthy. Also smart, lawyer-y—she lets her hair down— a goddess. The one who can get us out of any trouble that arises. And me. Super sexy, confident..." She trailed off.

Olivia jumped in. "The creative one. The one who deter-mines the plot."

Elle managed a small smile, but it was the first time she was devoid of confidence. "I'm not really a writer. Just an aspiring one. I haven't had any success. I work reception during the day. Like I said, I bring down the group average. All I offered was poop on the ring and carpet. Poop jokes are obvious, not clever at all."

"You're a writer," Olivia said, just as I admitted, "If you're not really a writer, then I'm not a chemist. I haven't proven any of my hypotheses, and I probably won't get a job when I finish my postdoc."

I'd never said those last words out loud, not even to Tucker, because the thought was too painful. But after everything that had happened this week, I felt completely naked and vulnerable (and not just because my left boob had been out for all to see).

Elle forced a smile. "Thanks for trying to make me feel better."

"So what does your writer brain say about our revenge plot?" Olivia asked.

Elle paused for a second, and some of the confidence returned to her eyes. "Well, my first thought is that everything we're talking about is so small. So nice. I mean, what he did to you two...that piece of shit excuse for a human has no balls, which is ironic because he has *huge*—"

"What were you thinking, then?" I interrupted.

Elle narrowed her eyes. "You have to get him where it hurts."

And with those words, it came to me. "His balls!"

Elle laughed. "Too on the nose. I meant you should find something specific to him."

"Exactly!" I exclaimed. "We'll cut up his precious underwear. No more special pouch for his balls."

Olivia and Elle burst into laughter so loud it drowned out the twinge I momentarily felt at the fact that they knew his underwear intimately, too. But the image of Tucker with his precious underwear unpouched was too hilarious to dwell on anything else.

We were decided.

Elle motioned for us to get in a circle and put our hands in. It felt silly, but it also felt right, especially for this trio.

"Ladies," Elle said, her voice full of conviction. And the three of us finished the next sentence together as if we had one brain.

"Tucker Jones—"

"Must—"

"Die."

Metaphorically, of course.

Dish Served Hot Podcast Transcript— Episode 11

(aka the Horse Dildo episode)

[Podcast theme song plays, sung by creator, host, and star Mandy Thorne]

MANDY THORNE: Hello, hello, my dear, dear listeners! You're lucky to be here with the one and only Mandy Thorne. You might know me from my influencer work or my stint on the reality TV show *Love Hut*, or from this brand-new but already award-winning podcast, where we only dish revenge out hot.

My guest for today is the incredibly fabulous and foxy Genevieve— code name, of course, for privacy—thanks for joining us today, Gen!

GENEVIEVE: My pleasure, Mandy, thanks for having me! And by the way, can I just say, you're the perfect host for this show, not only because you're you, but because your last name is Thorne.

MANDY: Thank you, thank you, I take that as a huge compliment. I for sure am a thorn in many people's sides, as are my guests, but they've earned that right. Like Genevieve here, who found her no-good, dirtbag boyfriend of *eight years* in their bed with his secretary. I mean, creative much? And she was a genius who quietly broke up with him—

GENEVIEVE: Very kindly, might I add.

MANDY: *Too* kindly, but not for long. Two days later, she signed him up for a newsletter about horse dildos, then put horse urine in his cologne.

GENEVIEVE: But only a few drops because I didn't want him to know.

MANDY: I gotta ask—why all the horse stuff?

GENEVIEVE: Well, Mandy, I'll tell ya, there *is* a reason. He hates horses. I don't really know why—it's such a weird, random thing, isn't it?

MANDY: Maybe he was jealous because they're known for, you know, having gigantic penises.

GENEVIEVE: [laughing] Well, as much as I hate to admit it, he doesn't need to be jealous, though, I mean, no human can be quite *that* endowed. But yeah, he unfortunately had no problems in that area.

MANDY: Unfair.

GENEVIEVE: I think maybe he had a traumatic experience with a horse when he was younger? At a kid's birthday party or something?

MANDY: Maybe it kicked him in the head.

[laughter]

MANDY: Well good for you, using that fear of his. There's no way you just had access to horse urine, though. How hard was that to get your hands on? Well, not your hands—I hope you used gloves.

GENEVIEVE: My god, it was so difficult to get! I had to call in, like, five favors! And even with gloves, some of the urine got on me, which really sucked. It's so pungent. Like pee that got left in the sun for a week. And since I only used a couple drops in the cologne, I was left with all this horse pee. So I poured it into his humidifier.

MANDY: Brutal!

GENEVIEVE: Yup. By the time he traces the smell to the humidifier, it's going to be in *everything*—on the walls, on every surface, in the carpet—

MANDY: He has carpet? Perfect!

GENEVIEVE: And that wasn't all I did.

MANDY: Spill! The tea, not the horse pee. Is this also horse- or pee-related?

GENEVIEVE: Yes.

MANDY: [laughs] Do tell!

GENEVIEVE: So there I was, standing next to the humidifier, and this thought occurred to me: I couldn't let the horse have all the fun now, could I?

MANDY: Oh my gods, you didn't.

GENEVIEVE: I did.

MANDY: What'd you pee in? The humidifier?

GENEVIEVE: Yup. And...

MANDY: And what? His shampoo? His sugar?

GENEVIEVE: [laughing] I'm bold but not *that* bold. Sugar is too much.

MANDY: Is it?

GENEVIEVE: Maybe next time.

MANDY: So then...

GENEVIEVE: You're close. But I wanted to be even closer to him than that.

MANDY: Closer than shampoo? Yikes. [pause] Was it his shaving cream? Aftershave?

GENEVIEVE: Ding ding ding!

MANDY: Is it less satisfying that you didn't get to see his reaction or how it all played out?

[beat]

MANDY: Oh! Ladies and gentlemen, Genevieve is smiling on the video chat! She's got a secret! Do tell us, you sly fox.

GENEVIEVE: I stalked the secretary's social media. Annnnd they broke up pretty soon after. I also saw that she liked a post about men smelling bad and beards being dirty.

MANDY: Winner winner chicken dinner! That's my girl!

CHAPTER 6

York Beach turned out to be the perfect place to heal a broken heart, and having Olivia and Elle with me made it more fun than I could have imagined given what we'd just gone through.

This was my first beach town, and I finally understood what the hype was about: cute New England houses; ice-cream stands; adorable cafés; jewelry, lotion, and craft shops that ranged from kitschy to chic; and so much water and sand. It had something for everyone, even an eclectic (though perfect-for-crime) trio like us. Olivia couldn't get enough of the local art scene; Elle couldn't get enough of the locals, breaking away from our group at night to blow off some steam in her preferred way; and I couldn't get enough of the ocean. That salty smell, the rhythmic, crashing waves…I was in love.

Except I hated that word now.

I was in deep, deep like.

Jesus, was I five?

Regardless, it was hard to leave.

Since Tucker had driven back on his own at some point, stranding Elle, the three of us packed into my old clunker for the road trip back. We were armed with gas station snacks and drinks as well as some York Beach taffy, all of which we began passing around immediately.

"I'm telling you," Elle said through a mouthful of Cheetos,

"when you're ready, getting under someone else is a great way to take your mind off things. I know it was different for me than the two of you, but, you know..."

"Don't knock it till you try it?" I filled in for her. (Referring to doors: don't knock on one until you've tried the knob first.)

"Exactly. Tinder's great."

Olivia snorted. "Can't wait to get on there and match with Tucker. Or find another cheater pretending to be single."

Elle laughed. "Okay, good point." She started waving orange-dusted fingers at us. "Oh my god, speaking of Tucker and Tinder, you both have to see this." She pulled her phone out to show us Tucker's Tinder profile.

Olivia began howling.

"Ah, hang on!" I exclaimed. A second later, we pulled up to a red light and I grabbed the phone. Then I laughed so hard my eyes began to water.

It was a shirtless ab-focused photo with his face just out of frame.

"Did you see his bio?" Elle asked, reaching over and using two orange fingers to enlarge the screen for me. "I didn't think much of it at the time, but now, holy shit."

Married and looking for some fun. Just kidding. Only about half—you figure out which half. Speaking of halves, I'm showing you the less impressive half of my body.

"Elle!" Olivia screeched. "You slept with him after seeing this?"

"I thought he was funny! I didn't know he really was in two serious relationships!"

"Okay, that does it," Olivia said, pulling her phone out and typing away.

"What're you doing?" Elle asked.

"Contacting Mandy Thorne. We're scheduling a podcast appearance for after we get revenge on Tucker."

"Wait, are you sure?" I asked.

Olivia paused. "I won't if you don't want me to."

I chewed my lower lip. Now that there wasn't any alcohol in my system, I didn't feel good about any of that.

"It'll be anonymous," Olivia reminded me. "I'll even make a new email account to contact her."

"Are you saying no to the revenge or the podcast?" Elle asked.

I didn't know what I was so afraid of, but I knew I felt scared. "It's not a no…"

"What if we come up with some pranks you're more on board with?" Elle suggested.

"Yeah, it doesn't have to be all horse pee and whatnot," Olivia said. "What if we tear out the last chapters in his books so he doesn't know how they end? You know he loves his mysteries."

I didn't know if I could bring myself to damage a book—I didn't even like to use bookmarks for fear of damaging the spine, so I folded my own origami ones that tuck onto the corner of the page.

Elle said, "We can put up a craigslist ad with his number that says, 'Free alpaca. Español por favor.'"

Olivia and I laughed.

"Let me just think about it, okay?" I said, and they both nodded.

I didn't know how to tell them that after this weekend, I was feeling so much better, and I didn't want to move backward. Olivia and Elle were the two unexpected cherries on top of a shit sundae, and that was enough for me for now.

• • • •

Later that night, less than an hour after I dropped Olivia and Elle off at their homes—the former at a gorgeous townhome and the latter at the duplex she shared with two roommates—a knock sounded at my door.

I looked through the peephole and saw a basket containing the cutest tan-and-white baby Mini Lop being held up in a way where I couldn't see who was doing the holding.

Damn it. Tucker Jones knew me better than I wanted to admit. Because he showed up with the one thing that could make me open the door.

But not yet. "What are you doing here?" I called out.

"Kat! I brought you a token of my love. Please, let me in."

I hesitated, but after a moment, I cracked the door an inch. The basket had *Cinnabun Junior* written on the side.

So fucking perfect.

"Hi, baby," I cooed to Cinny.

"Hey, babe," said the most clueless man in the entire universe.

I tried to reach out and take Cinny fast enough that I could close the door on Tucker, but he was ready, pushing past me and rushing into the apartment.

"Kat, baby, you have to help me."

The balls on him. If Elle were here, she'd comment on how, yes, his balls really were huge, and I couldn't decide if I hated or loved that I knew that about my boyfriend's regular hookup. And why was I thinking about his balls so much more now than when we were together?

I tried to settle Cinny Junior's basket on the couch. With every adorable flop of hers, toys lining the bottom of the basket jingled and squeaked. Worried she'd topple the basket and fall out, I picked her back up.

"I'm in trouble," Tucker blurted.

I laughed, and the surprise that registered on his face made me laugh harder.

"No shit you're in trouble! What'd you think would happen when your three girlfriends met? You did this to yourself."

Tucker looked confused for a moment. Then he shook his head. "No, I'm not talking about that. I'm...in danger. I got myself into some financial trouble. That's why I couldn't end things with Olivia. She's been giving me legal advice pro bono because of our relationship, and, Kat, please, you have to believe me, my situation is serious."

"You think I'm going to believe a single word coming out of your lying mouth?" It was hard to be angry while holding a baby bunny, but I found a way.

Then, relenting to the fact that I wasn't getting Tucker out of here this instant, I went and settled Cinny Junior into Cinny Senior's old but clean cage.

"I lied before," Tucker said, "but this right here, what I'm telling you, is the truth. I needed money. Need, present tense," he corrected. "I fucked up. And I just kept digging a bigger and bigger hole, and now I'm in over my head. I got involved with some really bad people."

"Who?"

"I can't tell you. For your protection. Kat, my life is in danger. For real. I think they've been *inside* my place. I'm desperate. Please, let me stay here for a little while until I figure this out."

I was starting to believe him, but thank god he said that last sentence. It was all a ploy, once again, to get what he wanted. Finally, I was beginning to see through his bullshit.

"You are not getting back into my life this way."

He dropped to his knees, which only reminded me of the last time he kneeled. "Kat. It's me. The one who you and Cinnabun fell in love with at first sight, as you used to say. Remember when I met Cinn? She rubbed her chin on my finger. You said that meant she was claiming me as hers, and then you rubbed your chin on me."

How dare he try to use that memory to help him now.

"But you aren't mine," I said coldly. "You never were. None of what happened between us means anything in light of all your secrets. And you're *still* lying!"

He stood and held both hands up. "I swear I'm not anymore. I'll prove it to you—ask me anything right now."

This wasn't fucking Reddit. But here was my chance. Not to give him a second chance, but to prove that I wasn't wrong about every last thing. Because my gut told me he hadn't changed a cell.

"How many girls were there?"

"Just you three, I promise."

I guess I didn't have proof otherwise, but there wasn't a single part of me that believed him. "No one else looked good on Tinder, huh?"

"I'm not on Tinder," he said, cool as a fucking cucumber.

"Get out." I started pushing him as hard as I could.

"Kat, wait! Please! Don't do this!"

We were just a couple feet from the door now. A couple feet from my freedom. "Goodbye, Tucker. Forever. I won't be opening the door next time no matter how many bunnies you bring, so don't bother."

"Kat, I'm telling the truth, I promise. It was always you. Elle and Olivia, they don't mean anything, not the way you do. I know you saw me propose to Olivia, but that wasn't real. She gave me an ultimatum—she wanted to move in together—but, well, I couldn't do that, and like I said before, I couldn't lose her legal help, so I didn't have a choice. I *had* to propose." His excuses grew more and more pathetic as I leaned all my weight on him to push him out the door. I couldn't put the garbage out fast enough, especially given the garbage spewing from his lips. "Kat, you're my last hope. Please. If anything happens to me, it'll be on you."

"Ask one of your other girls for help."

"Baby, please! Can I at least get the ring back? I need it—my life is in danger."

It had never been easier to dropkick someone out of my life. Emotionally, that is. Physically, it took all my strength. But once I heaved him over the threshold, I shut the door, locked it, and pushed a chair under the handle for good measure.

And I immediately texted Olivia and Elle.

I'm in, for all of it.

No holding back.

I was more ready than ever. Despite my love of sayings, Olivia and Mandy Thorne were right: the dish was best served scalding hot.

CHAPTER 7

This was ridiculous. Ridiculous, over the top, borderline too much, but also oh-so exciting. We were dressed in all black—Elle's idea, of course, to "fit the part"—and each of us had a backpack full of supplies. Or should I say, surprises?

"Add *badass* to Olivia's movie intro," Elle said with a low whistle as Olivia pulled out a lockpick set and knelt by Tucker's front door.

"You said you could get in!" I whispered.

"I can! And we will!" Olivia slid two slender tools into the lock.

"She's like a female Double-oh-seven," Elle said.

"Except she's the victim, not the cheater," I pointed out.

Elle laughed and pushed my shoulder. My heart swelled a little.

"I want to be you when I grow up," Elle told Olivia.

"Me too," I added.

The door clicked open.

We were doing this.

"You're sure he's not home?" I asked again.

"I'm sure," Olivia said. "He's in Phoenix for work."

Why was I so nervous? What was the worst that could happen? He comes home, sees us, and tries to propose to all of us at the same time? I kind of wanted to see what Elle would do if he dropped to one knee and yelled out his prepared generic proposal to no one in particular, ha.

"Ready, ladies?" Elle asked as we stepped inside and closed the door behind us. "I sure am." She put rubber gloves on and retrieved a tied-off plastic bag from her backpack. Even with the tie, the stench escaped and wafted right into our nostrils.

"My god, Elle!" Olivia cried.

I plugged my nose. "What is that?"

She looked at me as if I had just asked what H_2O was. "It's poop."

Of course. Sometimes a spade was a spade and poop was poop.

"Didn't you say poop jokes are obvious?" Olivia asked, also plugging her nose.

Elle shrugged. "Sometimes it's good to just own who you are."

I opened my mouth, about to tell her that, unlike us, Tucker couldn't smell anything, but...the girl brought a bag of poo. That takes commitment, preparation, and determination. No need to take her fun away now.

"And I thought we agreed it was best to be subtle," Olivia added, referencing a video chat we'd had earlier in the week.

"I couldn't think of anything else to do," Elle said. "So, you know, beggars, choosers, whatnot."

Olivia smiled. "You mean, beggars can't pick their poison?"

"Wait," I said, my mind perking up at the sound of beloved idioms but pausing on the unfamiliar turn.

"It's a malaphor," Olivia said, and I gave her a small shrug. "You haven't heard of those? How is that possible? You're the reason I started looking up origins of sayings, friend." My insides couldn't help warming a little with that word. "Malaphors are two or more sayings mashed together."

And the fact that she had started searching origins on her own and found something I hadn't even heard of...I weirdly wanted to hug her, which rarely happens to me.

We shared a long, borderline mushy smile.

Elle stepped between us. "Look at us sister wives…sister cuckolds… Why isn't there a female equivalent of *cuckold*?"

"There is," I said. "It's *cuckquean*."

Elle's eyes lit up. "That's perfect. So, my queens, my cuck-queans…" Olivia and I chuckled. "Shall we get to it?"

"Straight to the underwear for you?" Olivia asked me.

"Not just yet," I said, gesturing to my overstuffed backpack.

"Do we finally get to see what you've prepared, Science Guru?" Elle asked. I'd been secretive about my plans thus far.

With a shit-eating grin (possum origin, believe it or not), I extracted an item from the backpack—with difficulty, but not enough to lose my *ta-da* moment.

Olivia screamed. Elle took a step back in shock but then leaned closer once she realized what I was holding.

"Hi, buddy," she said, waving at the frog in my hand.

I got the idea from Genevieve talking about her boyfriend hating horses. Tucker had been creeped out by frogs since he saw a bullfrog eat another frog as a kid.

"Is that—" Olivia started, keeping a few feet between her and the amphibian.

"From the biology lab next door. Don't worry, he's retired. They all are. And I think they deserve to have some fun, don't you?"

"They?" Olivia leaned even farther away.

I let Frog #1 go as I retrieved Frog #2 from the ventilated container inside my bag. Then I scattered some dead insects around the condo. Food for the frogs and a bit of revenge in their own right. Two birds, all that. Or I should say, two frogs.

"You labeled them?" Elle asked, noticing the lab tags I'd swiped and attached to their legs. "What, to keep track of Kermit versus Speckles? Is one of them carrying disease? Warts?"

Olivia cringed.

"No, that's not why," I said cryptically. I was enjoying this.

Elle crossed her arms over her chest. "Well, maybe we don't care, then."

I shrugged. "Okay." I started toward the stairs.

Elle threw her hands up. "Fine, you win! Please tell us!"

"I have one frog left," I told them, retrieving the third frog from the bag and holding him tightly in my hands.

Olivia gasped when she saw it.

"What?" Elle asked.

Olivia pointed to the tag on his leg.

Frog #4.

They both started laughing, presumably imagining Tucker scouring his condo for a nonexistent Frog #3.

With a smile, I started up the stairs. "And you're going in the bed," I said to the frog. "Tucker's a cuddler."

Upstairs, the struggle began. Frogger #4 (really #3) turned out to be a slippery bugger. I made it to the bedroom, but he jumped out of my hands as soon as we got there. In my effort to snatch him back up in the dark, I tripped, slamming my forearm against the dresser.

I flicked the light switch, turning the lights and ceiling fan on at the same time, the latter making it harder for me to locate the frog since I couldn't hear him anymore.

"Where are you, buddy?"

He popped out momentarily, and I lunged. After a few minutes of gaining more cuts and bruises while feeling like I was suddenly in a cartoon, I gave up. Really, it didn't matter. Even if I had placed him in the bed, the chances he would stay there until Tucker got home were slim.

"You okay in there?" Olivia called out. A moment later, she appeared in the doorway, followed by Elle.

But unlike Olivia, Elle barely noticed me as she made a beeline for the bed. Without batting an eyelash, she dropped her pants, squatted over his pillow, and farted.

"Sorry to interrupt," she said, pulling her pants up as quickly as they had come down. "That one was time sensitive, you know?"

Olivia howled while I stared in shock. Then I started laughing, too.

"You know," I said, "there's a Chinese saying, buyao tuo kuzi fangpi—don't take your pants off to fart. Meaning, don't do anything extraneous."

"I want him to get pink eye," Elle said with a shrug.

"I thought you had that covered with your special bag," Olivia said.

"Just wanted to be sure."

The three of us were laughing as we piled into the master bathroom.

"Time to hit him where it hurts," Olivia said. From her backpack, she pulled out a bottle of Nair, which she promptly poured into his expensive high-end shampoo. Tucker cared about his hair almost as much as his pouched underwear. And unlike the underwear, everyone could see his hair, which was why he spent hundreds of dollars on his haircuts and hair products.

Elle opened her poo bag with one hand and grabbed Tucker's toothbrush with the other.

"Wait." I hated Tucker, but this was too much, right? I mean, ew.

"What?" she asked innocently.

I pulled something out of my ass (which felt fitting given the current situation). "That'll be too obvious."

"Not if I rinse it after." She began to lower the toothbrush into the bag.

"No, Kat's right," Olivia said as she rescrewed the top onto the shampoo bottle. "Here, let me."

She took the toothbrush from Elle's outstretched hand and scrubbed it in her armpit.

"Are you sure that's the best idea?" I asked, thinking about how many germs the human mouth had and how she was rubbing that all over herself.

Olivia's eyes widened. "Oh, shit, you want to up it a notch? Your butt crack?"

"Oh my god, no!" I yelled as Elle nodded a hearty yes.

"No, you're right," Olivia said, seeming not to hear me. "Butt crack is better. Here. You should do the honors. And put some floss up in there, too. Then his loofah."

"No, I'm not putting his bathroom down my pants!" I exclaimed, taking a step back. The idea was just too disgusting, and brushing my ass crack did not sound like it would be any more pleasant for me than for the poor toothbrush.

"Fine, whatever," Olivia said, already undoing the waist tie of her sweatpants.

Why was I the only one not willing to drop trou on a second's notice? I guess Olivia *has* seen me popping out of my bra already, so, tit for taint.

"You've got this covered," Elle said to Olivia. Then, with a wink, she added, "Guess I'll go cover his office." She and her gross bag left abruptly.

Sometimes it felt obvious why Tucker liked all three of us and other times (like right now), I wondered how in the world that was possible.

I didn't feel like staying with Olivia or joining Elle, and that was when I remembered: I still had my pièce de résistance (French origin, the principal dish of the meal).

It was time to destroy some underwear.

I crossed the bedroom and inched the walk-in closet door open.

And was immediately hit by the scent of rotten eggs. Was that a beta-mercaptoethanol ghost coming to haunt me? Or did it really smell horrible in here? Maybe one of the girls brought actual rotten eggs to the condo?

Leaving the closet door cracked, I went to open the bedroom windows. "Do you smell that?" I called out to Olivia.

"What?" Olivia yelled back.

I joined her in the bathroom and turned the vent fan on. "Do you smell that? The rotten eggs?"

She sniffed. "No."

I realized I didn't smell it anymore either. Maybe it had been in the closet. Or in my head.

"Oh my god, what are you doing?" Tucker's rinse glass was in her hand and she was trying to pour its liquid contents into his mouthwash. *Yellow* liquid.

"Maybe this is what you smelled," she joked. "But I'd like to think it's not as bad as rotten eggs."

"Olivia!"

She cackled. "What? Do you want to add yours in, too? It's not too late."

"That's so gross!"

"So is having three girlfriends. And let's be honest—I'm being nice. I *wanted* to put coffee in here to stain his precious teeth, but that would've been too noticeable."

I'm glad Olivia hadn't asked me for an invisible chemical to damage his enamel. Suddenly, the pee didn't seem so bad, though it was still too much in my opinion, even after what Tucker had done. Olivia, on the other hand, was going for Tucker's jugular. His loves in life (other than all the women) were his hair, his teeth, his underwear, and—the only one we didn't have plans for—his money.

We were interrupted by Elle calling out to us from the office. "Did either of you know that Tucker has a safe?"

Olivia and I shared a puzzled look.

"Let's go," I said, glad Elle had distracted us.

Olivia nodded. Then she poured the entire contents of the cup into the mouthwash in one fell swoop (Shakespeare origin, has changed meanings since).

We walked into the office to see poop smeared on the bookcase, carpet, and built-in wall of cabinets. The trail led to the bottom left cabinet, which was open, revealing a small locked safe.

Elle's eyes gleamed. "What do you think he has in there?"

"Only one way to find out." Olivia flexed her fingers.

She set to work by first pulling her shirt over her nose. "God, Elle, you couldn't have waited to do that?"

"I wouldn't have found the safe otherwise!" she said in defense, but she also went and opened the office windows.

Still, I needed to pop my head into the hallway and gulp a breath of fresh air, which I held for as long as I could.

As Olivia tackled the safe, Elle retrieved something from her pocket. I couldn't tell what it was until she went across the hall to the dryer and poured it in.

"Glitter?" I said with a laugh. She beamed. Somehow that made sense. Her two pranks put together were how I would describe her. Elle could get down and dirty, but she was also fun, the life of the party, the person you brought to add the sprinkle of glitter on top—the strip club version, not the crafts one.

"I'm in," Olivia said, pulling the safe door open.

"That was fast," I said, impressed.

"I told him not to do this, but does he listen to me? No. The combination was a birthday."

Of course he'd used Olivia's birthday.

She stood. "Yours."

"Mine what?" I asked.

She was already grabbing the leather notebook in the safe and scanning through it. Without looking at me, she said, "The combination. It was your birthday."

"But how do you know…" In the car. I told her my birthday when she asked me what my sign was. "You remembered?"

She shrugged. "I remember stuff like that—numbers, dates. Comes in handy as a lawyer, and apparently for breaking into ex-boyfriends' safes."

Why did Tucker use my birthday?

No. It shouldn't matter. It didn't.

Olivia frowned at the notebook. "Everything in here is shorthand. Just letters and numbers. Do you think it's some sort of code?" She looked up. "What do you think this is about?"

"His diary about all his girls?" Elle (partly) joked. "A way to keep track of what I'm sure was a hectic schedule?"

I glanced over Olivia's shoulder. Letter combinations like *CA*, *NJ*, and *LSU* jumped out at me.

"Are those locations?" Maybe California, New Jersey, and Louisiana State University? Though that last one was an outlier. Not to mention, the other letter combinations on the page didn't appear to be obvious locations. Other than *US*, which felt too broad.

"And the numbers?"

They varied. *CA* was beside *35*, *NJ* with *45*, *US* next to *15*, and *LSU* alongside *150*. Most were between 10 and 200.

Tucker's words from the other night popped into my head. *I got myself into some financial trouble. That's why I couldn't end things with Olivia.*

Had he been telling the truth? He couldn't have been... could he?

I could ask Olivia. Though this didn't seem like the time. And I didn't want to admit that I had let Tucker in the other night, even if Cinny Junior had been involved. What would I even say? *Hey, Olivia, did you help our shared ex-boyfriend with some shady financial shit?*

"Um, could the numbers represent money?"

Olivia looked intrigued. "What, like a ledger of some sort?"

I shrugged. "Maybe."

"That's certainly plausible. And hella shady."

Elle nodded. "Especially given that it's the *only* thing in his safe."

"Holy shit," Olivia said. "This could be it. If we found evidence of anything illegal—"

"It'd be the ultimate revenge," Elle finished for her. "*And* we'd be doing some good."

There it was, the last item on Tucker's Favorites list that we hadn't attacked yet: his money. But soon, if things went according to plan, we'd have taken everything from him.

"Should we—" I started to ask, but Olivia had already begun snapping photos of the ledger's contents with her phone.

"There might be stuff in here, too," she added, going over to his laptop.

Unfortunately, the laptop required a password. Olivia cracked her knuckles. "Alright. I've learned a few things from the PI at work. And now that we know Tucker was a complete idiot through and through... Elle, when's your birthday?"

I left them to return to my pièce de résistance. They didn't need me anyway. If any one of us had this, it was Double-Oh-livia.

Maybe I also left because I didn't want to know if Elle's birthday was the password.

When I returned to the bedroom and opened the closet door a little farther, the rotten egg smell was gone. I sincerely hoped I wouldn't be getting whiffs of rotten eggs randomly as an aftermath of the beta-mercaptoethanol spill. Or maybe the fan and open windows had dissipated whatever it was. Or maybe my nostrils were permanently filled with the scent of Elle's poop bag. But as I took a step just inside the doorway, I smelled rotten meat. That might sound similar to rotten eggs, but it's different. As a chemist who uses both beta-mercaptoethanol and the aptly named putrescine, I promise there is a difference.

I flicked the closet light switch on.

And screamed. The most gut-wrenching, horrible scream of my life.

There was a limp body on the floor. Sprawled. Unmoving. Familiar.

CHAPTER 8

I couldn't stop screaming.

Once, twice, over and over.

I instinctually retreated, backing away from the body while bloody-murder screams continued to erupt from my mouth—the first time I could aptly use that phrase, though I guess I had no idea if it was bloody or murder.

Olivia and Elle rushed into the room, an open tube of glitter in Elle's hands. Olivia spotted the body first. Her screams joined with mine. Suddenly, a burst of glitter filled the air in a dense, shiny cloud as Elle's hands flew up to her face. Olivia's and my screams turned to coughs as we inhaled the surprisingly sharp pieces. The whole scene almost looked like a bizarre celebration.

"Is that…"

"Is he…"

"I don't know," I said truthfully.

None of us moved. My mind was completely blank. Overloaded.

Elle's hands were still covering her mouth. "He…he can't be."

"He's so young, healthy," Olivia stammered. "How could—" Her eyes widened in horror.

But I was barely paying attention. Because they were right.

He couldn't be. Which meant now was not the time to be frozen in shock.

I ran to him, the only thought in my mind being, *Save him!*

When I reached the body, I screamed.

Olivia and Elle rushed in after me.

I fell to my knees.

I'd known it was him—who else could it have been? It was his condo, his closet. But seeing his splotchy purple face and perpetually open and cloudy eyes staring at me...that was a whole different story.

It was too much—too upsetting, too horrifying, too everything.

But there was no time.

"Do either of you know CPR?" I asked.

Their yells filled the air, confusing and scaring me. I made out a *Don't touch him!* and subsequently decided to tune them out. This was on me, apparently.

I put my hands over his sternum, trying to imitate what I thought CPR was supposed to look like. Olivia and Kat continued yelling, but the noise was dulled now. I was in the eye of the storm. Bits of facts came back to me from random parts of my life—a TV episode here, a college class there. I pushed. As hard as I could. As if Tucker's life depended on it, because it did.

"Stayin' Alive." That was the song to keep the beat of compressions. How fitting.

My hands were covered in glitter from earlier. Now Tucker's chest was shiny and rainbow-colored.

Ah, ah, ah, ah...

Bee Gees, glitter—this wasn't a disco.

Stayin' alive, stayin' alive...

Was I actually keeping him alive? Or was this all for nothing?

He smelled bad. Like putrescine. Bodies didn't smell until they were dead.

But I couldn't stop—what if he wasn't dead?

I heard his ribs cracking. Someone screamed. A blood-curdling, ear-ringing scream.

Oh, that came from me. After I felt his bones break beneath my palms. *Because* of my palms.

Pain shot through my arms and shoulders and chest from pushing so hard.

Suddenly, I wasn't pumping anymore. My torso was in the air. Olivia's and Elle's arms were around me, pulling me off Tucker. I saw red.

No. I couldn't leave. He needed me.

I struggled.

I was also so tired.

Ah, ah, ah, ah…

Staying alive. We were trying to stay alive.

Olivia and Elle helped me down the stairs. Then out the door and into the car.

This had not gone at all how it was supposed to.

Tucker Jones ~~must~~ has died.

CHAPTER 9

I should have known the worst was yet to come. My laws promised that. Bad luck stays in motion, and the beta-mercaptoethanol was still pouring down.

The problem was, how did I make it fucking stop?

Kathryn's Unforeseen Fourth Law of Luck: Sometimes the universe is just out to get you, and then you're fucked no matter what you do.

Olivia, Elle, and I were hunkered down in Olivia's townhome living room, shades drawn and lights off. I barely remembered the ride over. I spent most of it trying to keep myself from vomiting.

Olivia was on the love seat with her head in her hands, Elle was in the armchair pulling a blanket tight across her shoulders as if she were trying to give herself a hug, and I was sitting on the floor, which was the farthest I could make it.

When I finally spoke, my throat was so raw I sounded like I'd been smoking for fifty years. "Why did we leave?"

Olivia and Elle both turned to gape at me.

"We don't know—" I choked on my spit. "What if he— Why didn't we— I should've checked his pulse—"

"Kat." Olivia's voice was gentle. "He's gone. Tucker's gone. He was bloated and smelled and—" She swallowed loudly, her fist coming up to her mouth as if she was trying not to throw up.

"We should've called the paramedics. I could've kept doing CPR—"

"Kat." This time, it was Elle trying to comfort me. "You did what you could."

"Why did we leave?" It still didn't make sense. Tucker couldn't be gone. He was young, healthy, just like Olivia had said back at the condo. Right before her eyes went wide. "You were scared," I said, bits of it coming back now. "Of what?"

"Of whatever—"

"Whoever," Elle interjected.

"Might have, you know." Olivia couldn't seem to say the words out loud.

"You don't think…" I couldn't say it either.

"What else could have caused…it?" Olivia asked. "An unknown health condition that just, *bam!* Gets him out of nowhere while he's changing clothes? That's highly unlikely!"

"But I didn't see signs of…" I started to say, but then I realized I couldn't remember anything except the feeling of sheer panic and desperation. I hadn't been looking for wounds or blood or signs of foul play. I'd been laser-focused on his sternum, partly to be efficient and also because I was scared I'd lose it if I looked anywhere else.

This was too much to take in. "So you're saying we might have been in there…with a *murderer?*" I couldn't wrap my head around it.

"I don't know!" Olivia's thin veil of control finally slipped. "I just knew we had to get out of there!"

"You were right," Elle said, jumping in. "And besides, it doesn't matter, we're here now. Even if he's not."

And then it hit me all over again. "He's dead." We had wished him dead, but we hadn't meant like this. We had wanted him to hurt like we had, not *die.*

"What now?" Elle asked.

"We call the police," I said immediately. "Right?"

Olivia shook her head. "If we do, we would for sure be their number one suspects. But if we don't, that's a crime."

"We've already committed a crime," I argued, the gravity of our situation starting to sink in. "We left the scene. Which we shouldn't have. My god, what have we done? We broke in and smeared our DNA everywhere!" I turned to Olivia and exploded. "Why did you have to put the entire bathroom down your pants?" Then I turned to Elle. "And why'd you have to smear poop on every goddamn surface?" If we'd just done my ideas like the underwear—oh, I didn't even get to the underwear. Somehow that was upsetting even though, wait, WTF, that didn't matter anymore. But if we had just done my pranks, we wouldn't be in this mess, would we?

"None of that matters now!" Elle exclaimed. "What's done is done. We need to talk about what's next."

My pleading eyes turned to Olivia. "You're the lawyer. What do we do? What would you tell your client to do?"

"I…" She closed her eyes, squeezing tight. When she opened them again, they were brimming with tears. "I don't think we should call the police," she said, her voice just loud enough to be audible. "I've been on the inside long enough to know that the system is flawed."

"But if we just tell them what happened—" I began.

Olivia shook her head. "That doesn't always work. The truth doesn't always win out, especially when the evidence is stacked against you, and when you don't have the exact backstory they want."

"That happened to me," Elle added, her voice small now, too. "Abusive ex, fight that escalated, police didn't take my side."

"I'm sorry," I said to both of them.

"And just because we may not be in the same place as a murderer now doesn't mean we're completely in the clear,"

Olivia added. "If something horrible truly happened, we might still be in danger being connected to Tucker. That's… what happened to one of my previous clients. He had shady connections as a drug dealer, but he didn't commit the murder he was charged with. But the eyewitnesses were scared of retribution from whoever was actually guilty, so they lied and convinced the jury. That case almost killed me. I couldn't sleep for months after. It still haunts me now, years later, as I continually fail to get him out of jail."

Olivia's words brought to mind what Tucker had said to me back at my apartment the last time I saw him: *I'm in danger. I'm in over my head.*

Had Tucker been telling the truth that day? Could I have helped but, by turning him away, let this happen? Was this my fault?

If anything happens to me, it'll be on you. That was one of the last things he said to me.

"Olivia," I said so suddenly that she startled. "Tucker said he was in financial trouble and dug himself in deep with some really bad people. And…you were helping him with that?"

"Wait, that was about him? He told me he was helping a friend." She paused, putting the pieces together in her head. Then she narrowed her eyes at me. "When did he tell you that?"

I cringed as I admitted, "He stopped by the other day begging me to help him, saying he was in trouble."

"You let him in?" Olivia said, shocked.

"He brought me a bunny!"

"I don't care if he brought you a tap-dancing unicorn!"

"That's not what's important right now!"

Elle jumped in, trying to keep the peace. "So you think whoever he was in trouble with came after him?"

I shrugged. "I mean, maybe? He was scared when he came over and asked to stay with me, but I assumed it was just a lie to get back in my life." I hugged my knees, willing the nausea away. I didn't know. I couldn't have known. It wasn't my fault that he'd cried wolf too many times. Right?

Olivia sighed, then came over and put a hand on my knee. "This isn't your fault, okay? And maybe you're on to something." She hesitated, then got up and retrieved her backpack. "We might be able to find out more in here," she said as she pulled Tucker's laptop out. "I couldn't hack into it and I slipped it in my backpack before everything went to shit."

I lost it. "Jesus, Olivia! So we dressed like burglars, broke in, put our DNA and feces everywhere, and then *stole evidence*." We were so supremely fucked it wasn't funny.

Elle dropped her head in her hands. "How can a group of ladies this smart make so many bad decisions? None of this is on me, though, since I'm the group idiot as previously discussed."

"The DNA," Olivia repeated, her eyes opening with just as much horror as they had back at the condo when she thought there might be a murderer present. "Our DNA is still all over Tucker's condo!"

"Well, we *are* his ex-girlfriends," I pointed out. "It's not unusual for our DNA to be there, right?"

"But it *is* unusual for there to be poop, frogs, and glitter everywhere."

"Fuck!" Elle yelled.

"Why did we have to do that?" I cried.

After a beat, Olivia said bravely, "I'll go clean the condo."

"What?" I asked, not sure I'd heard her correctly. That seemed like the worst idea ever.

"I'll go to his place and clean up the pranks and wipe our DNA."

"Isn't it too late?" Elle asked.

Olivia shook her head. "They haven't found Tucker yet—how could they have? We're all here, and there's no one else to find him."

"That you know of," I argued. There could have been five more women for all we knew.

"Well, I'll take that chance. I'll be in and out, no breaking and entering necessary. I swiped a spare key as soon as we got inside," she said as she pulled it out of her pocket.

"Why?" I asked.

"I don't know, more pranks? I thought it could help. Just be grateful. So what do I have to do, Kat? What should I use to clean, and will regular scrubbing get rid of DNA?"

I sighed. "I'll go."

"You don't have to," Olivia said.

"I'm the scientist." I could do this, right? I just had to pretend Tucker wasn't in that closet. "I'll go tomorrow." And that was when I remembered. *"Dish Served Hot!"* I blurted.

"I think Tucker was served the hottest dish, being dead," Elle said dryly.

"No, we're scheduled to record the podcast tomorrow!"

Olivia's eyes widened in panic. "Oh shit."

"We have to cancel," I said.

"Won't that look suspicious?" Elle asked.

Olivia held her hands up. "Wait. No. This could be good. We can use this to our advantage. It's a chance for us to tell the narrative we want. We go on there and declare that we didn't do anything, that we forgave him, that revenge isn't the best action or whatever. The police likely won't even know it's us on the podcast—it's anonymous—but if they do figure it out, our story will point to our innocence." Elle was nodding along, but I didn't feel as convinced. "Kat, while you're cleaning the condo, Elle and I will do the recording. I didn't tell Mandy that there are three of us, so it won't be a problem."

The two of them looked at me expectantly. After a moment, I nodded.

"Okay," Olivia said, handing me the key. "We have a plan. Elle, download a voice modulator, just in case, for when we call in to the podcast. And then tomorrow morning, during the recording, all we have to do is be really convincing that we're over Tucker. He wasn't worth any more of our time. Supersmooth, easy peasy. Good?"

Elle shrugged. "How hard could it be?"

Dish Served Hot **UNAIRED**
Podcast Recording Transcript

MANDY THORNE: Okay, do I have the best episode for y'all today. The tea for this one is hot! Steaming, bubbling, scalding hot! It just may be THE juiciest, most hilarious revenge story we've ever had on the show, Thornies! Are y'all ready? Y'all aren't ready. But I'll tell you anyway.

Two girls realized they were dating the same asshole because one of them stumbled into the other's proposal. For reals! And I believe one of them was naked? The one who stumbled in, not the one being proposed to. That'd be weird, a naked proposal. Anyhoo, how does that even happen? I can't decide if I'd rather be the naked one discovering my boyfriend proposing to someone else or be the one being proposed to and having a naked girl tumble in. Actually, I *can* decide. When I say it like that, it's obvious. Better to be the *not* naked one. Gods, what I wouldn't give to have been a fly on that wall!

And wait. Just wait. That isn't even the best part. Guess what they decide to do? No, they didn't murder him, though it's still not too late for that. They say fuck him, and then they go on vacation together! On a trip that one of them had previously planned with the scumbag!

[explosion noise]

Is your mind as blown as mine? These two are queens! That feels like the ultimate revenge, doesn't it? Hey, jerk, we're dumping your sorry ass and the two of us are going to be best friends. A few mailing lists or stealing all his left shoes wouldn't hurt either.

So to hear what additional revenge they've done since, I bring to you—anonymously, of course—Queen Victoria and Queen Elizabeth.

Welcome, Queens. What an honor it is to have you on the show.

QUEEN VICTORIA: Hi, Thornies! Hi, Mandy! Oh, I can't believe I'm talking to you. I'm such a fan. Thanks for having us on the show!

QUEEN ELIZABETH: Hey, Mandy, what are your DMs like? Is it just, like, a 24/7 candy shop?

MANDY: Wouldn't you like to know.

QUEEN ELIZABETH: Oh shit, I knew it.

QUEEN VICTORIA: *Anyway*, what Queen Elizabeth and I have learned is that despite your fantastic and wonderful show, we've found that instead of serving the revenge dish hot or cold, the best dish of all is one never served.

MANDY: Uhhh—

QUEEN ELIZABETH: Yeah. What she said. Don't serve it.

MANDY: Come on—

QUEEN VICTORIA: As much as we like your show—because of course we do, Mandy, we're as Thorny as cactuses—

QUEEN ELIZABETH: Cactuses aren't horny.

QUEEN VICTORIA: *Thorny.* Anyway, our story is wild, but we didn't do any revenge. Not a single thing.

QUEEN ELIZABETH: Nope, not a lick. Licking was for before he became a cheating fuck.

QUEEN VICTORIA: [nervous laughter] So, um, sorry if we led you astray when we first wrote in.

MANDY: Well, it's still early. Maybe the dish can be served lukewarm.

QUEEN VICTORIA: No, no. No dishes needed. In fact, we've forgiven him. Because we found each other. Right, Queen Elizabeth?

QUEEN ELIZABETH: Yeppers. Chicks before dicks. Puss before wuss.

[pause]

MANDY: Are y'all serious right now?

QUEEN ELIZABETH: Super.

QUEEN VICTORIA: Yes.

MANDY: Really? This sucks! Y'all suck! The juiciest story ever, and it turns out y'all are a bunch of cowards? Come on, let me help you. I have plenty of ideas. For starters, I'll make a Lost Dog poster of him and spread it all over the internet. I promise it'll feel great.

QUEEN VICTORIA: No, no, we're good, thanks.

MANDY: You know I can't air this, right?

QUEEN VICTORIA: Oh! That's okay! No problem, we get it. Have to stay on brand and all that. Sorry to waste your time.

MANDY: Just a heads-up that I'll be doing my own episode about what happened. Maybe episodes, plural, depending on what I dig up.

QUEEN VICTORIA: No, you can just air what we've said. We thought it would be so interesting for your listeners, don't you think? A different perspective for them to chew on.

QUEEN ELIZABETH: Yup. They'll chew it right up. You got us, right, Mandy? Lasses before asses?

MANDY: Nah, I think I'll do the other thing. Bye, girls!

QUEEN VICTORIA: Wait! We don't give you permission to use our—

[end call]

CHAPTER 10

While Olivia and Elle called in to *Dish Served Hot*—and I was sure they were killing it—I set out on my mission. First, I stopped by the lab to prepare some cleaning solutions. Luckily, no one paid me much attention, so I was able to finish quickly without having to explain the empty backpack coming in and full backpack going out. And I didn't have to tell anyone I was sick or leaving for the day—no one liked me, so no one would miss me. Never thought that would be something I was grateful for.

Back at Tucker's, outside the front door, I put gloves on and tightened an N95 over my face until it hurt. Then I popped earbuds in and cranked the music so loud I couldn't hear my own thoughts.

With a deep breath, I entered.

The pranks looked so different in this light. Petty. Childish. But none of that mattered now. The only objective today was cleaning. No sweat (both meanings, because sweat could pick up skin cells and leave a trace amount of DNA).

I pulled my gloves tighter and, after telling myself to pretend it was just another day at the lab, I got to work.

One would think having a single goal would make it easy to focus, but it only meant my mind wandered. I tried not to think about Tucker or the fact that he was dead, but how could I when I was here? Everything made me think of him.

Even with the N95, I'm getting a whiff of poop. Tucker couldn't smell anything. And he definitely can't smell or see or do anything now.

I switched over to a *Dish Served Hot* episode, which required just enough of my brain to do the trick.

Scrub, scrub, scrub as if our lives depended on it. Because they did.

· · · ·

Upstairs, it became more difficult to forget Tucker. Because as I walked into the bedroom, I realized the closet door was still open (as were the windows, which was a blessing).

Without allowing myself a second to think, I closed my eyes and inched forward, my hands out in front of me. Soon, I contacted the wall, then felt my way over to the closet door, which I swiftly shut.

Out of sight, out of mind? Maybe?

I hurried into the bathroom and closed the door behind me, trying to put more distance between me and the body. I heaved over the toilet for a few seconds until the nausea passed.

Then I focused. This was the most important place, with Olivia's DNA everywhere. I cranked the volume even higher on *Dish Served Hot* and went to work.

And finally, I did it. My mind grew so numb I cleaned in a trance, only thinking about how there were fingerprints on the counter and toiletries, which solution to use for that, et cetera.

An unknown amount of time later, I felt a tap on my shoulder.

I screamed into my N95 as I flung my rag and spray bottle into the air.

CHAPTER 11

My first thought: Was Tucker alive? Maybe we'd been wrong. Or maybe Tucker had come back as a zombie.

I whirled around, ready for anything. Or so I thought. Turned out, I was wrong.

I came face-to-face with a badge. The person behind it was using his free hand to cover his nose with a handkerchief because of the smell.

I felt stupid. This was a much more reasonable conclusion than what I'd been thinking. And this was so much worse than Tucker, even Zombie Tucker.

I suddenly felt faint. Was it from the cleaning solutions? Oh wait, I had a mask on. No, I was just panicked out of my mind.

Primary goal by a long shot: keep him away from the closet. I couldn't do it so forcefully that it backfired, signaling that I knew about the body, but also, I could not, under any circumstances, let him discover Tucker's body after he'd just discovered me masked and gloved and cleaning with bleach—if that happens, I might as well walk myself into the jail cell.

His mouth moved, but all I could hear was the podcast that was still playing in my ears. Christ, I couldn't let him see what I was listening to.

I removed my gloves, then juggled them with my phone

and earbuds, trying to pause the podcast, only to play it on speaker instead.

"TODAY'S EPISODE IS A PERFECT EXAMPLE OF OUR PODCAST NAMESAKE, WHY REVENGE IS BEST AS A DISH SERVED HOT—"

And of course it was still blasting. Fuck. Could this get any worse?

Before he or I could say anything, Frogger #2 jumped between us, and he stepped back in alarm, his hand and the handkerchief dropping to reveal his face.

Of course the detective was hot. Because I was forever the universe's punchline. The man here to bust me for a murder I didn't commit but admittedly looked super guilty for just had to be tall, buff, and handsome. Not dark, though—he had dirty-blond hair that was so fluffy and ruffled I wanted to run my hands through it. The sleeves of his ivory button-down shirt were rolled up to reveal his defined forearms. Maybe I wanted to run my fingers along those, too, right before moving on to the sharp angle of his stubbled jaw.

"Do you live here?" he asked. Even his voice was hot. A deep, sexy but smooth baritone.

"No, my boyfriend does," I answered in a high, squeaky voice. Should I have said he was my ex? Or would that make me look even more suspicious?

"I'm Detective Birch."

Birch, like the tree. He certainly looked like a tree. And I would definitely climb that tree.

Oh my god, I needed to focus. This was a make-or-break situation. Life or death.

Stop thinking about trees. Stop thinking about his name. Call him something else, anything else. Detective McSpicy? He wasn't a McDonald's special. Detective McMoist? Oh no. What was wrong with me? McHottie? No. Birch. He was Detective Birch.

And Detective Birch was looking at me expectantly. I didn't want to introduce myself. Did I have to?

"Nice to meet you," I said in lieu of any information. "What can I do for you?"

"We received a flood of calls about bad smells emanating from this unit"—a body and feces everyfuckingwhere will do that—"and also about a lot of people coming and going."

Oh shit, did the neighbors see us coming in last night? Wait, could they have seen the killer?

"I was sent to check things out," he continued. "Do you know where your boyfriend is?"

Time to pull something out of my ass (and not Tucker's floss or toothbrush, both of which I'd cleaned). "I haven't heard from him either. That's why I stopped by. I have a key because I'm his girlfriend. I didn't break in, and he's not here, definitely not"—*get it together!*—"and then when I saw how filthy it was, I started cleaning for him."

He breezed past my incriminating awkwardness and asked, "Is this level of filth normal for him?"

What was I supposed to say? *No* would make it clear something was off, and *yes* would be inconceivable—I mean, there was an open bag of feces next to me.

"Is this normal for anyone?" I countered, hoping it was a good, innocent, in-between response that didn't give much away.

"Any idea what happened here?"

I gestured in the direction Frogger #2 had hopped off. "The frog."

"Frogs don't produce that much fecal waste."

Of course I got the one detective who knew about frog pooping volume and frequency. I shrugged. "He has a lot of frogs."

"What, a thousand?"

"Maybe he got a new puppy recently?"

"Are you guessing? Isn't that something you'd know?"

How could things be unraveling so quickly? I had to end this, now.

"We were in the process of breaking up."

His brow lifted in surprise. "Yet you're cleaning his condo for him?"

"Just because we're breaking up doesn't mean I can bear for him to live like this," I tried to say convincingly.

"How long has it been since you heard from him?"

"Several days."

"Does he do this often? Disappear?"

"I mean, yeah. It's partly why we're breaking up. Everything is always on his timetable, whatever he wants." What days we met up, how many girls he was sleeping with...

You know, I was doing pretty well if I could say so myself. Things were lining up.

"Could you come with me to the station and answer a few more questions?"

Shit yeah, I could. Whatever got him out of here quicker. I nodded, trying to do it in a normal way, though I suddenly couldn't remember what normal was. What was the right tempo? How many ups and downs were average? Thank god I still had my mask on—at least that covered most of my face, which felt stiff and fake despite my best efforts.

"Thank you..." He paused as if waiting for me to fill the space with my name, but I didn't want to, not if I could help it.

Instead, my mind rapidly formed a plan. If I went with him to the station, there were a million excuses to leave abruptly once there: family emergency, bathroom emergency, fake burst appendix. And then, yes, there were still a thousand more problems to solve, but at that point, Olivia and Elle could help. For now, my number one goal was to get this man out of here, and he'd handed me a way to do that on a silver platter.

I hurried out of the bathroom. And breathed a sigh of relief when the detective followed. Fifty steps to freedom.

But then, in the bedroom, he paused. "Did you hear that?"

I hadn't—my heartbeat was so loud it was in my ears—but I stopped moving and listened.

A soft thud sounded...*from the closet*.

I almost gasped but managed to bite my cheek instead. What the fuck—was Tucker alive? Was Zombie Tucker trying to get out?

Thud. The sound emanated from a spot close to the ground.

Oh no. It was even worse than that. I must have enclosed a frog in there. And unlike Tucker, frogs can smell, and this one did not like being stuck in an enclosed space with him, for good reason. Which meant I was thoroughly fucked.

The detective had already pivoted toward the closet. Each one of his steps was a step closer to my downfall. The fucking frog was the Jenga piece that would topple it all, and Detective McHottie was about to yank it out. I'd done this to myself. If I hadn't been petty, none of this would have happened.

Was there anything I could do to stop the oncoming tsunami? If I refused to let him open the door or if I stood in his way, it would only support my guilt. I could rush past him and crack the door just enough for the frog to hopefully hop out, but if he saw the body, again, it would only make me look more suspicious.

I needed a miracle. Something out of this world to save me. How could one person have this much bad luck in such a short amount of time? Wasn't I due for some *good* luck?

I held my breath.

The detective reached a hand toward the doorknob.

Kathryn's Fifth Law of Luck: Everything that can go wrong will go wrong. And no one's coming to save you.

CHAPTER 12

"I didn't hear a thump."

It was a terrible argument, maybe the worst one I could have thought of, but that was what came out of my mouth. No one was coming to save me, but I still had to try something, anything.

His hand continued reaching for the doorknob.

"But if you did hear one, it was probably just a frog. Like I said, he has a bunch of them. All over the condo. Free-range frogs—you know, like free-range chickens? Tucker's an animal rights activist. He likes to save the frogs from my lab. Well, not my lab. I don't have a lab. And I don't work with frogs."

Finally, McHottie paused and turned to face me. "You work in a lab? What kind of lab?"

Oh shit. I wasn't supposed to be revealing any personal information. I had to start thinking before I spoke despite my brain having turned to congee. "A lab at Harvard," I said simply, hoping it made me sound like I was a respected scholar and not a would-be murderer. He didn't need to know I was just a postdoc, and a failing one at that. I especially tried to sound scholarly as I said, "You know, you probably shouldn't go in there. Frogs can be dangerous, especially toward strangers."

He raised an eyebrow at me and I couldn't help noticing a

pale scar above it. "Are you sure you have your facts straight?" Again, had I gotten the one frog-enthusiast detective? But he apparently wasn't suspicious of me, not yet—there was no reason to be other than the poop everywhere, which isn't a crime unless he could prove intent to smear—because he followed up by saying, "Maybe the frogs are just scared of *you*."

He smirked, and I grabbed the lifeline with both hands and feet.

"Well, yeah! Probably because I'm scared of them! Deathly! Another reason we were in the process of breaking up! Just leave the frog in there, okay? He's fine."

Leaning into my performance, I darted forward, grabbed the human tree's hand, and pulled him away from the closet. "Don't make me confront another frog today. Please." I poured my desperation into that last word.

He laughed as if we were teasing each other, borderline flirting, and in any other situation, I would have been thrilled.

His eyes softened and I thought I'd won, but then he said, "Sorry, I can't leave him in there. Just one sec, okay?"

Great. He was a frog rights activist just like I pretended Tucker was.

Thus far, I'd been pulling the detective millimeter by millimeter, but it was only because he was letting me. As soon as he decided he had to let the poor frog out—which, fine, made him a good person—he became the birch that he was, suddenly immovable.

He took a step, this time pulling me with him easily like I was on wheels, as though it took no extra effort to move with a desperate person trying to anchor him in place. One who was fighting for her freedom.

The universe was giving me the finger now.

He opened the closet door. I screamed—not entirely sure why, but luckily, it matched my I'm-scared-of-frogs cover story.

The door was barely ajar before the frog hopped out. I

screamed again, this time partly from relief. Maybe he wouldn't open the door the rest of the way. Maybe my bad luck had finally run out.

"Okay, let's go," I insisted, running away from the frog and toward the hallway. "I've had enough frogs for today."

But the detective didn't follow. He wasn't even looking at me. He was...sniffing.

Oh no.

My N95 was still on, but I hadn't been able to get the rotting smell out of my head since we found Tucker's body.

It was already over. The detective knew that smell better than most. He knew exactly what was in there.

I had a narrow window in which to craft my narrative here. What would Elle the author do? Forget that—what would Gillian Flynn do?

The detective was opening the door wider. I couldn't pull him away again. That would be too suspicious.

I thought that in moments like these, time was supposed to slow. You were supposed to become superhuman, your brain flipping into overdrive, your fight-or-flight survival instincts kicking in. But my world sped up. My mind was too slow and muddled to do anything about the incoming shitstorm.

The door opened the rest of the way, creaking on its hinges. From where I was, I couldn't see inside. But I could see Detective Birch's eyes widening, then focusing on me as he turned in my direction slowly. Suspiciously.

If there was ever a time to call upon my acting skills, it was now. I tried to think about neutrons, pH 7, Switzerland—anything to help my face look neutral.

He was staring at me. Studying me.

"What, did you find another frog?" I managed to say with only a slight tremble in my voice. I hoped he'd think the wobbles were from my fear of frogs.

The detective continued to wait silently. He wanted me

to make the next move. His eyes casually traveled from my N95 to my now ungloved hands, then back toward the bathroom, where my plethora of unlabeled cleaning supplies were waiting.

I didn't have many options. And so, as if Agatha Christie herself was pushing me, I did the only sensible thing I could think of.

Pretending to be curious and confused, I took a few tentative steps sideways until I could see inside the closet. As soon as the corpse was visible, I screamed—a bloodcurdling one even louder than when I had seen Tucker for the first time, no acting necessary.

Then I ran straight for the body, tripping on the carpet and falling face-first into it.

CHAPTER 13

The falling was not part of the plan.

Because even with the mask on, that almost made me throw up. But I didn't because there wasn't any time.

I had to administer CPR. To get more of my DNA onto the body, to react how a normal semi-ex-girlfriend would upon seeing the corpse of her semi-ex-boyfriend, to explain any broken ribs and other evidence from the first time.

But like yesterday, strong arms pulled me backward, only they did so now before even one compression.

This was life or death, much too literally. This was for my freedom.

With more strength than I thought possible, I swung my arms down and pushed my hips back, the force and surprise breaking my body free from the detective. I lurched forward with no control, which was exactly how I delivered the next two compressions.

But two was all I managed before he pulled me back again.

Would the detective notice he didn't hear any ribs cracking even though the autopsy would show they were broken? Were two compressions enough to break bones?

I struggled against his hold, an act at first, but then the walls began closing in. The terror that had appeared with the frog's thumps was now consuming me.

Tucker is dead. Even more so today, his body stiffer, colder, and more bloated. The only man I'd ever loved, truly gone. Maybe a piece of me still believed up until this moment that I'd been mistaken, and maybe after we left, he'd stood up and made a sandwich, took a shower, then went to bed.

My vision was blurring. It was all too much. My face was soaked with tears I hadn't even realized were coming down. I gave in to it, crying and heaving as the detective pulled me out of the closet and down the stairs.

Then the self-damning accusations flooded in.

I wished Tucker dead, and now he is. Maybe it was even my fault. I didn't listen, didn't believe, didn't let him stay when he said he was in danger.

It wasn't hard to let the sobs, the dark thoughts, the ghost of Tucker consume me.

CHAPTER 14

I was operating in a numb zombie state that had been ironically brought on by the absence of Zombie Tucker.

When the detective walked me into the police station, everyone looked over at us, staring. I wasn't sure why—I wasn't in handcuffs.

And thank god I wasn't given the circumstances, though I *was* now in an interrogation room—harsh fluorescent lighting, a two-way mirror, an incessantly ticking clock. And despite having just stumbled upon my ex-boyfriend's body, they didn't bring me a blanket or snack, not even a cup of water—a bad sign.

The situation couldn't be worse if it had been planned by my mortal enemy. I had motive, my DNA was everywhere including on the dead body, and we'd stolen evidence from the crime scene. I was fucking killing it, wasn't I? Killing everything except for the victim. All I had to do now was keep the detective from learning the pieces he didn't already know.

Which only reminded me he knew about the DNA and sort of knew about the motive, so…I was already in deeper doo-doo than the crime scene was.

Kathryn's Fifth Law of Luck: proven. Statistical significance: way too fucking high.

And since everything that could go wrong was going to, all I could think about were the places I hadn't cleaned yet. Now there'd be cops crawling all over picking up everything we left behind—I could already see CSI holding up one of my long, black hairs with their tweezers.

I almost jumped out of my skin when Detective Birch spoke for the first time since we left the condo.

"Can you please remove your mask? I need to ask you some questions."

My palms immediately grew damp with sweat as I took the N95 off. I suddenly felt naked, even more naked than when I'd interrupted Olivia's proposal.

But his first question wasn't what I was expecting.

"How are you holding up, Ms…?"

Was there any way to avoid saying my name a third time? Maybe I could still use my acting skills to get out of here. Which side was the appendix on again? How could I remember the name McBurney's point from anatomy class but not where it actually was?

When I'd concluded there was no way out, I finally answered. And I already knew where this was going. "Hu."

"You."

No, that's a different Chinese surname.

"You were asking for my last name. It's Hu."

"Oh. Of course. And your first name?"

I couldn't lie, could I? He'd figure that out soon enough and it'd look suspicious. "Kathryn."

He nodded. "Kathryn, Ms. Hu, what's the best number I can reach you at?" He retrieved a notebook from his front pocket and flipped it open.

Again, seeing no way out, I answered, and he wrote each digit down carefully.

"Can I get a DNA sample from you?"

"Why do you need that?" I replied before realizing how incriminating it sounded.

"Standard procedure. Nothing to worry about."

He'd expect to find my DNA on the body and around the condo, so maybe I was fine? And since I really hadn't done the crime, wouldn't this only help me? "Okay."

When he produced a cotton swab, I obediently opened my mouth and hoped I wasn't shooting myself in the foot (origin: WWI, when a soldier would shoot himself in the foot to avoid battle).

"Thank you." He stowed the completed sample, then returned to his notebook. "When did you arrive at the condo?"

I figured I could be truthful in answering that. "Maybe about thirty minutes before you got there?"

His tone didn't change as he asked, "Did you know the body was in the closet?"

I didn't want to lie if I didn't need to, but I also didn't want to implicate myself by wording things too weirdly, like, *Explain what you mean by the word "know."*

"Body? You mean Tucker? That was Tucker, wasn't it? Is he okay? Did you call the paramedics?"

His face was completely devoid of any emotion as he said, "Ms. Hu, your boyfriend is dead."

What was I supposed to do? Scream? Cry? Faint? I tried to pretend like I'd just found out. A tiny part of me felt like I had since it was the first true confirmation that Tucker was gone.

"He can't be." I shook my head over and over. "He's young. Healthy. He worked out all the time." *By lifting weights, and by weights, I mean girls, other girls that he was having sex with.*

"Ms. Hu, did you know the body was in there?" he asked again.

I continued shaking my head.

Satisfied, he pivoted seamlessly, no change in expression or tone. "Where did you get those cuts and bruises on your fore-arms?"

Shit shit shit. Did they look like defensive wounds? I snatched my arms back, only to realize it made me look suspicious. So I stuck them back out.

Should I talk about a boxing class? That was easily verifiable. I slipped and fell? A weak and obvious lie.

I blurted out the truth. "The frogs. I was chasing them around and banged my arms." I pointed to the cut on my left wrist. "Edge of the nightstand. And, um, the dresser." I pointed to a bruise just starting to darken on my right forearm. There were more, but I hoped that would be sufficient.

"I thought you were scared of the frogs. Why were you chasing them?"

Why did I think I could do this? I couldn't. I should have let Olivia clean the condo like she'd offered. Because then she would be the one sitting here. She was the craftiest, the most poised, the best bullshitter. The lawyer. The one who could find her way out of this. Though if I had gone on the podcast instead of her, I would have botched it. So at least we had that going for us. Thank goodness, too, since I was royally bungling my end of things. And at least I was only hurting myself, I suddenly realized. I'd been the only one caught, not Olivia or Elle. No need to drag them into this with me. Maybe Tucker hiding his relationships and avoiding social media would ironically benefit us in the end.

"Ms. Hu?"

Don't say we. "I hated that the frogs were all over the condo. I used a broom to try to corral them into one place so they couldn't keep surprising me."

"You thought trapping them in the closet was better? And you didn't see the body in the process?"

"I didn't put that frog in there. I was trying to corral the others in the office."

It was only a matter of time before he asked me the question we'd been circling. The one I should be able to answer with certainty, no hesitation or guilt, but I wouldn't be able to because I'm me.

In elementary school, when the teacher was trying to figure out who had eaten a bunch of Jenny's birthday cupcakes before they were passed out, my ears turned pink and my face flushed even though I hadn't done it. Luckily, Jason had eaten so many that he'd vomited pink frosting all over the carpet, which was much more incriminating than my pink face. But because of my behavior, Mrs. Price thought I'd eaten one or two, so I still had to get a note signed by my mom. My mother had said at the time that this trait of mine would be the death of me. It had been annoying, for sure, but the *death* of me? I thought she'd been laughably wrong.

Until now.

"Did you have anything to do with his death?"

My palms were already sweaty. My cheeks hot. And when he asked that question, my body turned into a furnace.

"No. Absolutely not." Yet somehow it sounded like I was saying the exact opposite. It was the cupcakes all over again. Except this time, I might be the one vomiting all over the floor.

Unsurprisingly, the detective didn't look convinced.

Desperation only made my cheeks hotter, my palms damper.

"I'll take a lie detector test," I blurted out. There were questions and answers that would make me look even guiltier, but that didn't matter. What mattered was, lie detectors don't work. They're gameable. And as a scientist, I knew how to game them.

"She will *not* be doing that," a voice called from the doorway.

I turned to see Olivia enter, her sensible dark heels clicking away as she hurried toward me in a sleek updo and chic pantsuit.

No. I wanted to protect her. What was she doing here?

Detective Birch stood. "May I help you?"

"I'm her attorney."

Maybe this was okay. If she was here as my lawyer, the detective wouldn't necessarily figure out her connection to Tucker.

"How did you know she was here?" he asked. That was a question I was curious about myself.

"You should have allowed her to call me before she even stepped foot in this room," Olivia countered.

I relaxed, my shoulders lowering. It was going to be okay. I hadn't admitted to anything and Olivia was here now, taking over.

"We're leaving." She gestured to me and I stood.

Detective Birch held a hand up in protest. "We're not done—"

"Are you charging my client?"

"Well, no—"

"Good day, Detective."

"Detective," I said, bowing my head in his direction as Olivia held the door open for me. I just barely managed to not add *McHottie* at the end of it.

"We'll know more sooner or later, Ms. Hu," McHottie called after me. "It'll be better for you if you tell us now."

Olivia ushered me out the door before I could say anything.

• • • •

I followed Olivia to her shiny silver Lexus parked outside.

"I can't believe he let you go," she said with an exhale.

"What? You seemed so confident—"

"And that was my only strategy! You were in such hot water!" (From the 1500s, likely having to do with throwing boiling water down on castle stormers.)

Why *had* he let me go? One would think he had enough to arrest me on the spot. But Olivia changed the topic swiftly as she reached for the driver's side door.

"Why is that detective so hot?"

"Is he? I hadn't noticed."

Olivia smirked. "You're blushing."

"Hot detective? What?"

"Hi, Elle," I said just as she poked her head out, leaning over from the passenger's seat. Guess I was relegated to the back.

"We were already together when we realized you were down here," Olivia explained as she got in.

"And how, by the way?" I asked as we buckled up.

"The podcast was a disaster, so we were debriefing," Elle said with a wave of her hand.

A disaster? Well, shit. "Not how you got together," I said. "How did you know what happened to me?"

Olivia started the car and pulled out. "You weren't responding to my texts. So I checked Tucker's security footage and saw the detective—"

"Wait, wait, wait," I interrupted. "How did you get access to that? Did you get into his laptop?"

"Yeah, just this morning. The password was a combination of his and your name, the word *forever*, and your birthday," Olivia said with a shudder.

"What?" I had too many questions.

But Olivia wasn't listening to me, just rambling on about the password. "So predictable. Just as stupid as can be. How was I even with this guy?"

Elle piped up. "Send me a copy of that footage so I can see this hot detective."

"No, we're obviously deleting all of the footage so it doesn't incriminate us," Olivia said matter-of-factly.

"Wait—" I started.

Olivia answered my question before I asked it. "I already checked and the footage from before our frog and fecal spree was deleted. A whole week is missing. But it picks back up two days before we get there."

Damn. This was looking more and more like murder. "Did

the killer know his password? Because that could narrow down—"

"Maybe, but the footage was also accessible with facial recognition. Which we didn't use for obvious reasons. But maybe they did."

"Before or after they…" I couldn't say it.

"I don't know."

After talking over each other nonstop, silence finally descended. Until I realized, "We could show the detective the footage from just today. Show that I didn't go in the closet before he got there."

Olivia was already shaking her head. "Then we'd have to admit we have his laptop. That's a crime in and of itself, and they'll think we killed him and deleted the missing chunk of footage."

"Right, of course." I needed to turn my brain on.

The car slowed to a stop at a red light.

"So now what?" Elle asked.

The light mixing with the fog cast an ominous glow over Olivia's face as she turned to us and said, "We solve the murder before Kat goes down for it."

This should have been the clincher, the turning point when we banded together, came up with a group name, cut our palms and shook with a blood pact.

"No," I said.

Olivia's foot pressed harder on the brake in surprise. "No?"

The last thing I wanted was to face this alone like I've had to face everything else, but— "No," I repeated.

The car was silent as the red light turned green, now bathing us in a bright, eerily optimistic glow. I took it as a sign that I was doing the right thing.

Concerned, Elle started to ask, "Kat, are you—"

"Please don't."

I didn't want her to ask me if I was okay because I was most certainly not. I wanted to claw my skin off, jump out of the car, and run down the street screaming. This day had been one unbelievable, excruciating event after another, and now that my adrenaline was coming down, reality was crashing in and my mind wouldn't stop. Why hadn't I gone to the condo immediately last night, right after we'd settled on the plan? The detective likely wouldn't have come in the middle of the night. Why hadn't I cleaned faster, gotten out of there like my life depended on it—which it turned out, it kind of did? Why hadn't I just forgotten Tucker to begin with, putting him out of my life forever? It wasn't like those pranks made me feel any better. Why had I even talked to him in that hot sauce aisle that first day? I should have listened to my gut telling me he was too good to be true. Everything good always was.

A loud honk made me jump so high it felt like I was popping up out of my body and my soul was looking down into the car. We'd been sitting at the green light too long. Olivia took her foot off the brake but merely crossed the intersection and pulled off to the side of the road. The car behind us zoomed by with a finger out the open window.

"Fuck off!" Elle yelled.

Then Olivia's car was silent again except for the ticking of the blinking hazards.

Neither Olivia nor Elle seemed to know what to do. Which, ironically, was precisely why I was spiraling. There was nothing to be done now.

"It's over," I said. "I give up. But it's only over for me. You two can save yourselves."

Surprise filled their faces.

Then Olivia looked at me warily. "It's not over."

"And we're not leaving you on your own," Elle said with an eye roll. "You can't get rid of us that easily."

"But there's no reason—"

"Kat, you were just about to sacrifice yourself to save us," Olivia said. "What makes you think we wouldn't do the same for you?"

I turned to Elle. "You were barely even involved with—"

"We're in this together, whether you like it or not."

Before, I didn't even have anyone to call on a bad day at work, and now I had two friends willing to put themselves in danger to save my ass from going down for a murder I didn't commit? It was too difficult to comprehend, especially when my mind was already mush, and the overwhelming emotions had no choice but to form into tears that embarrassingly ran down my face.

Olivia and Elle both turned and leaned into the space between the seats.

Again, with even more resolve this time, Olivia said, "We're going to solve the murder. Together."

Our eyes met. Similar to yet completely different from that moment in the bar when we'd declared revenge on Tucker. This time, though, we were trying to save our—my—ass. And this time, we didn't need any words. All three of us nodded in agreement. A pact to keep each other's secrets and to dig into Tucker's clandestine life as a team.

Unfortunately, we didn't know at the time that in doing so, we would also be digging our own graves.

Dish Served Hot Podcast Transcript— Episode 88

[Podcast theme song plays, sung by creator, host, and star Mandy Thorne]

MANDY THORNE: Okay, do I have the best episode for y'all today. The tea for this one is hot! Steaming, bubbling, scalding hot! It just may be THE juiciest, most hilarious revenge story we've ever had on the show, Thornies! Are y'all ready? Y'all aren't ready. But I'll tell you anyway. You will not see the twists and turns coming for this one!

So! Here's the scoop. Two girls realized they were dating the same asshole because one of them stumbled into the other's proposal. For reals! And I believe one of them was naked? The one who stumbled in, not the one being proposed to. That'd be weird, a naked proposal. Anyhoo, how does that even happen? I can't decide if I'd rather be the naked one discovering my boyfriend proposing to someone else or be the one being proposed to and having a naked girl tumble in. Actually, I *can* decide. When I say it like that, it's obvious. Better to be the *not* naked one. Gods, what I wouldn't give to have been a fly on that wall!

So, back to the girls, what do they decide to do? ABSOLUTELY NOTHING! So then why are we featuring them on the show? Just you wait. You'll want to listen to the end for this one.

Please welcome Queen Victoria and Queen Elizabeth.

[music]

MANDY: Welcome, Queens.

QUEEN VICTORIA: Hi, Thornies! Hi, Mandy! Oh, I can't believe I'm talking to you. I'm such a fan. Thanks for having us on the show!

QUEEN ELIZABETH: Hey, Mandy, what are your DMs like? Is it just, like, a 24/7 candy shop?

MANDY: Wouldn't you like to know.

QUEEN ELIZABETH: Oh shit, I knew it.

MANDY: So, girls, do tell. What kinds of delicious pranks did you pull on this bastard?

QUEEN VICTORIA: Despite your fantastic and wonderful show, we've found that instead of serving the revenge dish hot or cold, the best dish of all is one never served.

MANDY: Are you kidding me right now? *You* contacted *me* about being on *Dish Served Hot*, just so you could come on with this boring baloney?

QUEEN VICTORIA: We found each other. Right, Queen Elizabeth?

QUEEN ELIZABETH: Yeppers.

MANDY: Wait, are you saying—

QUEEN VICTORIA: We're—

QUEEN ELIZABETH: Horny. Licking puss.

MANDY: Whoa, okay. I know this show isn't PG, but still. So you're saying you two got together instead? That's hot! What a story! I guess you came on the show not because you wanted to share about your nonexistent revenge, but because you found love out of it? How sweet!

QUEEN VICTORIA: We thought it would be so interesting for your listeners. A different perspective for them to chew on.

QUEEN ELIZABETH: Yup. They'll chew it right up. Lasses before asses. Chicks before dicks. Puss before wuss.

MANDY: That's beautiful, ladies. And I'm sure I speak on behalf of all Thornies when I say congratulations. We already ship you, and we hope you'll come back with an update sometime. Fuck that guy!

[music]

MANDY: Okay, wait. Stay with me, Thornies. You thought that was the final twist? Well, it wasn't. I'm about to play for you what happened once we stopped the official interview for the show. But I always keep recording, and thank gods I did. Because what we got will shock you. And don't worry—while they didn't want to share it at first, I went back and asked them to reconsider, and after I guaranteed their anonymity, they agreed. I'm sure you've noticed they're using voice modulators, so, yeah. And obviously their names have been changed. So sit back, relax, and listen to this…

[music]

MANDY: And we're clear. [beat] Thanks for coming on the show, even if it was to pass on the *boring* lesson of forgiveness. Though that other twist was a fun surprise.

QUEEN VICTORIA: Sorry. We led you astray.

MANDY: About what? Hold up…did you lie about getting revenge?

QUEEN VICTORIA: Yes. The best dish of all is one served hot.

MANDY: Oh my gods! Why did you lie? Wait. [gasp] What did you do?

QUEEN VICTORIA: Sorry. I can't.

MANDY: Don't you want to tell me? Just a little bit?

QUEEN VICTORIA: We're good.

MANDY: Oh shit, it must be *really* devious if you don't want to share even off the record. How could you keep this from me? Especially after it seems like my show inspired you, did it not?

QUEEN VICTORIA: Yes. I'm such a fan. But I'm sorry. We can't.

MANDY: You're really not going to tell me anything?

QUEEN VICTORIA: No. Sorry.

MANDY: Are y'all serious right now?

QUEEN ELIZABETH: Super.

QUEEN VICTORIA: Yes.

[click]

MANDY: So that was the end of our discussion, but I think you all heard what I heard. There is so much more to this story than meets the eye. It's the iceberg that sank the Titanic. So much more underneath, ready to kill even the most innocent love. Jack and Rose forever, am I right? So! Guess what? Y'all are in for a treat! We are doing so many unprecedented things with this episode, and it's only the—you guessed it. Tip of that doggone iceberg. But this is an iceberg you'll like. Like iceberg lettuce—delicious, cheap, keeps you trim. Instead of doing my usual episodes, this season is going to be something new. Something so frickin exciting I can barely hold it in anymore! [squeal]

This season, *Dish Served Hot* is turning into an investigative series. We are going to figure out what Queen Victoria and Queen

Elizabeth did, and we will be reporting back to you wonderful Thornies about *allllll* their salacious deeds. I'm gonna be a journalist, y'all!

I'm already working on the next episode, and you *don't* want to miss it. This gets so juicy you're gonna need a bib!

Stay tuned! Love y'all, Thornies! Kisses and hugs.

CHAPTER 15

"One per person," Elle said as she passed burner phones to first Olivia, then me.

We'd stopped at a gas station on the way home, and we were now huddled in Olivia's townhome with the curtains drawn. Since her garage was attached to the house, we slipped inside without being spotted by anyone.

Holding the shiny black flip phone in my hand brought me back to when I was a child with my first emergency cell phone from my parents, which I was only allowed to use "in case of kidnapping," as my mother always said. Which only emphasized the gravity of our current situation.

"The first official meeting of the Ex-Girlfriend Murder Club is in session," Olivia said in complete seriousness.

"Ex-Girlfriend Murder Club?" Elle asked.

"That makes us sound like we're planning to *commit* murder," I couldn't help pointing out. "That just makes me—us—sound guilty."

Olivia tutted. "Don't either of you read mystery books? Murder Club implies that we're trying to *solve* the murder, not commit it."

Elle shrugged. "I hear the other meaning, too."

Olivia waved a hand. "Whatever. I like it. But moving on, first order of business, the detective suspects you, Kat."

"Anyone would suspect me, let alone a trained professional. I mean, *I* would suspect me if I didn't know the truth!"

Unruffled, Olivia remained calm as she asked, "Did you lie or mislead him at any point?"

I shook my head even though I wasn't sure. I suddenly couldn't remember any details from earlier.

"Good. That would be a crime." *Just another one to add to the list*, I couldn't help thinking. Oblivious to my thoughts, Olivia continued. "It's your right to say nothing. And that's what you should do, always, the whole time. Otherwise, he'll assume you're telling the truth for the questions you answer and you're hiding something when you're silent. Just say nothing. Both of you."

"We won't get to that," I said with more confidence than I felt. "It's just on me right now." Hence the burner phones and the extra steps to avoid being seen together. We didn't want them to connect the three of us, didn't want them to find out about Tucker's cheating. Keeping the motive a secret was our top defense (along with finding the real murderer).

Elle shook her head. "It's on all of us. You're not alone."

Olivia nodded. "We will get you out of this, Kat."

With a wicked grin, Elle added, "It's not rocket surgery."

Olivia's mouth also quirked up. "As easy as shooting a piece of cake."

Each malaphor felt like a hug, but I didn't share their confidence. I couldn't. Had they forgotten? We three were the same girls who had gotten ourselves into this mess to begin with. We were *inside Tucker's home* releasing frogs and glitter and smearing our DNA and poop everywhere while his corpse was rotting upstairs.

Yet, at the same time, a small part of me thought we might be able to pull this off. After all, Elle had called us the ultimate trio. Sure, that had been in the context of us *committing* a crime. But maybe if we put the lawyer, the writer, and the scientist together, we'd also have the necessary skill set to solve one. Besides, who knew Tucker better than the three of us?

Maybe we truly were the Ex-Girlfriend Murder Club. Maybe we could figure this out.

Regardless, there was no time for doubt. The clock was ticking—on my freedom, on our chance to save ourselves. We couldn't let Tucker screw us one last time from beyond the grave.

"Where do we start?" I asked.

• • • •

The answer to that was our only lead: his financials.

Which also opened a can of worms (possible fishing origin) that Olivia might have been trying to keep shut. But maybe the guilt from my taking her place to clean the condo or her desire to figure out what happened to Tucker had loosened her lips, because she willingly released the worms.

"I'm still working on getting into Tucker's bank account, and in the meantime, I've been racking my brain trying to remember everything he asked me. It honestly didn't stick in my mind because I didn't know it was about him, but I've written down what I recall." She passed a leather journal to me and I opened it as she continued talking. "Basically, I think he was in debt. A lot of it. And trying to claw his way out."

I was grateful for the summary because her notes were in shorthand.

"Most of his questions were about what was legal and what wasn't, but I don't know if he was asking that to make sure he was staying above the law or figuring out how to skirt it."

"Probably the latter," Elle muttered, and I nodded.

Since Olivia was so freely giving up information, I took the opportunity to ask one of the questions plaguing me. "Is it true that you gave him an ultimatum?"

"He told you that?"

I forced a nod. Then, figuring I would want to know if I were her, I added, "He said he felt stuck because he couldn't end things with you on account of your help—"

"Dick," Elle interjected.

"And then with the ultimatum—"

"*That's* why he proposed? Because he was using me for legal advice and didn't want to lose that?"

"Well, that's just what he told me," I said, knowing he would've never admitted if he indeed had strong feelings for Olivia. But she wasn't listening.

"It wasn't even an ultimatum! I just...wanted to know what we were doing. It had been two years, and..." She shrugged. "I just told him I was questioning his commitment, which, in retrospect, I don't know if I feel smart or stupid about. Like, I was right, but I also wasn't bright enough to see just how right, you know?"

"Stop it," I said, both to her and to myself because I was having similar thoughts.

"This is all on him," Elle said adamantly. "No blaming ourselves for anything, got it?"

Olivia sighed. "When I saw the rose petals and candles that night, I remember feeling dread." She laughed. "I hoped he was just going over the top to ask me to move in, which is laughable now, knowing he would have *never* done that—"

"On account of all the cheating," I said through bitter, gritted teeth.

"Given how I was feeling, I honestly wasn't expecting a proposal. Nor was I expecting his half-naked girlfriend to interrupt."

"Twice," I added, sharing a look with Elle, who raised an eyebrow and said, "You know, Liv, I think it's only fair if you pop a titty right now."

Olivia laughed, then said to Elle, "To be fair, we didn't actually see any of your goods."

Nope, just mine.

"Isn't lingerie weird?" Elle mused. "Like, on *Love Island*, the girls sit around all day in barely there bikinis, then when they go to the Hideaway, they put on lingerie that covers up even more than their swimsuits. Sometimes it feels like a whole thing to squeeze into those complicated webs just for him to take everything off. Let's go back to trench coats."

Olivia and I chuckled.

"And rant over," Elle said quickly. "Back to the financial trenches."

Olivia nodded. "I think the place to start is Tucker's work. Based on the questions he was asking me, I suspect he was doing something shady there, possibly to cover his debts. Maybe we can find out what that was."

"Meaning?" I asked, already knowing where this was going and dreading it.

"I have a plan…"

• • • •

Ten minutes later, I found myself saying, "No. This is a terrible idea." I was 100 percent against Olivia's plan.

"What do you mean? It's brilliant."

"Please, do tell me what's so *brilliant* about it."

Olivia perched a hand on her hip. "It's the best way to get the information we need."

"At huge unnecessary risk to the two of you." There had to be another option.

Elle, who had been mostly observing until now, piped up. "I'm in. It's not that big of a risk, Kat."

"And it's a good plan," Olivia added.

If anyone else had said those words, I would have joked,

Of course you think that, it's your plan! But when Olivia said it, I weirdly felt comforted, even if it was coming from one of the three mistress stooges. Though how much were we even to blame for what happened when it was the universe and the bad luck laws at fault?

"Kat, we're doing this," Olivia said.

"We *want* to," Elle added.

I looked from one to the other, taking in the determined set of Olivia's jaw and the fire in Elle's eyes. I would do the same for them. So why was I resisting?

"Okay," I said, jumping on the bandwagon (origin: when bandwagons would carry musicians and politicians to a rally with the intent of getting others to follow). "Thanks for doing this."

Olivia clapped her hands together. "Let's divvy it up, then—who's stalking who?"

"Whom," Elle corrected, an instinctual response.

"Whom is stalking who?" Olivia amended.

Elle laughed.

"We're not *stalking* them," I felt the need to add, mostly to ameliorate my own guilt at what we were about to do.

"Research, recon, befriending," Olivia offered up instead.

"And maybe more," Elle said seductively. "I can take Tucker's boss. He seems like the kind of person who I might be able to use my special skills on." She waggled a lascivious brow.

"No, that..." *feels like we're using you for your body or something.* I couldn't say it out loud.

Elle shrugged. "I don't mind. Have you seen him? I'd be benefiting, too, babes." She turned her phone screen toward us, where his company photo was already pulled up.

"You don't have to do that if you don't want to," I said, even though she'd just said she was okay with it. But it felt like there was something else going on.

Olivia cleared her throat. "Sometimes when I'm at work, I

feel like I have to act a certain way, partly because I've done x, y, and z before and I feel like I have to stay consistent. But every situation is different."

I nodded, then added, "And I often feel pressured by social norms and what people expect of me to the point where it affects how I act." Did this even have to do with Elle anymore? "Anyway, you don't have to worry about that kind of stuff with us."

I would never have said anything if Olivia hadn't first, but I was glad we had when Elle let out a nervous laugh.

"Why do I feel like you two can see right through me?"

"The power of sharing a penis?" Olivia suggested.

Elle shook her head. "No way. Fuck his penis."

"We did. That's why we're here," I deadpanned.

They laughed. When it died down a second later, Olivia and I kept looking at Elle.

"I'm okay with it, really," she said slowly. "And I know I don't have to. I don't know why I do that. Except I also do."

She paused.

"You don't have to tell us if you don't want to," I said. Olivia nodded.

"No, I want to. I just…haven't told anyone this before. The reason I'm so…me…is because of my parents, and also a past relationship. Don't get me wrong, I like the way I am—"

"As you should," Olivia interjected.

"I just wish my journey to get here was different." Elle took a breath. "My parents were…absent. Cold. I don't think they wanted me if I'm being honest. I still remember the first time I realized it, when I was five, and I went to a friend's house for a sleepover and saw her parents not only hug her good-night, read her a bedtime story, and make her breakfast, but they did it for me, too. Whatever she asked for—*play cards with us, make us chocolate chip pancakes*, even *write me a new bed-*

time story with a princess, a talking hedgehog, and a pirate, they did it all, and happily. I just..." She trailed off, a rare moment of vulnerability showing through the wall of confidence.

I nodded, trying to signal to her that I knew where she was coming from. I couldn't bring myself to reach a hand out like she or Olivia probably would have, but I hoped she knew that the nod was my version of that.

"My whole childhood and as a teen, I was always on my own. I had to figure things out for myself—how to deal with assholes at school, how to do my hair, makeup, shave. I just felt so *alone*."

I nodded again, feeling these words even more. The reasoning may be different—for my parents and me, part of it was we didn't know how to communicate, the other part was a cultural gap—but the effects sounded the same.

Elle turned to me. "You too?"

I swallowed. "Yeah. And that's brutal as a kid—not feeling like you have anyone to turn to, to ask for help, to have your back."

Elle's eyes grew misty. "Exactly. That's why, when a cute guy showed interest in me, I fell hard. I leaned on him because I didn't have anyone else." Her face scrunched in disgust. "Fucking Chad turned out to be a steaming pile of abusive shit, but I stayed longer than I should have because I felt so dependent on him, you know?" She was clearly still beating herself up about it even now.

"You were young," Olivia said, her voice breaking. "And it's that asshole's fault, not yours. Just like how all of this is Tucker's fault."

"Completely," I said.

Elle closed her eyes and placed a hand over her heart to signal how much she appreciated our words. "Anyway, after Chad—"

"Fucking Chad," I said in support.

Olivia of course took it one step further. "No one good is ever named Chad."

Elle suppressed a smile. "Well, I didn't want to let anyone have that kind of power over me again. So, no serious relationships. All fun, no feelings. Makes Elle a happy, not-dull girl." She paused. "Is there a name for that? Changing the words of a saying?"

"I think that's just being a writer," I said.

Elle smiled—a rare genuine one that lit up her entire beautiful face.

"I'm sorry about Chad," I said.

"I think..." Elle sighed. "I think that all this stuff with Tucker has affected me in weird ways I'm still trying to understand. I feel like I shouldn't say that because it's so much worse for the two of you—"

"Elle," Olivia interrupted. "Your feelings are just as valid as ours."

I nodded. "And you *should* talk to us about it. We understand better than anyone else."

Our words seemed to get through because she said, "I thought I knew what I wanted, but I'm now realizing a lot of that was me trying to protect myself after an asshole. And it didn't even work! I didn't protect myself from the next asshole." Her eyes cast downward as she said, "Maybe I feel lost now, not knowing what I want."

"Maybe you don't need to know that right now," I said.

Olivia gave her a sad smile. "I sure as hell don't."

A comfortable, supportive silence fell over us.

Then, suddenly, Elle said enthusiastically, "There is something I know I want, though—to save Kat's ass!"

"Which we will," Olivia said with the utmost confidence. "Because we're the Ex-Girlfriend Murder Club."

I groaned, but the name was secretly growing on me.

In the end, we divvied up the targets as such: Olivia would try to befriend Tucker's boss since she could use her firm's connections to get to him; Elle would try to find a way to bump into the colleague Tucker worked with most; and I would see what I could learn from Tucker's secretary.

We were all going undercover.

Olivia ended with a piece of advice: "Subtle, ladies."

"Of course," I said.

Elle rolled her eyes. "No doi."

What could go wrong?

CHAPTER 16

I needed a baby. Not one of my own, thank god—that would take at least nine months—but it turned out, finding a random baby to borrow for a couple hours was a problem I never thought I'd have and didn't know how to solve.

I did the only thing I could think of: I answered an online ad looking for childcare. My intentions weren't the best, but they weren't the worst either, I tried to rationalize. The biggest question was, should anyone be leaving a child in my care, let alone a baby? Though new parents didn't have to pass a test to do it.

As soon as I arrived to pick up little Charlotte, I realized just how much of a hole I'd dug myself into. The crying had started before I arrived, and within three minutes of the handoff, I had snot and boogers in my hair, which Charlotte was tugging on with more force than seemed possible from those tiny hands.

People…want these? Why? As an only child, I had never been around babies, and as an almost perpetually single woman in her twenties, I hadn't thought about it much before. It just seemed like what one had to pursue when the time was right. But now, with this fluid-and-noise-producing bundle in my arms, I was wondering how the population managed to procreate, and so much.

"I'll just be taking her to a baby class," I told the mom, Hazel, who was barely listening as she tried to escape.

"Great, great, sorry, I'm late to—" She ran off before she'd even finished her sentence.

Just as well since I was holding Charlotte in front of me like a kettlebell. Then she started to squirm, and I had no choice but to hold her close to keep her from popping right out of my arms.

"Okay, okay," I repeated over and over in a panicked tone, the same way I talked to myself when I was working up the nerve to catch a spider in my apartment (a more common occurrence now that Tucker wasn't around).

I bounced up and down slightly like I'd seen on TV, but Charlotte only cried louder.

"Great," I muttered as I speed-walked the hundred feet to the Babyland Center I had never and probably would never set foot in again.

"Oh, poor thing is having a tough day, huh?" a voice said from behind me.

I couldn't help but think, *she's* having a bad day? All she has to do is eat, sleep, and poop. What I wouldn't give...

But maybe the arrival of this person was the start of my luck changing. My hope lifted as I turned around to face my new friend.

But it wasn't Tucker's secretary. Of course not. That would have been too easy. It was a mom heading into the same class as me, though, and as soon as she directed her attention onto Charlotte, the crying stopped. The relief was so overwhelming I didn't even care that Charlotte seemed to hate me. After all, I couldn't say I was her biggest fan either.

"First time?" the other mom asked, and I nodded. "Well, this is Maya, and I'm Anika."

I introduced myself and Charlotte distractedly, wondering if having a new friend would be an obstacle in my mission today. A mission that was feeling more and more ridiculous with each passing second.

This was too much, even for the Ex-Girlfriend Murder Club, right? What was I doing? And what if Olivia had gotten Tucker's secretary's schedule wrong? After all, I hadn't even known he had a secretary, much less that she had just gotten back from maternity leave and timed her lunch break so she could take her baby to this class.

But then, hallelujah, the first time in the last few weeks that anything had gone my way: a redheaded woman dressed in business casual approached, waving to Anika.

Anika made introductions, confirming this was the woman I'd been waiting for: Lacey Williams.

I shook her hand a tad too eagerly, then reined it in. Unfortunately, the class was starting, so we hurried inside.

The next hour was worse than when I got my first period during a presentation about our changing bodies. Look, maybe there was scientific research to back up the benefits of these baby classes. Or maybe these people were running a scam where you paid them to listen to terrible nonmusic while dancing with your baby—or a stranger's, in my case.

Or maybe it was different when it was your kid. Watching Lacey and Anika sway with their babies like there was nowhere else in the world they'd rather be did make me feel something.

Envy, I eventually realized. It had nothing to do with hypothetical kids of my own. It was the recognition of a mother-daughter relationship that could have been, with a mother who was actually excited about her child instead of having one out of cultural and societal obligation. Maybe this was what it looked like to be wanted, this swaying and connection and mommy-and-me time that no longer seemed as ridiculous as when I first got here. Maybe that conversation with Elle and Olivia the other day had stirred up a lot of long-buried feelings.

But there was no time to unpack that right now. Class was over, and my window was small. Lacey would need to drop her baby off at day care, then race back to work. At least Charlotte was more used to me now. We weren't best friends, but she wasn't howling bloody murder anymore. Maybe there really was something to these classes.

Sticking to Lacey and Anika like a shadow, I smiled and nodded as they talked about teething and Ferberizing and first words.

Lacey had to leave. I could tell. She was trying to find an opening to say goodbye as Anika chattered on obliviously.

"Maternity leave," I blurted. "Am I right?"

It was the only thing I could think of that could tie babies to work.

"Excuse me?" Anika said politely.

"Too short," I rambled. "It's so hard to go back to work. Especially if you don't like it. How do you feel about that? What do the two of you do?"

"Oh, I work at the city clerk's office! It's such an interesting job…" My brain tuned Anika out as she animatedly told us about all the boring documents she worked with. Lacey waited for her turn to answer, but Anika just loved her job too much. By the time she paused to take a breath, it was too late.

"Sorry, but I have to—" Lacey started to say.

"My boss just died," I burst out.

Crap. *I said subtle!* I heard Olivia yell in my head.

There was no time for subtle. Also, this was sadly the best I could do. My lack of social skills did not make me an ideal undercover agent.

"I'm just so distraught," I continued, which didn't require much acting. "It's also really confusing—just so many different conflicting emotions. He wasn't the best person, you see." All painfully true words.

Lacey had frozen when I'd first started talking, and now, she took a step closer. "How did it happen?"

"Tractor accident."

"What kind of work are you in?"

"Pharmaceuticals, but he worked on his family farm on the weekends, trying to ground himself." Wait, he was supposed to be a jerk. "I think he was stealing from them, though."

Yikes, this was already falling apart. Especially because Lacey's face remained neutral, barely reacting to my last statement. Did that mean she wasn't aware of Tucker's shadiness at work?

Time to try another route. "It's hard to know the real person, isn't it, even when you see them daily?" Still nothing. So I focused on the only thing I knew was true for her. "It's just so jarring to lose someone you worked closely with so suddenly." At that, finally, some emotion registered on her face. So I kept going. "It's hard to realize you're not going to see them every day, you'll never get to talk to them again, you'll never—"

"My boss died, too," she interjected. "So I get how you feel. I—I don't want to talk about it, though."

I wanted to blurt out, *you can and you should!* But I didn't want to come across too eager. Luckily, Anika jumped in. "He died? I'm sorry, Lace, I didn't know. That must be so hard on you." The deep sympathy in those last words hinted at a more-than-professional relationship.

Of *course* that was what was going on. I should have guessed that from Tucker by now, but here I was, still giving him the benefit of the doubt when he didn't deserve it.

Lacey's gaze met Anika's. "It is. So hard."

They had a conversation with their eyes, and in any other circumstance, I would have backed away silently. But I couldn't today, and I felt disgusting for it.

I opened my mouth to ask Lacey to go on, but then I closed

it. What kind of person was I becoming? This wasn't worth it. Maybe I should just go.

"Sorry," I said too loudly. "Sorry. I should— Sorry."

But before I could leave, Lacey circled my wrist with her hand. "Let's go talk."

• • • •

Lacey and I said goodbye to Anika, then buckled the kids into their strollers. (Lacey had to help me with mine.)

"Want to go to a coffee shop?" Lacey asked.

I gestured to the bench outside the class. "Oh, um, how about we talk here?" I didn't want to miss Hazel coming to pick up Charlotte.

After we settled in, Lacey asked, "So how are you feeling?"

"Shocked. Still processing. And you?"

"Same."

Now was as good of a time as any. "Did you ever notice your boss doing anything shady at work?" Her eyes whipped to me, upset, as if how dare I even suggest such a thing. "It's just that mine was—like I said earlier, stealing from the company— and I don't know how to feel about that."

"I thought you said he was stealing from his family farm."

Goddamn it, Kat. "And the company, too. Do you, by chance, have any experience with that?"

"Not at all," she said, and I completely deflated. This was going to be trouble. "He was incredibly kind, the one who would bring my favorite pastry every morning, who gave me extra maternity leave, who was the most understanding whenever Evie was sick or I needed to duck out early. And it wasn't just with me—he always brought cupcakes when someone was having a bad day, threw celebrations for recent promotions, and organized the office to chip in for flowers when someone was in the hospital."

In light of everything, I'd forgotten that side of Tucker. Or maybe I'd just recolored it, seeing it as a way for him to get on people's good sides and then into their pants. Because that was all it was, right?

None of that mattered. What mattered was that I didn't see a way to get through to Lacey. Not without...

"I was dating him," I admitted.

"Your boss?"

"*Your* boss. Tucker Jones."

"What? No—what? I don't believe you." Except she did, because how else would I have known his name? "Why are you here?"

"I'm sorry I lied to you. I..." I forced myself to swallow all comments about her and Tucker. "I think Tucker was stealing from the company. And I was hoping you could help me prove it. Did you ever notice anything suspicious? Or anything that didn't add up? Please, it's important. I hate to be the one to tell you this, but...he wasn't a good person, and just my association with him has put me in danger. I'm sorry to—"

Lacey stood, disbelief on her face. At that moment, Hazel arrived, handed me some cash, and grabbed Charlotte.

"Thanks for watching her!" She sped off, leaving me with a gaping Lacey.

"Oh, yeah, um, that's not my baby."

Lacey grabbed her stroller. I slipped a business card into her purse just before she fled. The fear in her eyes would haunt me forever.

I was the villain here. And I was thoroughly fucked.

CHAPTER 17

I was the only failure out of the three of us. No surprise there.

"I wasn't even trying to go the seducing route and he wouldn't stop staring at my tits!" Elle exclaimed a few nights later over thin-crust pizza at Olivia's. I felt bad we were always at her place, but her townhome was the biggest and offered the most cover. Elle had two roommates (a couple who owned the place and were renting her room out to her), and my place was so small we couldn't fit comfortably. And maybe I was embarrassed for them to see it, too. Olivia didn't seem to mind hosting, though. Elle and I already had favorite mugs here—*Big Dick Energy* for her (an office White Elephant gift Olivia got stuck with) and a baby chick with an eggshell cover for me (a gift from Celeste).

"So you got whatever you wanted out of him?" Olivia asked Elle, taking a sip out of her *For Fox Sake* mug in the shape of a wolf. I didn't really get the joke—I mean, I did, I just didn't get why it was so funny—but Elle had belly-laughed when she saw it.

Elle nodded as she broke a long string of cheese with an acrylic nail. "Whatever we need, he'll tell us. And he would've even if he didn't like my tits. I just mentioned the name Tucker Jones and he started ranting and raving."

Elle had found out what country club Tucker's coworker, Blake, belonged to, and she'd "waltzed right in," as she said. According to her, as long as you looked and acted like you belonged, no one would question you. She had been at the bar when he'd finished his weekly round.

"Unsurprisingly, Tucker was an asshole at work. Stealing clients, doing whatever it took to come out on top. Which, I mean, he did that in all aspects of his life, right? Always had to be on top, in control, even after I told him I can't finish unless I'm the one on top—"

"Aren't assholes usually rewarded in that line of work?" I interrupted. I still wasn't at a place where I could talk about *that.* Judging from Olivia's face, neither was she, though I was always the one to interrupt.

"Yeah, which is why Tucker was promoted over Blake."

"And he had a lot of leeway in the company," Olivia added. She'd had a meeting with Tucker's boss the other day. "But I'll get to that later—finish yours."

"So bossy." Elle raised an eyebrow. "Wonder how it worked for you two in the bedroom."

Olivia rolled her eyes, but I could see the doubt swirling beneath just like it had when I told her about the hot sauces. She was wondering if that was something Tucker secretly didn't like about her, if it had contributed to his cheating.

I gave her an awkward but firm pat on the hand. When her gaze met mine, it felt like we were connected, and I could feel her sadness and grief, and also her gratitude for my understanding. *Power of the penis*, I heard Olivia say in my head, but again, that wasn't right. Fuck the penis. *Power of friendship*, I thought with a smile as Olivia's mouth mimicked mine.

"Sorry," Elle said, looking from Olivia's face to mine. "I can stop with those jokes if you want."

"No," Olivia said immediately. "They're funny. And I want to be able to laugh about it. I'll get there."

Elle nodded and returned to the task at hand. "So, the lead I got from Blake: Balls In."

"What?" I said with a laugh.

"Balls In. The brand—"

"Of his underwear!" I finished, everything clicking together. "How could I forget?" That had, in a convoluted way, been the start of my troubles. If I hadn't wanted to destroy them so badly, maybe I wouldn't be in this mess.

"What about them?" Olivia asked.

"Tucker invested in the company. A shit ton. And was begging everyone he knew to also invest. Blake did, and he never saw his money again. He's convinced Tucker stole it."

"So did Tucker actually invest in Balls In?" I asked. "Or does Blake think it was just a front, a scam Tucker was running?"

"Actually, I think I can answer that," Olivia said. She stood and retrieved Tucker's laptop.

"You got into his bank account?" I asked, my heart leaping in excitement.

She grinned wickedly. "Last night. And not just his bank account, but everything. He has a password manager, but I needed the master password to get into that."

Having all your passwords in one place seemed like a terrible idea, though Tucker was not known for great ideas.

Elle asked the question I was wondering but didn't want to know the answer to: "What was it?"

"The password? What else from that idiot? It was my birthday mixed with Kat's name."

I shot a worried glance at Elle, who laughed.

"You think I'm feeling bad because I wasn't part of his password? I'd be worried if I was! We didn't have a birthday and anniversary kind of situation."

My shoulders relaxed. Honestly, I had mixed feelings about being part of his passwords myself. It was a sign that I did mean something to him, and that didn't make any sense with everything he did.

"I haven't had a chance to look at all this yet, but…" After a few minutes of typing, Olivia exclaimed, "Aha! He did invest in Balls In. And oh wow, yeah, it was a shit ton." She looked up from the laptop. "Leave it to Tucker to put all his balls in one basket."

I laughed.

Olivia continued scrolling. "I mean, we already knew this, but he was in massive debt. Humongous. Extraordinary."

"Over *underwear*?" Elle sputtered.

This is the next big thing, I could hear Tucker telling me in my head as he had many times. *It's going to revolutionize the underwear industry. Now, I know it's only for half the population, but still, once it gets out there, everyone's going to want it. I mean, your bra has a separate cup for each breast. Why not pouches for our junk?*

I'd thought he was partly kidding at the time. He'd been passionate, sure, but I thought he just really liked his underwear. I didn't think he was sinking his life savings into it.

"At least the name is kind of good?" I tried to joke. Balls In was better than Kangaroo or Pouch It or Cup Holder. Actually, scratch that. Cup Holder was kind of fun. Though I guess it wasn't a cup *holder*, just a cup—never mind.

"I mean, every company does something kind of random, right?" Olivia said. "No one's laughing at Squatty Potty now."

"Because they're successful!" Elle argued. "This isn't."

Olivia nodded. "Which is exactly why I think this is patient zero. Reason zero? Whatever, it's the root of all the problems. Ian, Tucker's boss, mentioned to me that one of his employees was losing a lot of money for them and it was looking suspicious enough that he was going to investigate, but then it suddenly wasn't a problem anymore. He was clearly talking about Tucker. So based on that, I think Tucker was scrambling to dig himself out of debt by doing some shady shit, including stealing from his company."

"All because of underwear," Elle said again.

Olivia sighed. "Do you expect anything else from our idiot ex-boyfriend?"

"No, no I do not," Elle said.

We chuckled. Mine cut off immediately when Olivia turned to me and asked, "So how did it go with Lacey?"

I deflected, not wanting to hear their disappointment yet. "The baby class was the worst. How do people go to those willingly?"

"Those are people who actually want kids, so..."Elle shrugged.

"You don't want kids?"

She looked at me like I'd just asked if she wanted to sleep with Tucker again. "Hell no."

Hearing her declare that opinion with such confidence inspired me.

"I don't think I do either," I said, surprising myself. But that was ridiculous, wasn't it? After spending just one class with Charlotte? Except this wasn't a new thing, not exactly. I'd never felt motherly instincts, never wanted to coo over a baby, and the idea of having someone depend on me made me sick to my stomach. Was there something wrong with me? Or did everyone have these feelings, but they changed once the child came along?

"When you grow up with parents who didn't want you..." Elle trailed off.

"Yeah," I said, so much more in that one word. It was starting to make sense. I would never do that to a child, have one when I wasn't sure, because I knew what that was like for the kid.

Elle came over and wrapped her arms fiercely around me. Then she turned to Olivia. "Kat and I are agreed. What about you?"

"I want kids," Olivia said. "At some point. Maybe not the picket fence—that's not trendy anymore—but yeah, two would be great."

I remembered her talking about willing Celeste into being. Of course she wanted two, not one. Funny how much our childhoods affected our futures.

Case in point, Olivia then said, "Celeste and I used to play house and we'd pretend we lived next door to each other and our babies were best friends. I know, so cheesy—"

"Not at all," I said. "It's sweet. And adorable."

After a moment, Olivia asked, "What are your thoughts on marriage?"

Elle didn't have to think before answering. "You think I can spend the rest of my life with one person? After the experiences I've had?"

Olivia chuckled. Then she and Elle turned to me.

I had always assumed I would want to get married if I found the right person, and I'd embarrassingly wanted that future with Tucker at one point, but now... "I don't know," I said honestly.

They both nodded, understanding my position as much as anyone could.

"Sometimes I wonder," Olivia started, then paused. "I wonder whether this was why I wasted two years on Tucker. Because I was thinking about the life I wanted, the marriage and the kids, and it felt like the time was now, the biological clock was ticking, and the next guy I was with should be it. I'm scared it made me ignore red flags."

"None of us knew," I said quickly, partly because I needed to hear it.

"I just can't figure out how I was so oblivious, you know?" Olivia continued. "And after all this blew up, I keep realizing more and more things I should have noticed sooner. Like how for most of our relationship, I was the one who made it so easy. I always paid for stuff, planned everything, came running whenever he needed something. And of course he gave back, too, just enough"—I knew exactly what that was like—"but how did I not see before that I was giving so much more? Yes, he gave me a new outlook on life and before him I didn't appreciate or live in the moment enough, but now I'm wondering whether that's the recipe for debt, danger, and downfall."

I shook my head just as Elle said, "Don't do that. You don't have to question everything. Just because he was the biggest dick doesn't mean he couldn't have helped you, too." The fact that she didn't make a joke about his dick size showed just how serious she was.

"We all had our reasons for ignoring Tucker's flags," I added. "Sometimes I wonder how much of it for me was because I was...lonely." Having Olivia and Elle now made me realize that Tucker and I were romantically involved, yes, but what I had valued most about our relationship was his support. His friendship. "I've always had a hard time making friends, and maybe that's what attracted me to him. He had such easy relationships. He charmed not only me but almost everyone he came across, and maybe I wanted to be able to do that, too."

Olivia nodded. "I get that. Except I was drawn to his zest for life."

"Zest for something else for me," Elle said, "but yeah, same idea."

"Do you think the shame of it will ever go away?" I asked. "Of trusting him, of not seeing the truth?"

"I hope so," Olivia said.

I sighed. "I guess it helps to understand it a little more."

"None of that matters now," Elle said. "What matters is that you, Kat, are deflecting."

"Huh?"

"Something clearly went badly with Lacey. Spill it."

I both loved and hated how well they already knew me. "I, um, may have had an underwear moment of my own."

"You accidentally invested all your savings in a tanking company with a ridiculous product?" Olivia joked just as Elle said, "You weren't subtle, were you?"

I bit my lower lip. "Does telling her the truth about me and my connection to Tucker count as subtle?"

Olivia's mouth dropped open. Elle didn't seem all that surprised. Then the laughter began.

I'd never felt this comfortable with anyone this fast, not even with Tucker. Maybe it was because all our secrets and shames (and private parts) were out in the open from the start.

Or maybe it was because even the worst storms can lead to a rainbow.

CHAPTER 18

It almost felt like a crime to be having fun with Elle and Olivia when I was possibly going down for a murder I didn't commit. Yet, they were helping me fight, and why not enjoy the few moments I could, especially given the uncertain future?

With a belly full of laughter and pizza, I arrived home to find a package in the lobby next to the welcome mat with the faded *l* turning it into *we come*. I should be excited—surprise package!—but I mostly felt dread. Given that we were looking into Tucker's murder, what if whoever had come after him was coming after us? *We come.* Maybe the mat was a warning.

The fear was replaced by annoyance when I saw who the package was from.

My mother. What ridiculous you-are-single gift did she have for me now?

After a cuddle and some treats for Cinny Junior, I sat down to open my anti-treat.

Even after receiving a handful of these, I was not prepared for this one. It was so weird it was hilarious, and despite not wanting to talk to her, I put my Bluetooth in my ear and called.

"Wei? You get my package?"

"Ma! This is for old people." As evidenced by the collapsed octogenarian woman on the Life Alert packaging.

"No, no, Yushan, I see it on TV. A woman fall—is so sad. She yelling, 'Help! Help! I fallen and I can't get up!' You single. You can fall and not be able to get up."

I didn't know whether to laugh or cry. "This is the strangest thing you've ever done."

"I pay for plan, you're welcome. Is active. My gift to you every year for birthday—you always complain I never remember your birthday, never give you anything. Well, now I give you this. For the rest of your life. Or until you get married."

"Stop wasting your money on this!" How could this be the woman who used the same rag to first clean the dishes, then the sink, then the floors, then the toilet? And *this* was what she chose to spend money on, a *Life Alert*?

Ironically, it was actually a *No-Life Alert*, purchased for me because I had no life.

"Yushan. You put on right now. Never take off."

"I can't wear this."

"Yushan!"

Nobody else had fights like this with their parents.

"Okay, Yushan. We meet in middle. Put on key chain. Okay? Then no one know what it is. Put next to your danger alarm."

"Okay," I lied.

"Now! Put it on now! I want to hear! Send photo after!"

"Alright, alright! Jeez." I put it on my key chain next to the alarm and jar opener, making as much noise as possible in the process. "Happy?"

"What you say now?"

"Thanks, Mom."

"Hmmph." I knew this was her way of saying *I love you*. Still, it was just so much. "You call Zhuang Ayi's son yet?"

"Yeah, we talk all the time. Nice boy. So you can stop sending me these gifts, okay?"

"When you marry."

"Bye, Mom."

"Be safe."

I moved to take the Life Alert off as soon as the call disconnected. My phone rang immediately. Does the Life Alert have a camera? I dropped the key chain like it was on fire, then picked up the call via Bluetooth.

"It's on the key chain! I wasn't going to take it off!"

"Um, is this Kathryn? Kathryn Hu?"

"Yes, sorry." I glanced at the screen to see a number that wasn't in my contacts. I refrained from making any Hu-who jokes as I asked, "Who's this?"

"It's Lacey. From the baby class. From, um, Tucker's office."

And to think, I'd expected the Life Alert to be my biggest surprise of the day.

CHAPTER 19

Later that night, on the other side of town, Lacey and I met at a hole-in-the-wall diner over matzo ball soups.

"Thanks so much for reaching out," I said—a toned-down version of what was really going through my head, which was, *Thank you for not telling the cops I'm borrowing babies to stalk my dead ex-boyfriend's coworkers.*

"I didn't know anything about Tucker's personal life," she said. "I didn't even know he had a girlfriend."

Or three, I wanted to say, but I kept that to myself.

For some reason, this fact both soothed and scared me. If Tucker could keep his personal life this quiet, if he was this good at hiding, maybe I shouldn't be kicking myself for not figuring it out sooner. At the same time, just how much was he hiding? How much trouble had he been in? Clearly a lot if it led to his murder. But the bigger question right now was, how much danger was I—were we—in? Should we be looking around, ruffling feathers? Should I be letting Olivia and Elle get so involved?

"I'm sorry I lied to you," I told Lacey.

She squirmed in her seat. "Thanks for telling me the truth. Eventually."

I nodded. Then waited. I didn't know why she'd wanted

to meet and the curiosity was killing me, but I forced myself to be patient.

"I didn't believe you at first," she said. "But then...I remembered the cryptic notations on his calendar, the hushed phone calls. And I need you to know—Tucker and I did... hang out. But that's all it was, because of Evie—who isn't his, by the way. Anyways, once I realized that was true, I couldn't stop thinking about what you said about the company, so..."

She took a breath. "I went through a bunch of his files. Which led me to other documents, which led me to—you get the idea. And, well..."

The anticipation was too much. I folded my hands together and squeezed until it hurt.

"It goes deep. Deeper than I could have imagined."

I scooted to the edge of my seat, the first time I fully understood and embodied that phrase.

Lacey glanced around. The only other person in the diner was an old man dozing in a booth in front of a half-eaten slice of pie. Still, she leaned forward before saying, "I found fraudulent invoices. For enormous sums, from vendors I don't recognize."

She reached into her purse and passed a folder to me. "Follow that money. It sure as hell didn't go to the company."

"Lacey," I said, my heart beating in my ears. "Thank you."

"Do you think—" she started, but then she shook her head. "You can ask me."

"Do you think he was with me just to cover up whatever he was doing, in case I noticed? Or do you think he actually— I shouldn't be asking you this."

All I could do was offer the truth. "I don't know. Regardless of the reason, he's gone, and you're better off for it. I'm sorry for your loss."

She waved a hand. "That's ridiculous. Don't—I'm sorry for *your* loss."

She stood. But right before she left, she said, "Don't let him hurt you again."

I was working on it. And with her help, we now had proof of Tucker's fraud. Next, we just had to follow that money and hope it didn't lead us into the same danger that had taken Tucker's life.

CHAPTER 20

We had the invoices, we knew they weren't coming from real vendors, and Lacey had told me to follow the money. But I wasn't sure how to do that.

I had someone I could ask, a person who wouldn't talk to the police or pose a threat, but there were other prices to pay.

"Hi, Ba," I answered the phone. "Thanks for looking at those invoices." I'd sent my father images of the files earlier, emphasizing how confidential they were before asking him to take a look.

"Yushan, aiyah, what kind of hole you in?"

Uh-oh. "What do you mean?" I asked as innocently as I could.

"This stinks. Of trouble. The companies on here are under trees."

"You mean they're shady?"

"That's what I said. Where you get these invoices from?"

"From...a class I'm taking."

"So you cheating? On homework?"

Oops, I hadn't thought of that. "No, these are just practice. Can you explain them to me?"

"Practice for what?"

It was time for my last resort, the only thing that would move this along. "I've been thinking about business school like you suggested." *Shoved down my throat* was more like it, but whatever.

He whooped. My father actually whooped, his excitement feeding my already crushing guilt. "I help you! We study together! Aiyah, the best news! We will get you into the best MBA program!"

I just wanted this to be over. All of it. The constant lies I've been forced to tell, my parents' perpetual disappointment in me, my disappointment in myself.

I swallowed the lump in my throat. "Thanks, Ba. The invoices?"

"Yes, yes, of course. We start the study now."

I'd never felt worse for getting exactly what I wanted. Well, except for when Tucker died, though I never actually wanted him *dead* dead. But as I was learning the hard way, the universe had a sick sense of humor.

• • • •

Thirty minutes later, thanks to my extremely effective lie and my father graciously answering all my questions, I'd learned everything I could about Tucker's under-the-tree invoices.

"Great job, Yushan. We schedule a talk every week?"

Was I a terrible person? I tried to remind myself that his excitement was coming from the fact that he didn't support my chemistry career, but my heart still felt like someone had reached into my chest and was squeezing it.

Then he said, "How 'bout six a.m.?" and I didn't feel bad saying, "Maybe, Ba. Thanks. I'll call you if I have more questions."

"Yes, yes. Anytime. Talk soon."

Child-of-immigrant guilt. A silent killer.

Just like whoever killed Tucker.

Time to focus.

I rubbed my eyes, then took a metaphorical and physical step back. I had to combine this new information with the old.

So, Tucker was massively in debt, which we knew, but what we hadn't known with certainty until now: he was stealing money from his company to dig himself out. He submitted fraudulent invoices from dummy vendors, and the company was unknowingly paying sketchy shell corporations with bank accounts in the Caymans—likely Tucker's accounts.

His boss suspected it, having said that Tucker was suddenly losing the company a lot of money, but as far as we knew, Ian didn't know the details. Even if he did, what was his incentive for murder? In fact, maybe it was better to keep Tucker around so the company could sue him, ask for the money back, whatever. Murder did not make sense. And this was the company's money, not Ian's own savings. Unless...would Ian be in trouble for letting this embezzlement happen right under his nose? Was there any gain from taking Tucker out of the picture so he wouldn't get in trouble? Perhaps, but not likely.

Blake the coworker, on the other hand—that was personal. The money he lost was his own savings, and he'd entrusted it to Tucker, who betrayed him. Much more motive there. Again, would Blake want Tucker alive to try to get his money back? Or was this a crime of passion?

We were getting warmer (hunting origin, believe it or not, based on tracking scents). Were things finally shifting in our favor, however small? I texted Olivia and Elle from my burner phone.

Calling a meeting of the Ex-Girlfriend Murder Club.

Dish Served Hot **Podcast Transcript— Episode 89**

[Podcast theme song plays, sung by creator, host, and star Mandy Thorne]

MANDY THORNE: Okay, Thornies, welcome back to *Dish Served Hot*, The Queens' Revenge edition! For the first time, we're going to be following the same case for a whole season, so if any of you missed the previous episode, well, you'll wanna get on that because it's juicy as hell and that backstory is necessary for this episode.

And for those who listened but need a refresher, we're following two anonymous queens—even anonymous to me!—who were dating the same disgusting cheater and then got together. They *claimed* they didn't do any revenge, but we got the true scoop. And have we got a doozy of a reveal for you today! My goodness, I almost wish I was a listener so I could experience what you're about to!

No interview for this episode mostly because what I'm going to tell you is all thanks to me putting on my detective hat—which I look fucking *fire* in, by the way, as I'm sure y'all can imagine. Check out my latest Instagram post to see. [whispering] And if you're one of my *special* listeners, you can see me wearing *just* the hat on my OnlyFans page.

[speaking at normal volume] So I had to use all my connections and resources for this one, but holy gods am I glad I did. We're talking private investigators, cops, nurses, but I shouldn't say more because I don't want to out my sources. Seriously, I should've gone into journalism! I didn't know it could be this awesome! Or easy, if you know people. And, you know, people have always loved telling me stuff, so that helps.

So. Remember how we originally thought Victoria and Elizabeth were losers because they claimed to forgive and not get revenge, but then we learned that they were lying? Well, I've uncovered *why* they lied. And holy hells, it is going to *blow your fucking minds*!

So. This lowlife cheater two-timed them. Not only do *they* get together in what I used to think was the ultimate fuck-you, but they actually did THE ultimate fuck-you. Like, I still can't believe it. Seriously, I cannot make this shit up. Are y'all ready?

Queen Victoria and Queen Elizabeth...

[drumroll]

They stole all his money, then fucking *murdered* him. They killed their ex! They did it together, then made love over his corpse. Okay, fine, I don't know that last part, but we don't know that they *didn't*.

So they came on this show to—what else? Rewrite their story. Because they went too far, so they had to convince the world they had forgiven him. They *used* me! They used my show! How dare they! And they kept the juiciest story from us in the process. Unforgivable!

So, I am obviously going to be giving you all the scoops on this investigation moving forward. And I know, this is the biggest bomb of all the bombs to have ever been dropped on any podcast in history. So obviously, with that comes the following announcement: we are becoming a true crime podcast. Not just a true crime podcast, but THE true crime podcast, the GOAT, the best of all time, the true crime podcast to take down all other podcasts.

Stay tuned, y'all. Detective Mandy is on the case.

CHAPTER 21

"That little ratings-hungry lying piece of shit!" Olivia screeched the next time we met up.

We had started with more important topics—like my dad's interpretation of the invoices, which helped us track down the name of a bank in the Caymans, which Double-Oh-livia then accessed through Tucker's laptop, which then confirmed the embezzling and also showed that the money had since been moved out. But once Elle told us about the latest *Dish Served Hot* episodes, Olivia couldn't focus on anything else.

"I thought you loved Mandy," I said.

"When she was stabbing other people in the back, not us!"

"That's what happens," I murmured to myself. I should've trusted my bad feeling about the podcast.

"In addition to splicing together our interview—and horribly, might I add—she has to be making everything else up, right? There's no way she actually knows anything?" Elle's worried eyes ping-ponged back and forth between Olivia and me.

"Then how did she get it right?" Olivia asked. "Well, not right—we didn't steal his money or murder him, but he's dead and Kat's a suspect. What are the chances of her guessing that correctly?"

Elle shrugged. "You tell me."

"Why aren't you freaking out?" Olivia asked me.

"I don't know. You two already are, so I feel like I have to hold it together for the group." *Even though* I'm *the one in the fucking hot seat.* "And I mean, yeah, this is a nightmare, but it's most likely just a coincidence, and she can't keep guessing correctly, can she?"

My words calmed Olivia down. "That's true. And it's not like she has proof, so she must have just gotten lucky once. Even a lying clock is right twice a day. We just have to wait her out."

"A broken clock," I couldn't help correcting.

"A lying clock could be wrong all day long," Elle agreed.

"You get my point! Just…a piece-of-shit clock that sometimes gets lucky!"

As Elle and Olivia chuckled, I couldn't help wondering if I should tell them that Detective Birch heard me listening to the podcast. That would only make them spiral more. No good would come from that, right?

But it did make my stomach lurch. Were we—and especially me—completely fucked?

• • • •

I'd known it was inevitable, but I wished I wasn't back at the police station *this* soon. But when the detective summoned, there wasn't much of a choice, not when you were a murder suspect.

Had he listened to the podcast? Had he found a piece of evidence that, like everything else, pointed to me?

This was more familiar than I'd ever wanted to be with an interrogation room. Or a detective, no matter how hot. Today he was wearing dark gray slacks and a pale blue button-up shirt with the sleeves rolled up again to showcase his forearms.

"How are you, Ms. Hu?"

"Oh just dandy," I said for some reason. His kindness and familiarity irked me—we weren't friends, weren't familiar. He thought I was a monster.

The side of his mouth twitched, but his face remained otherwise neutral. "Thanks for coming down on such short notice. Are we waiting for your lawyer?"

I had texted Olivia as soon as the detective called, but she hadn't replied yet. "Can we just get this over with? I left an experiment running."

"In the lab. At Harvard. Where you do…"

I was so tired. Of defending myself from a crime I didn't commit, of his trailing-off questions that always seemed to bite me in the ass. Did I have a choice, though? I had to answer. "Chemistry."

He nodded like he already knew that. "Do you work with dangerous chemicals?"

"Sometimes. I mean, lots of chemicals have the potential to be dangerous depending on how you use them. They could be safe in one instance but dangerous in another."

He continued nodding as if I were saying exactly what he wanted. Shit, I'd forgotten about keeping silent. "So someone who knew how to use chemicals—an expert, you might say—could do dangerous things with them. Including, say, murder?"

Fuck. I should have waited for Olivia. Though I didn't want to pull her in too far if I could help it.

I said nothing. Made absolutely no movement. But wait, according to Olivia, because I'd already answered one question, by not answering this one, I was now increasing suspicion. Crap! I'd messed this all up.

The detective made his next move. "Tucker Jones's autopsy came back."

I held my breath. Was he going to just tell me or…

"Where were you on the morning of September fourteenth?"

Oh god oh god. This was bad. The worst. I was screwed.

That line of questioning back-to-back… He didn't need to tell me. Chemistry had to be involved in Tucker's death, and since there hadn't been visible damage to the closet, it had to be some sort of caustic substance he'd inhaled or ingested and not an explosion. And I'd just gone from the girl who was suspiciously cleaning the condo when Tucker's corpse was discovered to the girl who definitely did it. Hell, I was even starting to wonder if I'd blacked out and somehow *was* involved.

Wait, the detective said September 14. They knew when Tucker died. That was a new piece of information. When was that? Counting in my head…that was three days before the pranking. This had to be good for me, right? I mean, he didn't die while I was cleaning the condo, and even if they found out about the pranking, that was after the fact, too.

I was on the verge of something, but Detective Birch interrupted my thoughts. "Ms. Hu? Do you know where you were that morning?"

"At work." I didn't want to say the word *lab* again and remind him I had access to a buffet of dangerous chemicals. And even though I wasn't sure of my schedule, if I wasn't with Tucker—which I wasn't, of course I wasn't—then I had to have been at work.

"Can you prove that?"

"Yes. With time-stamped swiping into the building, there are probably cameras, and you can ask anyone at the lab." Hopefully, they would ask more than one person in case Johannes decided to lie just to throw me under the bus.

The detective nodded. "And the two days prior to that?"

"The whole day?"

"Both days."

That didn't make any sense. Didn't they have a time of death? "I was at the lab—again, check the swipes. Why do I need an alibi for such a long stretch of time?"

He ignored my question and instead gestured toward the

two-way mirror. A moment later, a man entered. In his gloved hands was a red plastic bucket sealed inside a clear evidence bag.

"Does this look familiar to you?" the detective asked as the man placed the bucket on the table in front of me, then sat in a chair against the wall, his eyes never leaving the sealed bag.

I shook my head immediately. Not a lie. But then the fire-engine red poked at something in my brain like when you see someone you've met before but can't place when, where, or who.

If this was related to Tucker, then…

The closet. I saw red that day when my mind was imploding, when Elle and Olivia were pulling me off Tucker's body. That same fire-engine red.

What did this bucket have to do with what happened?

I looked at the detective, but he was studying me, trying to read what was going on in my head.

Which was, what?

If Tucker died by a chemical reaction, if this bucket was in the closet and produced what killed him, it likely wasn't something he ingested. And if it had been through inhalation…

The rotten egg smell.

"Oh my god." I couldn't hold it in. The realization had slapped me across the face.

I leaned forward and confirmed my suspicions by looking inside the bucket.

The detective stared at me, his eyes piercing. Watching me as I crumbled internally and maybe also externally.

"Tucker… My god… How… Why…" My breathing grew fast and shallow.

"What is it, Ms. Hu?" Detective Birch asked, but the calmness in his eyes only emphasized how he was steps ahead of me.

Even though he was chasing the wrong person, I had no path forward. But there also was no path backward. As Elle had said right after the snowball was set in motion, *what's done is done.* Through a series of events that I'd tried and failed to handle well, I found myself here, with yet another life-altering decision before me. Did I take the red pill and try to fight my way out of this, or the blue pill and just give up?

"Ms. Hu." His voice was growing impatient.

The time for saying nothing was over. Now was the time to beg, plead, and play every card I had. But the first words out of my mouth were the ones repeating over and over in my head since I'd been slapped awake.

"Hydrogen sulfide," I whispered.

His head snapped back in shock. "What did you just say?"

"Tucker died of hydrogen sulfide poisoning, didn't he?" That would also make sense with the detective asking about my whereabouts over several days. The time of death wasn't the only factor since the murderer may not have been present for the kill, thanks to the bucket.

"How do you know that?" he asked calmly, but his pupils were wide and searching.

"The bucket," I said, gesturing to it, "your questions—" *The rotten egg smell.* I couldn't tell him about that. I was wearing an N95 when we "discovered" the body, not to mention, the smell might have been gone by then.

I pivoted to what I could reveal.

"The bucket has bits of fertilizer in it," I said, gesturing. That was what I'd been looking for when I peeked inside earlier. "If it was a sulfur-containing fertilizer and it was mixed with an acid—which is easy to find, it could've been a common household cleaner..." My voice broke. I wasn't acting. I was truly devastated. What a horrible way to die. Even with everything Tucker had done, who would do this to him? Given the approximate size of the bucket, he likely collapsed within five minutes, then stayed unconscious on the ground as he slowly asphyxiated to death.

Tucker was *murdered.* We had heavily suspected it, enough to be investigating it as such, but this was the first confirmation.

And I was suddenly realizing just how out of our depth we were. And how deep in shit I was.

The detective's eyes bored into me, and I tried to stay calm as he continued interrogating. "How did you know it was hydrogen sulfide specifically?"

Was there anything other than the rotten egg smell I could point to?

Think. What else did hydrogen sulfide poisoning cause? Skin irritation. Respiratory distress. Serious eye damage.

Eye damage!

"His eyes were clouded over—the kind of damage consistent with hydrogen sulfide poisoning."

"You expect me to believe you figured that out on your own based on so little?"

This was my moment. To do what those geniuses do on CSI, NCIS, all the shows with letter names. I would tell the detective his entire backstory because I saw that he drank black coffee—even in the evening—out of a Stepping Stones Elementary mug, that he had a small protruded scar above his eyebrow, that he didn't have any photos of a wife, girlfriend, or kids on his desk. And I hadn't noticed all of those things because I was overly interested in him, no way. I was just a genius.

"Stepping Stones!" I burst out. Then I closed my eyes because, what the fuck.

His eyebrow with the scar rose as he said, "That's where my sister works."

"I knew that," I lied. "Your mug."

Shit, I was losing him.

"Okay, I didn't know it was your *sister*. But I did notice your mug. Also..." I then uttered the first thing that popped into my head. "You have a hard time trusting others."

It was simply a hunch, but his eye twitched ever so slightly. I was on to something. This was bigger than just me.

Think. I replayed our interactions, searching for relevant details. Flashes of information came to me, piecemeal, mostly because I'd been observing him because, well, because he was hot, okay? And I'd noticed plenty of details that had appeared insignificant at the time but were now adding up to a bigger picture.

"Your previous partner. Something happened."

His eyes widened so large I could see white above and below his irises. He didn't speak, so I filled in the silence.

"You work alone. You keep your distance from others in the station. When we first came here, I thought they were staring at me, but they weren't. They were staring at *you*."

I didn't break eye contact as I waited for him to respond.

He sat in silence for a few beats, then gestured to the man still watching the evidence, who then grabbed the bucket and left the room. That man might be the only person on earth quieter than the detective.

Once it was just the two of us again, Detective Birch leaned forward. "So are you some brilliant savant? Should you be working here instead of at the lab?"

Maybe I only notice things with you, I thought but didn't say. I just shrugged.

His eyes appraised me from head to toe, and I suppressed a shiver, one that wasn't born from fear.

"Or you're just smart," he said. "Perhaps smart enough to commit the perfect crime and cover it up?"

I shook my head as adamantly as I could. "Absolutely not. Please. I'm telling the truth."

Detective Birch leaned forward, and even though I knew I would hate what he was about to say, I had to fight the urge to move even closer.

"I have enough to arrest you. The evidence is overwhelming. Tell me, Ms. Hu, why I shouldn't handcuff you this very second."

Images of him handcuffing me and then pulling me across the desk flitted through my mind.

Jesus, I had to get it together. This was serious. As he proved when he started to reach for the handcuffs at his waist.

"I can help you!" I blurted out. My time was up. I'd been forced to choose a path, and I'd swallowed the red pill whole. "I didn't do it, but I have information."

His hands stilled.

Was I doing this? Did I have a choice? Should I request my lawyer first?

He was losing patience, though. And he didn't have to wait for my lawyer to arrest me, did he? And the most convincing motivation: I trusted him. It wasn't because he was hot—in fact, that should make me trust him less with my history. But there was something about the way he looked at me, looked *into* me, that made me believe he cared about the truth more than anything else. Otherwise, he would have arrested me that first day.

After being bottled up for so long, the details came pouring out of me. Tucker's debt, his fraud, the pranks. All of it except for Elle's and Olivia's involvement. Meaning, I didn't mention the cheating—merely citing a bad breakup as the reason for the pranks—and implicating only myself in the revenge plot.

"Again, that's why I had bruises on my arms. From chasing frog number four around, the slippery bastard."

"You let four frogs go in his condo?"

"Well, three. But they were labeled one, two, and four."

It didn't sound so funny out loud in the interrogation room, but Detective Birch chuckled lightly—only for a second before he covered it with a cough.

"You also smeared fecal matter everywhere?"

"Yup," I said with a straight face. "Seemed like a good idea at the time."

"Why were you so angry with him?"

This would not bode well for the detective seeing me as a potential romantic interest, but my freedom and protecting Olivia and Elle were more important. Chicks before dicks, after all, as Queen Elizabeth had said.

"Our relationship had turned sour. He was, well, he was a jerk. So many red flags."

"What were some of them?"

I tried to remember what I'd said to the detective that day we first bumped into each other. "Long stretches where I wouldn't hear from him, he was so weird about his condo and not letting me keep things there—"

"Did you suspect he was cheating, it sounds like?"

Crap. I didn't want him even near that track, but I also needed a reason why I'd been mad enough for that enormous volume of feces. "Maybe? I didn't have proof, so maybe not. He could've just been a jerk."

Detective Birch sighed. "Ms. Hu, I don't trust people easily—"

"Because of your previous partner."

He ignored my comment. "But my gut says you're telling the truth. So I have a proposal for you."

My heart leaped into my throat. *No more proposals*, I couldn't help thinking.

"Let's work together. I don't arrest you today, and you keep looking into Tucker's financials, his fraud, and let me know what you find."

"Seriously?" I wanted to jump up from my seat in relief.

"You can't leave the state, and you have to be willing to go along with any operations we may want to run in the future, like making contact with certain people or wearing a wire."

I couldn't stop nodding my head. Whatever it took to get out of this mess.

"Let's start with a list of potential suspects." He pushed his notepad and pen toward me.

I didn't have a ton of names, but I wrote down everyone I could think of. I wrote it down with gusto.

Kathryn's Sixth Law of Luck: If you're pathetic enough and past rock bottom, maybe the universe will eventually throw you a bone.

CHAPTER 22

"I cannot believe you talked to him without me!" Olivia boomed. "What did I tell you?"

"To not say anything and to not lie. I didn't lie."

"And that you should wait for me!"

"You never said that," I argued.

"That's true, you technically never did," Elle said. Olivia dropped her head into her hands.

I'd left the station, deal in hand, before Olivia arrived. Detective Birch's last words to me had been "be careful." It was now late in the evening and we were huddled in not Olivia's townhome but Elle's shared duplex. Where Olivia's townhome was upscale chic, Elle's bedroom was eclectic chaos. Romance books spilled out from bookshelves and piles on the floor, mismatched decorations brought pops of color to every nook and cranny, and sticky notes had been scribbled on and stuck to random surfaces. There was even some scribbling on the wall near her bed, maybe from when she couldn't find a scrap for her midsleep ideas.

"I got a deal, though, didn't I?" I said, defending myself. "It ended up working out okay."

"For now!" Olivia stood and paced back and forth. "We don't know if anything you told him is coming back to bite us in the ass. And we don't know his motives. Be wary, okay? The hot ones can't be trusted." I wondered if she was always this suspicious or if it was a new development since Tucker.

"Sorry," I said quietly, like a scolded child.

"Liv," Elle said gently from beside me on the futon. "Kat did what she thought was best. What's done is done."

Just like how they helped me back at the station, Elle's words flipped a switch in Olivia, draining the panic from her face and replacing it with regret. "Sorry. I have an unhealthy need to be in control. I...wish I could change that about myself."

"I wish I could change most things about me," I said, which in and of itself was a hint of change because I normally wouldn't admit that out loud.

"Why do you think I write?" Elle said. "I want to change everything—the present, the past, the future."

Our words seemed to inspire Olivia to share more. "It started when I was a kid. When Celeste was dealing with a lot of medical issues. She basically grew up in the hospital, in and out for UTIs—something about her anatomy being different—and I just felt this need to fix it. In whatever way I could. My parents were busy with nurses and doctors and insurance, so it became my job to cheer Celeste up as she went through tests, was bedridden, was in pain. I just...had to make it better. I tried to distract her and make her laugh, and it seemed to help. So I vowed to always do that. For the people I care about." She looked away, not meeting our eyes.

"You *have* been making it better for us," Elle said.

I nodded. "But it's not all on you. And we can't control this. It's a mess. It's covered in glitter and poop and too much DNA."

Elle leaned over and poked Olivia's knee. "And it doesn't help if the brains of the group falls apart, yeah?"

Olivia pulled her knee away. "I'm not the brains."

"Well I'm sure as hell not the brains," Elle said with a laugh.

"Then what are you?" Olivia asked.

Elle shrugged.

"You're the guts," I said, thinking about how Elle was always that last push we needed when we weren't sure. The one who believed in us.

"And Kat's the heart," Elle said.

I'd never thought of myself that way before. I would have guessed I would be the brains, the robotic non-emoting pile of neurons. But with the people I cared about, I did lead with my heart. And the way Elle had said those words with such admiration...maybe that wasn't something to be embarrassed about. While it was a mistake to miss the garbage parts of Tucker, maybe I could stop beating myself up someday for having seen the best in him.

Olivia's mouth finally curved up slightly. "You're right. The brains, the guts, and the heart—we're the Ex-Girlfriend Murder Club. And we can do this." Her spine straightened as she turned to me. "Kat, did you learn anything from Detective McStudly?"

Elle shook her head. "McHunky."

"You didn't even see him!" Olivia argued.

"Doesn't matter. McHunky just sounds better."

"Actually, now that I'm thinking about it," Olivia said, "he was more of a McBroody, wouldn't you say, Kat?"

"I've been calling him McHottie," I admitted.

"He is *your* detective," Elle said. "McHottie it is."

"That's a good one," Olivia added.

"Well, I landed on that only after McSpicy and McMoist came to mind."

We all started laughing at the same time.

"McMoist!" Elle screeched. "That's the one!"

It took us a little while to get back to business after that.

• • • •

Eventually, I told them what I'd learned from McHottie: the time of death and the chemical poisoning.

"Oh shit," Olivia mumbled when I mentioned the latter.

"I know," I said with a sigh. "It doesn't get much worse than the murder weapon turning out to be my expertise. What I'm still unsure about is how it all played out. There was a bucket involved, but there's still a lot unexplained. I mean, the killer couldn't have been there unless they were wearing a gas mask, but then Tucker would have seen them. So how did they get Tucker to be in the closet with the door closed precisely when the gas formed?" I started picturing a convoluted contraption with the bucket, maybe somehow connected to the door closing? It wasn't impossible. And the closet was smart because it had to be a small, contained space. But why didn't Tucker notice—

"Oh my god." My hand flew up to my open mouth.

"What?" Elle scooted to the edge of her seat as Olivia sat up.

I looked from one to the other, my gaze finishing on Olivia. "The killer knew that Tucker couldn't smell."

"What?" Elle asked.

"Congenital anosmia. He was born without a sense of smell," Olivia said robotically, almost flippantly. Because the wheels were churning in her head.

"Wait, really? He never told me that." After a moment, Elle's eyes went wide. "Wait, so all that poop I painstakingly collected—"

I cut her off, not wanting to hear more details about her collecting process. "I didn't want to ruin your fun that day."

Shoot, I suddenly realized. I would have to keep my knowledge of Tucker's anosmia from the detective. Because if he knew that I knew about it, my smearing poop all over the condo wouldn't make sense. Which would then lead him to deduce that someone else had been there with me.

This was getting complicated so quickly. There were too many details to keep straight, and it felt like just a matter of time before I slipped up.

"He wouldn't have even smelled it," Elle said mostly to herself, and it felt like we were watching her mind wrap around this new fact.

Then, after another moment, she shrugged. "Well, it still would've been a bitch to clean up."

"Yes, it was," I said with a pointed look, only half joking.

"Sorry." Elle's mouth pulled down in a guilty frown. "All I did was make it more miserable for us, huh?"

Just talking about it conjured up the horrid smells from that day—the feces, the rotten eggs...

Wait. The rotten eggs.

"You know what?" I said to Elle. "Thank god for the poop. Because it made us open the windows." And thank god Frogger #4 made me turn on the ceiling fan. And thank god I left the closet to ask Olivia if she smelled rotten eggs. "There was still hydrogen sulfide in the closet that day. If we hadn't dissipated it..." I trailed off.

Elle and Olivia grew somber. Elle's voice was barely above a whisper when she said, "So it could have...if we hadn't..." She couldn't finish her question.

"You were right that night," I said to Olivia. "About danger being present. You were right to make us leave."

The confluence of all those seemingly small things might have saved our lives. Or at least saved us from hydrogen sulfide toxicity.

Olivia leaned forward, grabbed Elle's and my hands, and squeezed. "We're okay."

Elle gently bumped her knee against mine. "You're the brains, too."

"This could narrow our suspect list down," Olivia said, her mind taking off as she let go of our hands. "There probably aren't a ton of people who know about his anosmia. Though how do we know if a person *doesn't* know a fact? You can't prove a negative. They could just lie."

"Lie detector test!" Elle said excitedly.

Olivia barely heard. Her eyes were unfocused, her mind calculating.

A moment later, she said, "You know who would know about his anosmia and maybe also have beef with him, especially if money was involved?"

Elle looked at me. I shrugged.

"People that none of us have met," Olivia answered. "Though I'm guessing they don't actually live in Canada."

I sucked a breath in. "His family. But will they want to talk to us?"

Olivia's eyes met mine. "Only one way to find out."

I nodded. "How do we find them?"

• • • •

"Did we know Tucker at all?"

Olivia said it, but we were all feeling it.

Searching for Tucker's family was proving exceptionally difficult. Turned out, there were a lot of Tucker Joneses in the world, and we were beginning to question everything he'd ever said, like, was he actually from Topeka? Did his parents currently live in Canada? Was his name really Tucker Jones? And his complete absence from social media and almost the entire internet wasn't helping. He also didn't have any emails to or from family, which was surprising and sad.

"I feel weird looking through his laptop without him knowing," I said.

"We're looking at your laptop!" Elle yelled down to the floor.

Olivia laughed. My jaw dropped.

"Sorry, too much?" Elle said, sheepish.

"Never," Olivia said.

Why was I the only one feeling squirrelly? Was it because I couldn't stop thinking about how Tucker had shown up at *my* door in his final days? And used my info for his passwords? Though he'd used Olivia's, too. But none of this mattered, my god.

Olivia yawned.

"Should we call it a night?" I suggested.

"Yeah, maybe." Olivia leaned over to turn off the lamp beside her, the one shaped like a dodo bird. But she couldn't find any buttons or switches.

"Oh, yeah," Elle said, coming over. "You actually have to…" She reached her long fingers up and into the ass of the bird, extracting a silver chain. After clicking it once, the bulb extinguished and the chain retracted back up and out of sight.

"Ouch," Olivia joked just as I said, "Poor bird."

"Gift from one of my roommates. Right after I told her she pulls things out of her ass too often."

We laughed.

"Does everything have a story in here?" I asked, my fingers lingering on four bookends that spelled out her name.

"Isn't that the best part, what makes everything special? Who are we but a summation of our thoughts and experiences?"

Olivia grinned. "You are so a writer, through and through."

I gestured to the scribbling on the wall. "Seriously."

Elle smiled shyly at us—maybe the first time she'd ever done anything shyly in her life. "Too bad my skills haven't helped us at all, unlike yours."

"Mine have only dug the hole deeper," I pointed out.

"And sometimes I wonder if mine helped or hurt," Olivia said.

After a moment, Elle's eyes gleamed mischievously. "What if I tried to use mine to help our situation with a certain podcast host and cretin?"

Olivia looked at her sternly. "No. That will only draw more unwanted attention."

Elle pouted. "Someone needs to put her in her place. She's ramping up."

"Wait, what now?" I hadn't had time to listen to the latest episode yet.

"Uh, it's bad," Elle said. "Bad for us, bad journalism, bad entertainment."

"Most of it is wrong, but there's enough right that I'm worried," Olivia said. "*And* it's getting so popular that my friends and coworkers are starting to talk about it. Like, what the fuck?"

"She guessed more details correctly? How?"

Elle looked at Olivia as she repeated her words from before: "Piece-of-shit clock?"

Olivia sighed. "There's not much we can do, but it's actually to our advantage she's starting to go off the rails. That should make it more confusing for the police and harder to figure out what's real and what's not. It decreases her credibility."

What she said made sense, but dread still pooled in my stomach.

"I still think we should mess with her," Elle said.

"Priorities," said the brains of the operation. Then she stood. "Good progress today. Let's keep trying to find his family. I'm also going to follow the money, and, Kat, let us know if the detective lets any other useful information slip."

Elle raised an eyebrow. "Or if he lets anything else slip...in. Or maybe you could slip *him* something first."

I knew exactly what she meant but joked, "Like a ten-dollar bill?"

Exasperated, Elle opened her mouth, but Olivia cut her off. "No more crimes!"

"No *more*? We haven't committed any!" I wanted to tattoo *I didn't kill anyone* on my forehead.

Olivia began ticking them off on her fingers. "Breaking and entering, not reporting the body, taking the laptop..."

Right. Whoops.

"No more crimes," I said. The ones we'd committed were part accidental, part out of necessity, I tried to remind myself.

"No more crimes," Elle repeated. "Unless it's to mess with little Miss Mandy Thorne," she added under her breath.

Olivia shot her a glare. Elle returned an angelic smile before saying, "But Kat getting to know McSexy on a better level, even biblically, isn't a crime, right?"

"I guess technically not, as long as it's consensual and not for the purpose of getting information on either end."

"Did you hear that, Kat? On *either end*." Elle gave me a *you're welcome* grin.

Even though I had been admiring McHottie—I had eyes and a pulse, after all—actually thinking about anything romantic or intimate with anyone, even someone that hot, made me dry heave. I quickly excused myself to the bathroom.

Just another unwelcome consequence courtesy of Tucker mothereffing Jones.

Kathryn's Seventh Law of Luck: Consequences of bad luck snowball ad infinitum.

Dish Served Hot Podcast Transcript— Episode 90

[Podcast theme song plays, sung by creator, host, and star Mandy Thorne]

MANDY THORNE: Welcome, my lovely Thornies, to True Crime: The Queens' Revenge. And a hello and thank-you to my many many *many* new subscribers. I'm so thrilled that you all see what's so fascinating and downright bonkers about this case we're covering. Welcome to the Thornie family. Y'all will fit right in.

Now, it's only getting more bonkers from here. Bonkers in the best and ugliest and worst way, of course. [cackles] You'll just have to stay tuned to see what I mean.

So I've been hearing that the police are bumbling this one so far. But I'm telling them and you right now that if they wanted to, they would be able to prove Queen Victoria and Queen Elizabeth's guilt in one second. Because these girls, they stole evidence. That's right. I know, with quite certainty, that they have in their possession, the laptop and phone of the deceased. If the police just did a search, they would find this irrefutable proof of their guilt.

How do I know this? Again, because I'm the best detective ever. I'm frickin Mandy Sherlock over here. And not only do these girls have his laptop and phone, but they have something *even more personal* of his.

Are you ready?

Y'all aren't ready.

They have…

[drumroll]

His *thumb*.

That's right. You heard me. They have his thumb. And why? So that they can get *into* his laptop and phone. Fingerprint entry, y'all. Frickin biometrics. That's how they stole all his money.

I'm telling ya, you just can't make this stuff up.

Stay tuned, because our next episode will be *even more bonkers*. I promise. Just you wait. Detective Mandy is still on the case!

CHAPTER 23

Going back to work amid all this felt as strange as becoming besties with my dead boyfriend's other girlfriends. Actually, stranger, because the friendships no longer felt weird.

As I measured, poured, and mixed solutions, a cloud descended over me that was even thicker than the precipitate in my flask. In the past, this had happened from time to time in the lab, but today was different. In addition to the usual fatigue and anxiety, there was something new.

Hopelessness.

What was the point? I was under suspicion of *murder*. And even if I wasn't, all the current data from my work in the lab led to a single conclusion: I was a failure. I hadn't accomplished a single thing since arriving. What was I even doing here?

Normally I would have texted Tucker, who would have known just the right thing to say, but now...

I may not have him, but I had someone else. Two someones.

Retreating to the break room, I sent a text with my burner phone. Less than a minute later:

Elle: Babes, you're the smartest person I know. Well, you and Brains, you two can share the crown, but still. You got this, okay? I have no doubt.

I had plenty of doubts, but it helped that she didn't.

A second later, my phone rang.

"Kat." It was Olivia. "Talk to me."

Just hearing her voice made tears prick at the corners of my eyes. I closed the door to the break room and let it all out: how I constantly felt like I didn't belong here, how things felt pointless, how I couldn't tell if I was rattled because of Tucker or because of something else.

Olivia listened intently, injecting *mm-hmm*s and *I know*s and *I'm sorry*s in all the right places. When I finished, I already felt lighter.

After a beat, Olivia asked, "Do you love what you do?"

"Of course I do."

"Take a second, and I'm going to ask you again. Do you love what you are doing right now in that lab?"

No. "I love chemistry. I just don't know if I love my current job or the lab I'm in. I did what my professors told me to at every step, and now I'm doing boring experiments with a bunch of people who don't like me."

I'd never thought about this before because it all happened so slowly, in steps, like how you don't notice someone getting taller if you see them every day.

But now that I was thinking about it, how did I get here?

Was this why I'd been struggling? I'd been questioning my ability and intelligence, but was it more about passion?

"As Elle said, Kat, you're the smartest person we know. You can do whatever you want. And you don't have to know what that is right now, but let yourself do what you need to in order to figure it out, okay?"

"Yeah, okay." I paused. "Liv?" It was the first time I called her that, partly because it was apt after that conversation, and also because I now felt close enough to her to say it. "Thank you. Seriously."

"It's nothing."

It was everything. It was the first time someone was thinking about me and my well-being. Someone who believed in me when I didn't. So it didn't matter that I still lacked an answer. Because for the first time in a long while...

I wasn't alone.

• • • •

After a slightly aimless day in the lab, I returned home to another package from my mom. I immediately groaned, only to be shocked to find value in both items she'd sent. The first was a self-defense tool called a Kubotan. I didn't know how to use the plastic marker–sized weapon with a tapered end, but I put it on my already-too-heavy key chain. Next, the body pillow in the shape of a muscular dude's arm and torso was embarrassing as fuck, but, um, I kind of liked it? The resemblance to a man was silly, but its size and plumpness made cuddling it, sadly, pretty nice.

But not as nice as cuddling my baby Cinny, who I let out of her cage. She immediately went to sniff the new body pillow.

"Cinny, meet..." My mind blanked on a name. I wasn't known for being creative. What would Elle name it?

Detective Birch.

I laughed out loud. No freaking way.

It was settled. No name.

"Meet No Name."

Cinny quickly lost interest and hopped over to the basket she'd arrived in. I hadn't touched it since Tucker died. With one graceful, effortless leap, she jumped in. While her front half cleared the side, her back half lagged, toppling the basket onto its side. Several toys spilled out.

Cinny grabbed a plushie carrot and darted off.

"That's the only one you're getting tonight," I jokingly told her. Despite the common association, carrots aren't great for rabbits, being too high in sugar, and thus were relegated to infrequent treats. It pained me since she loved them so much her entire body would vibrate with joy whenever she ate them. Maybe this plushie was a nice compromise, though it for sure wasn't as tasty.

Had Tucker remembered that fact? I'd told him about it once when he asked to feed Cinny Senior a treat. I let him give Cinny her monthly carrot, and after, she rubbed her chin on him for the first time, which bunnies do to deposit scent glands and mark something or someone as theirs. Like a naive dolt, I had thought it was a sign that we were meant to be. What a load of rubbish.

With a sigh, I grabbed the other two toys in the basket to cut the tags off. One was a plushie Easter egg (which was pretty cute, I had to admit) and the other was— I sucked in a breath.

A plushie sriracha bottle. A toy that was more for me than Cinny. I squeezed it tight, trying to push away the memories of the first time we met, of all the spicy meals we shared throughout our time together.

There was something in the middle. I glanced at the tag, which claimed it was a squeaky toy for dogs. Guess they didn't make hot sauce bottles for rabbits, though why would a dog want one?

And that wasn't the only thing that didn't make sense. The tag said it was a *squeaky* toy, but it hadn't squeaked.

I squeezed again. My fingers felt the outline of a rigid item inside, but again, no sound. Complete silence.

Was it broken? It was brand-new. And why would the squeak mechanism be so hard? Wouldn't that hurt the dog's jaw?

Before my mind had sussed out the answer, my fingers were already searching for the seam.

The majority of the stitching was a bright red that matched the rest of the toy, but a small stretch was lighter, closer to pink. Did Tucker know how to sew?

Yes, I remembered. He once asked me to fix a button on his precious Balls In underwear, and I'd jokingly called him sexist for asking, after which he'd proudly YouTubed it, then offered to fix all of my missing buttons.

I hastily dug through the kitchen drawers until I found scissors to cut through the lighter stitching. Reaching through the stuffing, I felt around until my fingertips grazed the hard object. Breathless, I pulled it out.

A USB drive.

Too many thoughts crashed into my mind at the same time. But I shoved them all away as I stuck the drive into my laptop. No use spiraling until I knew what was on it.

Moments later, a list of names and phone numbers popped up. Fifteen people in total. Some had the last name Jones—likely family members, though, just our luck, Jones was also one of the most common surnames in America. My eyes lingered on Blake Williams and Ian Zurling—Tucker's coworker and boss, the ones we'd talked to. Were these people Tucker owed money to? People who had reason to come after him, maybe kill him?

I couldn't fend the thoughts off any longer. They swarmed the dam, flooding in.

Tucker gave this to me because he feared for his life that night. He wasn't lying. This is a suspect list, and Tucker entrusted it to me.

He put his life in my hands, and even though I had reason to doubt him, I had kicked him out. Refused him safety and sent him home to be murdered. The guilt was so overwhelming I couldn't breathe.

A fuzzy nose booping against my bare foot was just enough to bring me back from the plane of despair I'd descended to.

Maybe Cinny knew how distraught I was because when I scooped her up, she nuzzled her face into my shoulder.

I heard Olivia and Elle in my head.

You didn't do anything wrong.

Of course you were right to throw him out. You should've let Cinny pee on him, too.

This is a good thing—we have new leads.

That was true. Tucker had handed us exactly what we needed to solve his murder. Had he known what was coming? Or was he hoping I would temporarily hold this sensitive information for him?

I guess, like so many things with Tucker, I would never know.

Even though my emotions were more muddled than an insoluble solution, I whispered, "I'll figure this out." Not just for me, but for Tucker, too.

CHAPTER 24

Hypothesis: Someone on this USB drive murdered Tucker. Or at the very least, they were people Tucker was scared of.

However, this hypothesis didn't have much supporting evidence other than my gut and the weird way in which Tucker gave me the information. And I guess it was suspicious that we couldn't find any of his family members in his contacts, but here they were, highlighted.

If this was indeed a curated list of suspects, fifteen felt like a massive number. Leave it to Tucker to piss this many people off.

I only recognized two names. And the more I thought about it, the less I suspected Blake and Ian. At least for now. Because the hydrogen sulfide information changed things. This was not a crime of passion or spur-of-the-moment, heated revenge. It was calculated, painstakingly planned, the details of which I still hadn't figured out. Was it possible that it was revenge so deep-seated and hot that it led to this level of planning? Or were there more complicated issues at play? This almost felt planned by a professional, an assassin who needed to get the job done but in the most elegant, least traceable way possible. Was one of these people on the USB a professional? Or more likely, had one of them hired a professional? But if Tucker owed them money, why would his death help, other than as revenge?

There were still too many details missing, but at least we knew where to look next.

· · · ·

"You know what prank we could've done to Tucker that would have been hilarious? We could've baked him brownies, half with laxatives, and half with pot—for shits and giggles! Get it?" said—who else?—Elle.

We were at Olivia's townhome. One of her recent clients owned a butcher shop and had sent over some prime grade beef, and since we needed to meet up anyway, Olivia suggested we come over for a home-cooked meal—"for shits and giggles," she had said in the text. I hadn't realized at the time that "home-cooked" translated to "cooked by the three of us, none of whom knew what they were doing."

The problem was, I grew up in an Asian household so I didn't know how to cook a giant hunk of meat, Elle was mostly vegetarian "not for the animals, but for my figure, but also, if that helps the animals, great," and Olivia "didn't cook very often," which I think was her way of nicely implying that she made a lot of money and could afford to eat out on the nights she wasn't expensing her meal.

Our cooking session had begun with Olivia poking the slab of ribeye with her glossed nail as we exchanged glances. But then I decided to own it and do what I do best: I looked up the science of cooking steak.

"I think we should reverse sear it," I said after a few minutes. "It makes the most sense, scientifically. We cook at a low temperature so the chemical and thermal reactions happen gradually, allowing us to cook the meat evenly throughout. Then we sear at the end for flavor and texture. Pretty cool, right?"

Elle and Olivia were both grinning when I looked up from my phone.

"What?"

"*That* is the passion that's missing from your voice when you talk about your job," Olivia said.

Elle nodded. "You're cute when you talk nerdy."

My cheeks grew hot as if I were being heated at a low temperature. This made sense, though—the chemistry of cooking was what had sparked my interest in the first place. Though it wasn't the cooking part per se, but how it connected me to my parents.

"I..." Memories popped into my head and warmed my insides—my mom teaching me how to fold dumplings, my dad showing me how to cook them gently so the skin wouldn't break open. "Food was the one language my parents and I shared. Preparing it, eating it—those were the only times we came together and felt like a unit. But I don't have intuition when it comes to cooking. All my creations were more Frankenstein's monster than culinary genius. We had one incident my parents call huoshan cai—volcano dish—when I added way too many chili peppers. And since we didn't keep milk in the house, it was, well, an epic disaster." I couldn't help laughing remembering the three of us stuffing our faces with rice to calm the heat. "Anyway, learning the science was the key for me." Though maybe now that I was thinking about it, some of our most fun memories were *before* I found my way around the kitchen. Maybe it wasn't skill we had needed—just the shared interest.

Maybe I hadn't been trying hard enough to find more of those with them.

"I think you're on to something," I said. "I've forgotten what first drew me to chemistry. Guess I need to go back to the beginning. And also figure out how to channel the passion into something that will make money."

Elle sighed. "Ah, yes. I know that problem well."

"Isn't that everyone's problem?" Olivia asked.

That surprised me. "I thought you loved being a lawyer."

"And it makes you buttloads of money." Elle gestured around Olivia's beautifully decorated townhome.

"I just...don't know if I went into it for the right reasons. Maybe I'm realizing now how much pressure I felt to just, I don't know, be a certain way. I do like what I do. It's just been hard accepting how little control I have, and how even when I try my best, it doesn't always work out."

A heavy pause descended where we weren't just thinking about her past client.

Olivia broke the silence by saying, "I won't let anything happen to you, Kat."

"Hear hear," Elle said, raising her *Big Dick Energy* mug of wine (she insisted on the combo).

Olivia raised her cup of coffee. "To the Queen of Bad Coincidences and Science."

That was me all right. I clinked my cup against theirs. "Okay. Let's use the science part, hope the bad coincidences stay away, and reverse sear a steak."

"Great. What do we do first?" Olivia asked.

"Um, we season it. With salt and...other stuff." I hadn't gotten to that part yet.

"YouTube!" Elle declared. "Taught me everything I needed to know about periods, sex, and now apparently steak."

"Periods?" Olivia asked.

"*That's* the one you're curious about?" Elle said with a laugh. "Yeah, taught me how to put a tampon in."

"My mom wouldn't buy tampons because she said using them would mean I wasn't a virgin anymore," I said with an eye roll.

Olivia stifled a giggle while Elle let hers out unabashedly. I furrowed my brow at them.

"C'mon," Elle said. "That's hilarious, no?"

It hadn't been at the time, but I guess now that I was looking back on it...

A small chuckle escaped my lips, and it grew until I was laughing with them. Maybe it was okay to acknowledge my parents' hilarity. Healthy, even. I certainly felt better after.

Once the seasoned steak was in the oven and we were feeling pretty fancy, Olivia turned to me.

"Kat, I got you something since your life isn't on fire enough." She reached into the cupboard and retrieved a tiny Tabasco bottle with a bow on top.

I squealed and hugged it to my chest. I loved it because it was Tabasco—which I was convinced made every dish better—but it also represented Olivia's progress. Not only was the hot sauce not making her question her relationship with Tucker, but she was even joking about it.

"I don't know if that goes with steak," Elle said.

I wanted to argue it went with everything, but okay, fine, maybe the steak wouldn't need it. "Are we making any side veggies?" I asked.

As we began chopping the random vegetables we'd scrounged from Olivia's fridge, we finally got down to business. I told them about the USB list and my hypothesis.

"Shit, Kat, good job," Elle said, looking up from dicing tomatoes. "A-plus sleuthing."

Olivia nodded, already deep in thought. "This is exactly what we needed. I have a feeling this will blow the case wide open."

Elle and Olivia both looked at me expectantly.

"You know," I said, "I don't know the origin of that one."

They watched as I googled it on my phone.

"No definitive history," I concluded. "Someone on Reddit thinks it might be related to blowing your nose to clear it." I put my phone away. "Sorry. Nothing too interesting on this one."

I was disappointed in the result, but happy that my friends automatically looked to me to learn about idioms.

"So what's our next step?" Elle asked.

• • • •

We were so distracted by the USB list that we forgot about the steak after we took it out of the oven. But the beauty of our chosen method was that we still had to sear on the stove, and by the time we sat down to our hot, charred pieces of steak, we also had our plan finalized.

"Are you sure we have to do it this way?" I asked one last time.

"You don't have to do anything you don't want to," Olivia said.

Elle nodded. "We're happy to do your part."

"No, no, of course not. Thanks." I hoped they knew I meant not just for this, but for keeping their noses in when they could have run and left everything on my scapegoat head.

Olivia raised her mug. Elle and I followed.

"To catching a murderer."

We clinked.

I tried to ignore the nausea in my stomach by drowning it in red wine and delicious, perfectly seared steak.

Dish Served Hot Podcast Transcript— Episode 91

[Podcast theme song plays, sung by creator, host, and star Mandy Thorne]

MANDY THORNE: The girls are getting desperate. Because Detective Mandy is on the case. They've dumped the victim's possessions, including the thumb—which, how do you dispose of a thumb? I guess no one's checking the trash for human digits. Gross.

I believe I've identified one of them. There will be more on that coming very soon.

And surprise of the week: we will be hosting a *live* show soon! An in-person recording! That you can attend! Details are linked in the show notes. Now, I can't tell you what we'll be discussing on the live recording, not yet, but you are not going to want to miss it, I promise. It will be worth every cent. So don't be scared by that price tag! And we suspect demand will be super high, so we've been beefing up our servers in preparation. Y'all are gonna want to be ready the second tickets go on sale.

And lastly, what you've all been waiting for, here's your juicy tidbit of the week: one of our queens is sleeping with a cop in the hopes that it'll help! She better be *really* good in bed!

CHAPTER 25

"Hello, is this Sebastian Jones?"

"Speaking. Who's this?"

"This is Kathryn, one of Tucker Jones's friends. I'm calling in case you haven't heard yet—Tucker has unfortunately passed away."

I hated talking on the phone. Especially with strangers. Awkward turtle times infinity. My antisocial ass was so introverted, I often made decisions based solely on avoiding phone calls. Dentist? Picked because of their fantastic online scheduling and email/text communications. Same for the doctor.

This was why I'd been resistant to Olivia's plan even though it made sense. I had asked, *Couldn't we match the USB list to Tucker's contacts and email them instead?* But she'd made a good point—not only were they unlikely to respond, but we wanted to hear their immediate reactions to his death.

The three of us had divided up the list, five contacts per person. Olivia had initially wanted to call the Joneses.

"He didn't introduce me while we were together, and I just...want to talk to them."

"Are you going to tell them who you are?" I asked, thinking about how I definitely did not want to talk to Tucker's family.

"You know, I didn't think this through. Actually, yeah, maybe this is too much."

"I'll take the family," Elle had said.

"I'll take the two Joneses unaccounted for," I found myself saying. As much as I didn't want to, I couldn't let Olivia do it.

Which was how I ended up here, on the phone with Sebastian Jones, the first of my five calls.

I had no idea what Sebastian's relation to Tucker was, how old he was, or whether he knew about Tucker's passing. I only knew there was a chance Sebastian was a suspect. And weirdly, I still didn't expect his first words to me.

"How'd you get my number?" He didn't even acknowledge Tucker's death.

"Tucker gave me a list of people to contact." *Closest to the truth when possible is best*, Olivia had coached us.

"So Tucker knew he was going to die?"

"No," I said, panicking. "I found the list after he passed."

"I think you're mistaken about what that's a list of, hon."

"What do you mean?" I hoped this was the opening I was waiting for.

"I just don't think he'd have cared if I knew."

"I'm sure he would have. Aren't you family?"

"I'm his uncle." There was a brief pause. "What happened to him?"

"We don't know, unfortunately."

"You said you were a friend?"

"Yes. I'm sorry for your loss."

He exhaled sharply. "I'm more sorry for yours. Seems you were closer to him than I've been." There was another pause. Then he admitted, "Tucker and I had a falling-out."

"You did? I'm so sorry to hear that. Do you mind if I ask what happened?"

"Yes, I do mind." He hung up.

Whoops. At least we had some confirmation. This was not a list of people Tucker was on friendly terms with.

We were on the right track.

The second person on my list didn't pick up and the third refused to talk to me. The fourth, Aurora Grant (née Jones), was angry enough to divulge without much prompting.

"Guess karma got him," she said right after I informed her of her cousin's passing. "He's nothing but a snake oil salesman, lying to his family members to get them to put their hard-earned savings into his business ventures. And all the money disappeared! Thirty-five thousand dollars! We can't prove it, but we suspect he pocketed it. Most of us cut him off, which to me felt like we were letting him win *again*. The money was already gone and now he never had to hear from us? So I sent him messages detailing our suffering—photos of overdue bills, the leak in the ceiling we can't afford to fix. My blood is boiling just thinking about it! I'm ashamed to be related to him."

I knew Tucker was terrible, but this hurt in a way I hadn't been expecting. Tucker was awful. I hated him for what he did to me, Olivia, and Elle. Yet I'd weirdly thought his faults were contained to cheating. Like maybe there was something undealt with there. But obviously he was just a shit person through and through.

"I'm so sorry," I told Aurora. Tucker was deep in debt, but if there was any money left anywhere, we would have to find a way to return it to the people he'd wronged.

"You shouldn't be. Be glad he died before he destroyed you, too."

I didn't have the heart to tell her he'd already done that.

Raymond Underwood, the last person on my list, picked up on the first ring. A drastic outlier from the rest of my calls, he was the only one distraught to hear about Tucker.

"Tucker *died*? How? He was so young!"

"Unknown, unfortunately. Were you two close?"

"Tuck and I were old friends, going back—goodness, has it been a decade now? We've had our ups and downs, of course, as any friendship would over that many years."

I wasn't sure how much to push, but this seemed to be an opening, and I had to take it. "Did he owe you money by chance?"

There was a brief pause, then Raymond—or Ray, as he'd asked me to please call him—exhaled in a laugh. "Is that what he told you? Is that all he thinks of me?"

"No," I said quickly, feeling bad for giving him that impression. "He didn't tell me that at all. I was just assuming."

"Tucker got himself in some trouble there, did he? Well, yeah, he borrowed some money from me way back when, but that's water under the ole bridge. I told him myself he didn't need to pay me back once I realized he was drowning." He sighed. "Is that what did him in?" I held my breath. "Did it get to be too much for him, maybe emotionally or mentally?"

And I exhaled. He hadn't been implying what I'd originally thought.

"Maybe," I said.

"That's downright awful. I should have checked in more. Is there a funeral?"

I...hadn't even thought about that. His family sure as hell wasn't throwing one. And who else did he have?

"I'll let you know if there is," I promised.

"You said you were a friend?"

"Yes."

There was a brief pause. "Maybe even more than a friend?"

I hadn't said that, but could he tell based on how I was talking about Tucker? I didn't answer.

"Well, Tucker's friend, thank you for calling. I hope he's at peace now."

I hadn't allowed myself to give in to this emotion since Tucker died, but Ray's words seemed to grant me permission to feel the loss untangled from everything else. "Me too."

I hung up quickly so he wouldn't hear me cry.

CHAPTER 26

Olivia and Elle turned up similar findings through their calls: lots of pissed off family members who were out a large sum of money (Elle), and other pissed off nonfamily members who were also out a large sum of money (Olivia). Elle's conversations had gone similarly to the one I'd had with Sebastian, though she also learned that Tucker's parents were swindled by their son, too, and weren't on speaking terms with him when they died several years ago.

"That's so sad," I said on our burner phone conference call a couple days later. "Why didn't he tell us that? Why say they were in Canada?"

"Maybe it was too painful to talk about," Elle suggested.

"Do you think they died from…heartbreak?" Olivia asked.

That could be a reason Tucker lied. Or maybe he just lied about everything.

I redirected our conversation so I wouldn't be eaten up by the rising emotion. "Good sleuthing, Elle."

"Why does it feel like everyone in the world wanted to kill him?" she lamented.

"Because he was a jackass," Olivia said matter-of-factly. Then she proceeded to tell us how three of her contacts were Tucker's golf buddies who had invested in Balls In, as well as a company she suspected Tucker made up so he could pocket the money. Another of her contacts was a business school acquaintance who had also invested in both, and her outlier was Atlas Barron, the CEO and founder of Balls In.

"Atlas was beside himself about Tucker's death," Olivia continued. "Said he was the company's most important donor and the person who believed in the product most."

"Why would he be on the list, then?" I asked. Ray's incongruity also popped into my head.

"Maybe they had a tiff over the money Tucker and his acquaintances lost," Olivia said. "Atlas wouldn't have told me if that was the case."

"Hmm." Elle paused. "Maybe we can get that out of him somehow? I totally have a way in, too. Get this—I pitch him, All Bits In. A revolutionary underwear that will keep all your lady bits in—"

"Isn't that just normal underwear?" Olivia interjected.

"Let me finish! It keeps your lady bits in *and* it stores all your bits. So, there will be a pocket for your credit card, another for your makeup..."

We spent the next fifteen minutes laughing as we expanded upon All Bits In before deciding our next moves: follow up with outliers Atlas and Ray, and continue trying those on the list who hadn't yet answered our calls.

• • • •

I decided on my own to share the USB list with Detective Birch. I would have mentioned this to the girls if I'd thought of it earlier, but it didn't cross my mind until the next day when the detective called asking for an update. And I had to feed him bits (ha) here and there to ensure I continued to roam free.

I hoped to avoid the interrogation room today. I wanted to be treated like a collaborator, not a criminal. As I approached Detective Birch's desk, the brunette talking to him spotted me in her peripheral vision, then turned to glare.

My pace slowed but without much other choice (except maybe to run for the bathroom, but that felt cowardly), I continued on my trajectory.

Her head followed me as I neared, the glare deepening. But before I reached the desk, she turned and stomped off.

"What was that about?" I asked.

"What was what about?" Detective Birch was looking around his desk, and he located a file a moment later. His poker face was impressive. "You said on the phone you had something to show me?"

"Oh, right." I pulled my purse off my shoulder to retrieve the USB. But, still rattled by that woman, I accidentally spilled the contents onto the detective's already messy desk. This was why I needed a purse with a zipper, but this large tote was my go-to since it was the only one that fit my laptop.

A pad, a tampon, and a pair of period underwear were what my eyes homed in on first. I shuffled those back in at breakneck speed. My mind was already preparing excuses—*I like to be prepared depending on my flow, like Goldilocks*—but Detective Birch was a gentleman and averted his eyes. As he helped me gather the rest of my things, I prayed to the universe that hated me, *Please don't let there be anything else humiliating or, worse, incriminating.*

The detective picked up my key chain, examining it for a moment. Luckily, he skipped past the more embarrassing items and singled out the Kubotan. "Are you feeling unsafe?"

My ex-boyfriend was murdered and I'm now tangled up in it. "I don't know" was all I said.

"Do you know how to use this?"

I shook my head.

"Do you need some tips?"

"Oh, um, yeah. That would be great."

He nodded. No elaboration.

Then he led me to the interrogation room. If he was trying to play good and bad cop by himself, he was nailing it.

• • • •

"You found this in a stuffed sriracha?" Detective Birch asked as he plugged the USB into a department laptop.

Why did I bother sharing that detail? It had seemed important at the time.

"I'm pretty sure it's a list of people Tucker was afraid of. And I called a bunch of them"—technically *we* called, but he didn't need to know that—"and Tucker owed money to a lot of them. He didn't seem to be on speaking terms with most of his family as a result."

"I see."

"Including his parents, who he was estranged from up until their deaths a few years ago."

"I see."

Was that all he could say in response to the golden information I was offering? I almost wanted to give him more to try for a bigger reaction, except this could be a ploy on his part. Or maybe he was just that grumpy.

"Do you not trust me or something?"

He looked surprised. "Why would you ask that?"

"Because you just don't seem to."

He didn't say anything.

"Is trusting someone that hard for you?"

His only reaction was to narrow his eyes. I knew exactly where he was coming from, yet it somehow felt different when I was the one in question.

"Yet you agreed to a deal," I pointed out.

No response.

"Are you ever going to tell me what happened with your partner?"

Still nothing.

"This feels very one-sided."

That got his mouth to tilt up slightly. "This isn't how your deals with law enforcement normally go?"

I wasn't going to dignify that with a reply. I could turn these tables, be the silent one for once.

But he didn't seem bothered.

Of course I caved first. "Can you at least tell me why you agreed to the deal?"

This one he finally answered. "You have access in a way I don't. My badge limits me. But you're already entrenched in Tucker's world. The perfect mole."

I knew he meant mole as in the animal, but for some reason, I pictured myself as a skin mole burrowed beneath Tucker's epidermis.

As if he could hear my thoughts, Detective Birch added, "And you have a different way of thinking. It's beneficial. As is the fact that your awkwardness and earnestness seem to hinder your ability to lie."

Except I had been able to keep things from him. Though just the thought of that was making my pits feel damp, pink-cupcakes style, so maybe he knew me pretty well after all. Maybe too well.

I couldn't help wondering, was that just his detective skills at work, or was he watching me in the same way I'd been watching him?

He finished writing something in his notebook, then retrieved the folder he'd found earlier on his desk. "Tell me what you make of this," he said as he slid a stack of photographs toward me.

The red bucket. Except these were photos of it in the closet. Tucker's socked foot could be seen from some angles, and I had to ignore it to be able to look at the rest of the image. The bucket was tucked away in the corner, in the shadows, easily missed if you weren't looking right at it, explaining why

Tucker hadn't noticed. There was a lid on top, which was a piece the detective hadn't shown me when the bucket had been brought out last time. And it wasn't a normal lid; there was a gaping rectangular hole in the center.

And another new piece I hadn't seen before: a strip of wire, lying on the floor. And attached to the end of it on the side closer to the bucket was a rectangular piece of plastic the same size and shape as the hole in the lid. And it had bits of fertilizer on it.

So what did we know? The bucket had fertilizer remnants inside when I saw it. If it was the medium in which the cleaner and fertilizer combined to form hydrogen sulfide, there had to be a way to trigger the reaction at the right time.

Given that the wire was connected to the rectangular piece of plastic with bits of fertilizer, that piece could have served, in essence, as a "trapdoor" that, when activated, allowed the fertilizer on top to fall into the bucket. If the bucket already had cleaner in it, the trapdoor opening would dump the fertilizer in and trigger the chemical reaction. But how to time that? And how to close the closet door? Unless they were connected, literally and figuratively, two birds, one stone. If the wire had also been tied to the door...

"When the door closed, the wire connected to it pulled the rectangular piece out from the lid, allowing the fertilizer and cleaner to mix," I said. "But what would make the door shut? I doubt Tucker closed it. Who goes into their walk-in closet and closes the door behind them?"

I quickly flipped through the photos until I came upon one of the door hinges. A spring had been inserted between the door and the wall. "When you push the door open," I murmured to myself, "it would engage the spring, which would then apply a force great enough to shut the door, which then triggered the wire and bucket contraption."

"Impressive, Ms. Hu."

I didn't feel impressive. I just felt sick to my stomach. This had been so meticulously planned. Who could hate Tucker this much?

"Do you think this was done by a professional?" I asked.

"We're exploring all possibilities."

I nodded. Then breathed deeply until the nausea passed. Before, I'd been in investigative mode, but now I was remembering this happened to someone I loved.

Detective Birch awkwardly patted the table space between us in support. Then he disappeared and returned with a Styrofoam cup as well as another folder.

I downed half the water in a single shaky gulp.

"I'm okay," I said.

The detective nodded, then shared two pages from the new folder: the first itemizing the residual chemicals identified from the bucket, and the second listing compositions of different cleaners and fertilizers.

I helped him narrow it down slightly.

Then I said, "If the killer was really smart, they would have used Tucker's own supplies." I didn't know if he had fertilizer—he didn't have a garden—but he probably had cleaners, especially since his condo was always immaculate.

"We have a list we can cross compare to."

Instead of sharing that list with me, Detective Birch leaned back in his chair, relaxed—a signal that the interrogation portion was now over, maybe because I'd passed whatever test he'd been giving me.

"You seem to trust me a little more now," I ventured, hoping my hypothesis was correct.

The corner of his mouth tilted up a millimeter. "Well, I doubt the murderer would have helped me figure out all these details."

"Or maybe I led you astray on purpose." Why did I say that? Was this another pink cupcake coming to bite me in the ass?

But he just chuckled. "It's cute that you think that." Immediately after the words came out, he flushed, then grabbed his handkerchief to cough into it. "Thanks for your cooperation today, Ms. Hu. We—the department—well, me on behalf of law enforcement, will be in contact with you shortly."

He exited abruptly.

Well. That was a new development.

But I couldn't let my defenses down. I could *not* let him in. I was never going to make that mistake again, not after the last time led to this clusterfuck I was *still* in. I hadn't seen the red flags then, and I wouldn't miss them now, not when my freedom depended on it. The detective's kindness and even compliments were just him playing good cop. He needed me since I was the "perfect mole," as he'd said himself.

But I also couldn't help thinking how maybe we had more in common than just our abnormal social behavior, slight grumpiness, and extreme awkwardness. Maybe he saw my intelligence, sense of humor, and weirdness—and maybe he liked it. Though I doubt he was calling me McCutie or debating nicknames with his savvy, sassy friends. (His loss.)

I was not sharing any of this with my savvy, sassy friends. Why give them the ammo to make fun of me with?

• • • •

Savvy and Sassy knew immediately without my saying a word.

"She's blushing!" Olivia exclaimed on our phone call that night.

"You can't see me!" Our burner phones were not capable of video calls.

"I can tell by your voice!"

"Oh my god, did you kiss him?"

"No!" I almost yelled. "I don't want to talk about it." Especially after Elle asked if we kissed. I would have sounded like a twelve-year-old if I'd said, *No, he just called me cute.*

I tried to change the subject. "What's the update on your end?" Olivia had asked for the call.

"Oh, nothing. We just wanted to ask about McHottie."

"You two."

I hung up, but I was smiling.

Dish Served Hot Podcast Transcript—
Episode 92

[Podcast theme song plays, sung by creator, host, and star
Mandy Thorne]

MANDY THORNE: First off, thanks for the record high
interest in the live show. We sold out in ten minutes! You Thornies
are the best, always showing up.

And speaking of, we've started getting tips from y'all, and I just
want to say thank you to everyone who reached out. When I tell
y'all I have the best resources, I am of course including all of you!
So please join me and put on your detective hats, too. We want
to hear *everything* you have to say. And if your information is good,
we'll have you as a guest on the show—yes, you!

And our first Thornie to grace the show will be featured today!

[imitating Mister Rogers's voice] Hello, Neighbor.

NEIGHBOR: [giggle] Hi, Mandy! I can't believe I'm talking to
you right now! You were my all-time fave on *Love Hut*! I think you
should've gone the whole way!

MANDY: I would have if the rest of them hadn't ganged up
on me. My awesomeness was too much of a threat! Anyhoo,
Neighbor, why don't you tell the other Thornies why we gave you
that nickname?

NEIGHBOR: Because I'm the neighbor of one of the murderers.
And you know how all the family, friends, and neighbors always say
they can't believe what that person's done, they've always been so
nice, yada yada? Well, I am *not* surprised AT ALL. I'm telling you, I
knew this gal was up to no good.

MANDY: How?

NEIGHBOR: I once saw her getting rid of a body in her backyard. It was a pig's, but you know what they say about starting with small animals and then moving on to humans. She had all these people come over, and they cooked it and ate it! Like cannibals! I wonder if they knew she'd been stringing it up, putting an apple in its mouth, and burying it before they arrived. My theory is that she was trying to get rid of it, realized she couldn't, and then found a way to eat the evidence!

MANDY: That could be when it all started.

NEIGHBOR: And then another time, I saw that she had a dog in her yard and thought, here goes the neighborhood. All that yapping, not to mention it ate everything in sight—*everything!* Kids' ice-cream cones, flowers, groundhogs. Then, do you know what happened?

MANDY: Tell me.

NEIGHBOR: The next day, the dog was gone! Vanished! Nowhere to be found! I think it made one wrong move and she *crrrrrk*, vanished him. The same way as that pig.

MANDY: There you have it, folks. Even more proof. And a good reminder to keep an eye on your neighbors.

NEIGHBOR: Binoculars help. And night vision goggles.

CHAPTER 27

I texted Ray, inviting him to coffee in the hopes of learning more, and he accepted.

Funny how that worked—the ones willing to divulge were either in a good place with Tucker or so angry they couldn't help themselves, like Aurora.

Ray suggested we meet at a mom-and-pop coffee shop across town with a decent online rating. When I arrived five minutes late, Ray was already there. He was a couple decades older than I thought—I'd assumed he and Tucker were close in age—but it had to be him because there were no other customers and he stood as soon as I entered. The barista barely looked up before returning to polishing glasses.

"Kathryn," Ray said in a booming voice like we were long-lost friends. "What a pleasure to meet you."

"Likewise." I went for a handshake, but he went in for a hug, which made me tense up. I forced myself to relax. This was what normal people did in social situations.

"I ordered for you." He pointed to the porcelain teacup across from him with white foam on top, no pattern drawn in it. I couldn't tell what beverage was beneath.

This was weird, right? It wasn't what normal people did? How would he know what I wanted? Though I guess it was nice that he paid?

"Thanks," I said as I slipped into the booth.

Ray leaned closer as soon as I was settled. "Kathryn, my dear, I hope you don't think me forward, but there are some things I'd like to know. You see, Tucker and I were once such dear friends, and I know he had difficulty with his romantic relationships"—had Tucker always been a cheater or was Ray talking about something else?—"and it would just ease my heart to know that he found something meaningful before he passed. Can you tell me about your relationship with him?"

All my alarms were sounding. And if my alarm system had been so bad it hadn't even foreseen Tucker's betrayal, did that mean something was very truly horribly wrong here? Or had my system readjusted too far after said betrayal and I now found everything suspicious?

I tried to deflect. "We were close, just like you and he seemed to be, before. How did you meet? When was the last time you talked to him? What happened between you two?" Maybe if I peppered him with enough questions, he'd back off or at least get distracted.

The warmth drained slightly from his face, just around his eyes and only for a second, but it was enough.

My alarm system was not overreacting. This was off.

I retrieved my phone with such shaky fingers I almost dropped it, but I tried to use it to sell my story. "Oh my god! I'm sorry, there's been an emergency. I have to go. Thanks for the coffee." Or whatever it was.

I started to slide out of my seat.

But as I reached the edge of the booth, the barista was suddenly there. One second he was behind the bar, the next he was looming over me, a brick wall blocking my way out. Up close, I could see scars and bulging muscles I hadn't noticed before.

"You're not going anywhere," I heard from beside me. Ray's voice, previously warm and familiar, had taken on a singsong, teasing quality.

Kathryn's Eighth Law of Luck: By the time you see the red flags, it will be too late.

CHAPTER 28

They didn't tie me up, mostly because there was no need. The barista—not a barista, let's be real. The nonbarista took my phone out of my hands, then continued to stand guard next to my side of the booth. Ray locked the front door and flipped the OPEN sign to CLOSED.

"Do you own this place or something?" I asked.

"Yes."

Well, shit. This was looking worse by the second.

Why hadn't I considered the danger more thoroughly before this moment? I'd been scared, sure, but it hadn't been enough to deter me or even make me second-guess what we were doing, as it should have.

Hadn't Detective Birch himself warned me to be careful? Given how few words he'd said to me in total, that should have signaled how many risks there were. At the same time, why hadn't he made a bigger deal about the danger? Why hadn't he given me a rundown of what could go wrong *and* taught me to defend myself? Speaking of, he was supposed to teach me how to use the Kubotan, but he never did because he got flustered over calling me cute. How childish that felt now. I did have it in my purse… Should I try to use it? Or would that only make my situation worse, especially since I didn't know what I was doing and the nonbarista most definitely did?

I should have taken more precautions, maybe told Detective Birch I was meeting with one of the names on the USB list. Why did I naively believe Ray's story about Tucker when my own hypothesis was that someone on the list killed him? When was I going to stop making the worst decisions?

Maybe all my bad-luck hypotheses were garbage, just like the rest of my research, and the problem at the center of it all was me. Wasn't that what the evidence pointed to? Taylor Swift was right. I was the problem, not him.

Ray's now creepily sweet voice broke into my spiraling thoughts. "Ms. Hu." Of course he knew who I was. The question was, who was he? "Do you have access? To Tucker's bank accounts, laptop, that sort of thing?"

"No." I hoped I'd said it convincingly. After all, it was the truth—Olivia was the one with access, not me. She had told me his passwords but I'd forgotten them all, truly. And since broken-clock Mandy had annoyingly stumbled onto that one true fact, that we had his laptop, Olivia had put it "in a safe place" that neither Elle nor I knew for our own safety.

The warmth leeched from Ray's face and voice. "You're lying."

"I'm not. I'm really not."

"Don't destroy an old man's dreams, Ms. Hu. I know you have the laptop. Or is it in the possession of another one of his women?"

So he knew there were others. But he might not know who. "Or maybe it's in the possession of one of the many people he owes money to."

"Come now, dear. We're all friends here."

"I'm telling you the truth. Why would I know anything? I wasn't the only one he was with, as you said. And I wasn't his favorite."

"Do you know where his favorite is?"

I shook my head. I was about to lie that I didn't even know who his favorite was when he cursed under his breath.

"That's been a problem for me, Ms. Hu, which means it's a problem for you. The reason I turned my attention your way is because I've been trying to find Tucker's wife and I've somehow come up empty even with all the resources at my fingertips."

I blacked out for a second. My heart stopped beating. The world stopped spinning.

I'd misheard him, right?

As I plummeted into a dark, upside-down abyss, Ray continued talking, oblivious to my crumbling.

"You see, my dear, our boy Tucker owes me money. A lot of it. He borrowed a hefty sum with the promise of a healthy interest—for my troubles—and he's very much past the due date. I haven't seen a single cent."

"You're a loan shark," I blurted out. There was too much coming at me all at once.

"Obviously, dear. Here I thought your PhD would have made you catch on a bit quicker. Might want to ask for a refund, though of course that's not how it works. There are rules in place for these kinds of things—with universities, banks, even loan sharks. Otherwise, the world would fall into chaos, would it not? Anyway, I thought getting my hands on Tucker's wife"— there was that word again—"would give him the proper incentive, but that has proven fruitless. And now that dear ole Tuck is dead, I have to get creative to get my money back."

He had to be mistaken, right? Did he wrongly think that Tucker and Olivia had gotten married, not just almost engaged? He didn't look like the kind of person who made mistakes, though.

"Tucker's wife," I repeated blandly, unable to form a proper question.

Ray's eyes widened in shock. "You didn't know? Here I am, being a dick, telling you that your boyfriend was married. How did you not know? That's it. I'm convinced. Our country's educational system is broken. But wait, you said you knew you weren't the only one." He started laughing. "How many mistresses did Tucker boy have? I didn't bother looking into it because I didn't think they'd know anything, but maybe I should have for fun. Is this why he needed money so badly? Women are expensive."

I wanted to punch him, claw his eyes out, but the non-barista was still breathing down my neck.

Fuck Tucker for being married. Fuck him for making the worst decisions ever, for being the worst person ever, for stealing and embezzling and cheating. And fuck him for giving me the USB! I thought he was trusting me, asking for help, but he was just putting me in danger. He was the problem. He was toxic nuclear waste that condemned every person he touched. And now I was drowning, unfairly paying for his sins.

"I'm sorry that Tucker stole from you," I said, using strong language to show I was on his side. "I wish I could help, but I can't. It's like you said—I'm just his mistress; I don't know anything."

Ray was silent for a second. Then his predatory eyes raked over me as he said, "You know, I'd just about given up hope recently. And then you called. I couldn't believe my luck. Your voice was just dripping with grief and pain and regret, and I knew immediately who you were to him. And since I couldn't find Lauren, I figured I'd see what you know. Now, I'm at my wit's end. If you don't come up with something..." He trailed off ominously.

"You can't hold me here," I said while tucking the wife's name away for later. "That's a crime."

He laughed, which sent shivers up my spine. I wasn't getting out of here, was I?

"I'm just an honest man looking for my money," Ray said innocently. "I'm upfront with every client that comes to me. That's not a crime, now, is it? Tucker boy was the one committing crimes. Adultery, breaking his contract with me, his financial mess."

Ray folded his hands in front of him. "Ms. Hu, I'm just looking for my hundred fifty thousand dollars. I don't even need all of it. Whatever you have is a good starting point."

Now it was my turn to laugh, but I held it in. "I don't have anything. Truly. I'm a graduate student."

Ray sighed. "I was afraid of that." He signaled to the nonbarista, who started to fold his long legs underneath the table so he could sit next to me. "As I said before, I do need something. Maybe my friend here—"

"Wait." Fuck, it felt like the nonbarista's giant hands were already closing around my neck. "I'll get you something valuable. It'll even be from Tucker. But I need a phone call, and you have to promise to let me and the other person go."

Ray gestured to the nonbarista, who pulled my phone out of his pocket and slid it toward me.

I wanted to use the burner phone, but I couldn't let him know I had that at the bottom of my purse—it might come in handy later. Her number wasn't in my contacts, but I knew it by heart.

Taking a deep breath, I dialed.

CHAPTER 29

Olivia picked up on the first ring. "Why are you calling my burner from your—"

"I'm in trouble." I tried not to look at Ray or the non-barista, who were listening to my call on speakerphone. Ray had, of course, insisted.

"Do you need legal help?"

"No, it's worse than that. I'm meeting with—"

Ray tapped the table with two fingers. He was smiling, but his eyes were stern, daring me to test him.

"Bring the ring. My engagement ring." I was hoping that Olivia would catch on to the hidden meanings beneath what I was saying—for her not to reveal who she was or that it was her ring. "To pay back number five." And hopefully now she would know I was meeting with Ray from the list and was in trouble. She and Elle both had his info. We just had to play this right.

I quickly gave Olivia the location. Then Ray gave me another look and I added, "Um, and don't tell anyone, okay?" I hoped she would know that meant to tell at least Elle if not more people.

Ray hung up for me and took the phone back.

Then, we waited.

• • • •

"How long had Tucker been married?" I asked Ray. The silence and curiosity were both killing me.

He just laughed.

Well, that was a clear enough signal. Silence it was.

Ten minutes later, Olivia arrived. Had she sped here and run every light? At least she was in one piece.

The nonbarista let her in, then locked the door behind her. Olivia immediately read the tension in the room, which was reflected in the clench of her jaw.

Maybe I shouldn't have brought her into this. But I also didn't see another way out.

Before she could say anything, I quickly jumped in. "Ray, this is my lawyer." Then I turned to Olivia. "Thanks for getting my engagement ring for me. My ex-boyfriend Tucker owes this man a lot of money, and I'm going to use the ring to pay him back."

Ray looked Olivia up and down hungrily, and I wanted to claw his eyes out even more than before. I shouldn't have called her. Yet I couldn't help feeling relieved that she, the brains, was here.

"I left the ring in a secure location, which I'll text to you once you let us go," she said.

Like I said, the brains. We would be okay.

Ray laughed. "That's cute, sweetheart. Hand the ring over. Now."

Olivia stood steadfast. "I don't have it."

"Then you and your friend are out of options." Ray nodded to the nonbarista, who took a step closer to Olivia.

By his second step, Olivia grabbed the ring from her pocket and flung it. "Okay, you got what you wanted. Kat, let's go."

I grabbed my purse and hurried to get out of the booth. But

the nonbarista was there in a flash, keeping me trapped. Ray picked up the ring, then retrieved a jeweler's loupe from his front pocket. Did he carry that everywhere? What was Tucker doing dealing with someone this shady?

As he examined the ring, he spoke to Olivia. "Who are you, my dear?"

"She's my lawyer. You said you'd let us go," I insisted, but only with my words. I was too scared to try to exit the booth against the nonbarista.

"This is fake," Ray said.

"What?" Olivia yelled.

No. She couldn't reveal who she was.

"What?!" I tried to exclaim with even more indignation.

"Tucker proposed to you"—Ray smiled at Olivia, having picked up on her secret—"with a fake ring." He smashed it on the table and the "diamond" shattered into a thousand pieces. Of course we hadn't examined it or gotten it appraised. "You think a man in debt can afford a diamond ring?"

Truthfully, I hadn't thought much about it. But deep down, I figured Tucker either stole it or bought it with money he'd embezzled.

Ray flicked two fingers and the nonbarista gestured for Olivia to take a seat next to me. "Girls, you two are in a bit of trouble here."

CHAPTER 30

"Run, Olivia!" I yelled. If she could get out of here before the nonbarista trapped us both in the booth, it was our only chance. Then she could get help.

She hadn't taken two steps toward the door before the nonbarista reached into the back of his pants and pulled out a gun.

My stomach plunged. Now what?

Olivia put both hands in the air and came over. The nonbarista moved to let her in, then resumed his guard position.

At least we were sitting together. Olivia's hand grasped mine the second it could.

"I'm sorry," I whispered to her. I shouldn't have asked her to come. Maybe from now on, I needed to do the opposite of what I thought was best. Turned out, I was part of the problem, too.

"Girls, girls, you're making this so difficult for no reason. All I want is a little bit of my money back. You're the ones forcing me to keep you here. Now, what kind of money can I get out of you two? I assume you have family members?"

That was his plan? To call my parents and ask for a ransom? I could see exactly where that would go.

"*Wei, who this?*"

"*We have your daughter.*"

"*Ay, thank goodness. You marry her? We pay you. How much you want?*"

"Fifty thousand dollars."

"Aiyah, so steep! You a doctor?"

"Ma'am, we have your daughter. We will keep her until you pay."

"Yes, yes, you keep. All yours."

I wouldn't even get to say goodbye. My mom couldn't even tell the cops what happened. *"Yushan get married, is all. Finally. You know she almost thirty? Can you believe!"*

It would have been funny if my situation wasn't so dire. Others could count on their moms to save them, and this was what I expected from mine in a hostage situation. Why couldn't I depend on my mom for anything?

Wait...

My mom. My mom!

My god, maybe she *could* save me. I still had a secret weapon that Ray didn't know about. If I could just get to it...

I tried to signal to Olivia that I had an idea and needed to be covert. Maybe needed a distraction, too. I had no idea if she understood what I was saying, but it was now or never.

My purse was already in my lap from before. I slowly started inching my hand inside.

Suddenly, Olivia started crying. Very loudly.

This was my window. I pretended to be startled and quickly made my move.

CHAPTER 31

Five minutes later, Olivia was still crying and my hope was beginning to dwindle.

Moments ago, when I had reached into my purse, grabbed the Life Alert, and pushed the button, it had felt almost comical. *Help! Help!* I heard in my head. *I'm in deep shit and I can't get out!*

The Alert contained a GPS tracker and my mom was supposedly paying for the subscription, so they would send help to the café, right? But this was taking too long. What was their response time supposed to be? All I could remember from the packaging was something about a monitoring center and 24/7 service—why hadn't I read the details more carefully?

Had my mom forgotten to pay? Or thought she had but messed it up? Honestly, neither of those would surprise me, and before, I hadn't cared enough to verify whether she'd set it up correctly. In fact, I would have preferred if she hadn't.

I couldn't bring myself to look at Olivia. Her presence here was my fault, and I was more upset at myself for that than anything else I'd ever done, including my relationship with Tucker, the pranks, and being in the condo when the detective arrived. Endangering her was completely different from endangering myself.

Ray hadn't been reacting to Olivia's crying, but now he was looking from her to me. He seemed to think something was amiss, and by the time I realized it was because I wasn't comforting her, it was too late. I started to put my arm around her shoulders, but he was already standing.

"Location change," he said to the nonbarista. "Back to headquarters." The way he said that last word was ominous. No one was finding us there.

Olivia and I grasped hands and planted our butts down firmly.

"No. We're fine here," I said more confidently than I felt.

"How much money are we talking?" Olivia asked, and I squeezed her hand harder, trying to tell her not to go there. "I might be able to pay."

I didn't want that. Tucker couldn't cost Olivia her heart *and* her savings. And her offer was premature. It wasn't like Ray was going to kill us. Though...second location, maybe he was?

Hopelessness crept in. Especially because my plan likely hadn't worked—about ten minutes had passed by now.

Ray snapped his fingers. "Let's go."

We still didn't move.

The nonbarista reached over and grabbed Olivia's arm so hard she yelped.

"Don't hurt her!" I screeched.

Ignoring me, he yanked her out of the booth and threw her over his right shoulder.

I quickly put my left hand up and slid to the end of the booth willingly, my purse in my right hand. "Put her down. We're coming."

He made no move to do so.

I only had a second to decide. Did I go with my gut or the exact opposite? Did I really make the worst decisions or had this all been a byproduct of Tucker being the worst?

No time to think.

As I prepared to stand, I committed. One swift movement, as fast as possible. No room for hesitation. My right hand dove into my purse and grasped the Kubotan, then I lunged at the nonbarista, aiming for the open left half of his body where Olivia wasn't.

I jabbed, over and over, into his shoulder, arm, stomach—wherever I could contact. The tapered end wasn't sharp but maybe if I used enough force, especially on sensitive areas, I could cause pain or at least surprise him.

When I managed to catch his side, he dropped Olivia. She immediately scrambled to her feet and grabbed his arm. He swung wildly, knocking her sideways into a wall. I forced myself to ignore her groan and continued attacking. But it felt like trying to drive a pencil into concrete. I was hurting him, but nowhere near enough. He quickly overpowered me and wrapped an arm around my neck. His other hand yanked my hair and subsequently my head backward so hard that tears streamed down my face. The force of it lifted me in the air, and I felt my feet swinging beneath me, trying to find the floor so my lungs could find air.

Out of the corner of my eye, I saw Ray grabbing Olivia. She fought back, trying to get to me with everything she had.

I wanted to tell her so many things—*Sorry; I'm so glad I met you; Don't let Tucker keep pulling you down*—but I couldn't talk. I couldn't breathe.

Right before I slipped out of consciousness, a gun went off.

CHAPTER 32

Sweet, sweet air. As soon as the gunshot sounded, the non-barista released me and I crumpled to the floor. Oxygen had never tasted so good, though it hurt going in.

The nonbarista backed away from me, arms in the air. My eyes were focused on him, my attacker, but once I realized I wasn't in imminent danger anymore, they swept the scene.

Just inside the doorway, inching toward me, gun drawn, was *Detective Birch*. How was he here?

Tears of relief flooded my eyes. I quickly wiped them away so I could see clearly.

Another officer came in and made the nonbarista lie on the ground so he could cuff him. One threat down.

But Ray was still holding a struggling Olivia in front of him, using her as a shield.

"Let her go," Detective Birch said calmly. "No one needs to get hurt."

He jerked his head toward me, then toward the door. But I couldn't leave Olivia. Especially not when I'd gotten her into this.

"I'll let her go if you let me go," Ray said. "She'll just come with me out the back door, you don't follow, and I'll let her go there."

"That's not how we're going to play this," Birch said. He jerked his head at me one more time, but I didn't move.

Another officer came in, gun also drawn.

My adrenaline was pumping. My brain was flying, trying to think of anything that could help.

Ray didn't have a weapon that I knew of. His nonbarista carried the gun. Maybe he had a weapon strapped to his body somewhere, but he was currently using both arms to restrain Olivia, his forearms looped through her elbows. His hands were empty. If she could get one good blow in, she could get away, and the worst he could do was punch her. Honestly, the bigger threat felt like Detective Birch's gun aimed at her. As long as he didn't shoot, Olivia should be fine.

"Everybody stay calm," I said, mostly speaking to Detective Birch. Then I turned to Olivia. "Liv, what was Tucker's most prized possession?"

She understood immediately. Her arms were locked, but her feet were free. She jerked suddenly against Ray's hold, the surprise catching him off guard and allowing her to create space between them. Swiftly, she kicked backward, driving her heel as hard as she could into Ray's balls.

Balls In. As in, kicked so hard they hopefully went inside of him.

Ray howled and dropped his arms so he could clutch his crotch.

Olivia kicked him in the same spot again just as Detective Birch ran forward. As one of the officers pulled Olivia back, Detective Birch restrained a whimpering Ray easily.

It was over. Olivia and I were safe.

Kathryn's Ninth Law of Luck: Maybe there were one or two people in the world who could save you, including yourself.

CHAPTER 33

"Are you okay?" the detective asked me.

I managed a nod. "Thanks for..." I circled my hands vaguely. "You know. Just, thanks, Detective Birch."

He hesitated before saying, "Adrian, please."

"Adrian," I said, trying it out. I liked it more than I wanted to. "Please call me Kathryn."

He smiled, then nodded.

We were outside the café. Ray and the nonbarista had been taken in by other officers. The parking lot was filled with flashing lights and uniforms. One of the medics had just finished examining me—get some rest, call my doctor if I notice any changes or abnormalities—and I was sitting in the open back of the ambulance, a blanket around my shoulders. Olivia was with another medic several feet away. I hadn't had a chance to talk to her privately yet other than to ask if she was okay, to which she'd only managed a brief nod. I wanted to go to her now, but I'd been instructed to let the medic finish in private. And Detective Birch—Adrian—was still standing in front of me, now handing me a handkerchief.

"What's this for?" I asked, quickly checking my nose with the back of my hand. Dry as a bone (origin connected to animal bones found in the sun—which I found misleading since bones in living vertebrates are wet).

He flushed. "Oh. Um. I'm not sure. I thought maybe you'd be sweaty? What you went through was..." He scratched the back of his hand absentmindedly.

This was a new side of him I hadn't seen before. He seemed...agitated. Lost.

I tried to lighten the mood. "I could have used that self-defense lesson."

"I am truly sorry," he said sincerely.

Guess I was awkward even when I was trying to be normal. "I was just joking. This wasn't your fault."

"It was." He said it confidently as if he'd instructed me to meet with a known violent loan shark. But now that I was thinking about it, I guess he had in some ways. He didn't know the extent of the danger, but he had told me to investigate.

"I should have never asked you to do this. It was bad judgment." The distress on his face hinted at something deeper at play, but I didn't know how to address it.

"Hey, I'm okay. You showed up just in time." Speaking of... "Um, how did you know to come?"

I wasn't sure if this was treading into dangerous territory—did Olivia tell Elle, who called the police?—but I needed to know.

Adrian gave me a sad smile. "You were smart to press your Life Alert."

Great. How did he know about that? Talk about embarrassing. Even though it had saved us, I suddenly wanted the earth to swallow me whole.

"Uh, that was from my mom. She worries." I was pretty sure my entire face was red. "Doesn't that go to some Life Alert monitoring center, though?"

He scratched the back of his head. "It does. I...saw it on your key chain when it fell out of your purse the other day, and I contacted Life Alert to request any notifications go straight to me."

Double great. "Did you do that because you were worried about my safety, or because you don't trust me and wanted to keep tabs on my whereabouts?"

He pressed his lips together. "Two birds?" He just had to use an idiom. (Unfortunate origin: slingshots.) "But I completely trust you now, okay? Though why didn't you listen to me?"

"When?" I honestly couldn't remember.

"When I told you to get out of there. You were free, you should have run."

"I couldn't leave my friend."

His eyes widened in surprise. "That's...very admirable." He paused, then said, "I thought she was your lawyer."

"She's more my friend than my lawyer." *Please don't look into her.*

"Well, loyalty is...hard to come by these days. That may be related to why I have a hard time trusting."

I wasn't sure if he'd go on—before, he definitely wouldn't have—and I held my breath as he walked over to sit beside me on the ambulance floor.

Was this finally it? Was he going to open up? If so, it only took my near death from helping him do his job, sheesh. But maybe he meant it when he said he trusted me now.

I considered prompting with a question about his partner, but I'd been around him enough to know I should just wait. He liked to take his time, and questions only distracted him.

"My previous partner screwed me over. We were working an assault case, and something felt off. But my partner, who was more experienced, told me it was in my head, he'd dealt with similar cases before, and to follow his lead. I didn't want to, but I felt like I had no choice. If you don't trust your partner..." He sighed. "You have to, with your life. By the time I started finding evidence of something larger at play, he'd already taken a hefty bribe and skipped town. It made me question everything and everyone. It's why I haven't been able to find a new partner, and it's why I don't ever ignore my gut."

"Yet you trusted me enough to let me go."

"Well, I had mixed feelings. I didn't want to believe you, but my gut also told me the evidence wasn't adding up. And you can't lie." A brief twitch of his mouth was the only hint that the last part was said tenderly. "I thought our deal would be the best of both. I could keep an eye on you and you could help me get to the truth, including if you were involved. Even if I was wrong and you were actually the greatest liar of all time, everyone cracks eventually. But again, I shouldn't have done that. I should never have put you in danger."

I wasn't sure what to say. There were too many emotions, and this wasn't the best time to sort them out.

So all I said was "I'm sorry about your partner. And I might know a bit about what you went through and how you felt."

"Yes, I know. I'm sorry about that, too."

There was a brief silence filled with understanding.

"So what's going to happen—" I started, but he cut me off.

"No more investigating."

"But—"

"No more. We're good. We have Ray. He likely had something to do with Tucker's death." I had told Adrian who Ray was in my statement.

"Why, though? What's his motive?"

"It could have been to send a message. Loan sharks have reputations, and Ray can't have his clients not paying him back. Rest assured, okay? We have him, and we'll be interrogating him. As soon as I'm able, I'll give you updates, but it might be a while before I can share any information. So just…stop investigating and relax. Recover. You've been through a lot."

I nodded slowly. He seemed pretty confident, though I wasn't sure how much was an act just to get me off the case.

"When you're feeling better..." He tilted his head to peer at me, the slightest curve to his mouth. "Stop by anytime for that self-defense lesson, Kathryn."

He stood and shuffled off, maybe to hide the fact that his cheeks were starting to flush. I wished he had stayed. Not because I wanted to flirt or know for sure whether he'd been blushing, but because I needed him to answer the question that popped into my head:

Am I still in danger?

CHAPTER 34

Olivia and I left in separate cars and went straight from the café to her townhome. Once we were both inside hugging throw pillows on the sofa, we sat in silence for a moment, too exhausted physically and emotionally to talk. Then, for the next five minutes, all we could do was continually ask each other, *Are you okay?* After that, we shifted into business mode and discussed what details we had and hadn't shared with the police. Our stories lined up, so all was good there. Eventually, I asked if Elle knew what had happened.

"No, she doesn't. I texted her on the way here telling her to come over, but that's it."

"You didn't contact her before you left for the café?" I asked, not able to mask the surprise on my face.

"You told me not to tell anyone!"

I thought our connection had been better than that. I tried to think of something positive to say since everything had ended up okay. "I guess, thanks for listening to me?"

There was an awkward beat of silence. Then Olivia, her voice small, said, "I didn't know what was going on, but I knew you were in trouble, and I was scared something bad would happen if I told anyone."

I hadn't thought about that. If the situation were reversed,

I could see myself doing the same thing. "Thank you. Truly. For everything. I'm sorry I brought you into it."

"I'm always here for you, Kat."

This time, the beat of silence was filled with affection, and I didn't have to worry about whether or not Olivia knew what I was trying to project.

A moment later, a smirk crossed her face. "So how did McDouble-Oh-Yes know to come?" Oh shit. That was fitting, especially after seeing him in action today. "Did it have to do with why I had to cry for way too long? I hardly ever cry, by the way."

More proof of why I shouldn't have doubted our connection. I reached into my bag, clasped nothing, then moved to hand Olivia the invisible object.

She opened her palm. "What's this?"

"An Oscar for Best Performance."

She laughed, closing her fist around the imaginary award. "Let's never do it again."

"Your distraction allowed me to use this." When I reached into my bag this time, I pulled out the Life Alert.

Olivia screeched and fell over. "Why do you have one of those?"

I never talked to anyone about my parents, but I suddenly wanted Olivia to know what it was like for me. As I told her about the jar opener and step stool and she howled, I couldn't help joining in.

"Of course it had to be this that saved us! Now I have to be grateful to my mom. But if I tell her, just imagine what's going to show up on my doorstep next!"

"What could be worse than a Life Alert?"

"A mail-order husband? Though maybe that wouldn't be so bad. If the movies and books are right, he'll turn out to be my soul mate. As long as he doesn't have other girlfriends, it'll be a step up."

"In life or on your step stool?"

It was the perfect distraction until Elle showed up.

Unfortunately, after she arrived, we had to fill her in on what happened, which meant reliving it.

Olivia and I talked in short bursts, finishing each other's sentences to get through it as fast as possible.

Elle looked flabbergasted. Which made sense—there was so much, and we'd thrown it at her in one go. But a minute later, she, not surprisingly, turned into Mama Bear, wanting to make sure her cubs were okay.

Now Olivia and I were wrapped in blankets, our hands around steaming mugs—hot cocoa for Liv, tea for me.

After Elle ordered Chinese food for us, she asked, "So the detective thinks this is over?"

I shrugged. "That's what he said, but I think he might have just wanted me to stop investigating."

"He feels bad for putting his crush in danger," Olivia said with a knowing nod.

I flushed immediately. "That's not true."

Olivia turned to Elle. "It is. I saw him with her. Don't believe what she says."

"About McSmokeShow? Definitely not."

I tried to throw a pillow at them, but my mug of tea was too full and the pillow barely left my side.

Olivia laughed, but Elle looked more serious.

"Why didn't you call me?"

I wasn't sure if she meant, why didn't I call her instead of Olivia, or why didn't Olivia call on her way to the café.

Olivia answered both questions. "Kat told me not to tell anyone. And she needed the engagement ring from me to pay the loan shark back. Though Tucker just screwed us yet again with that fake diamond."

Elle shook her head. "I can't believe he got involved with a loan shark."

"*That's* what you can't believe?"

I was barely listening because there was an unpleasant conversation we needed to have.

Band-Aid, I reminded myself. That first day meeting Olivia felt like a lifetime ago.

"There's something else I found out. And it's…a lot."

Olivia and Elle leaned forward. Even though I wanted to rip the Band-Aid off, my mouth was completely dry.

Olivia came over and put a hand on mine. Elle did the same on my other side.

"According to Ray, Tucker's married."

I had expected cursing, raised voices, anger. But it was dead silent.

Olivia spoke first. "Do you think Ray was telling the truth?"

"I can't think of a reason he'd lie."

Elle still hadn't spoken. I had expected her to react the strongest, calling Tucker names, cursing his soul in hell.

"You okay?" I asked her.

She blinked a few times before meeting my eyes. "I just… I don't know whether to laugh or cry or yell. All I can think about is how I should've known from the beginning."

Olivia and I both gave her confused looks.

"His Tinder profile! *Married and looking for some fun.* How is he *still* managing to make me feel like this is all my fault for not seeing what he was putting out there, like in that *Mr. Right* movie where Sam Rockwell keeps telling Anna Kendrick he's an assassin and she thinks it's all a joke. Was Tucker a genius or the dumbest person in the world?"

"Was it a joke to him?" Olivia wondered out loud. "Or a way to rationalize to himself that he wasn't the absolute worst?"

"What I want to know is, how did he have the time?" I couldn't wrap my head around it. Not only was there another woman, but a *spouse*?

"Maybe it's not true," Olivia said.

Guess we were switching roles today, because I became the brains and the guts by saying, "Well, let's find out."

Elle nodded. "Did Ray give you anything else?"

"Her name."

• • • •

We searched for "Lauren Jones" and "Lauren and Tucker Jones," but neither yielded much.

"Tucker knew how to wipe his presence," Elle said, exasperated. "Of course we're not going to find anything!"

"Why can't we find anything about the wife?" Olivia asked. "Why would she need to scrub herself off the internet?"

I unfortunately knew the answer to that. "Because of Ray. He was looking for her."

The air grew somber. We knew what Ray was capable of. I suddenly hoped Lauren was far, far away, somewhere safe.

"Maybe we should just let her be," I said.

"We're not looking *for* her exactly, are we?" Olivia clarified. "Just finding out if our cheating scumbag ex-boyfriend was actually married. I think we deserve to know."

"Right," I said. "Of course." I knew it would be healthier to move on and forget Tucker, especially now that I was no longer suspect number one, but I also needed answers, just like Olivia seemed to.

"Okay," Elle said, taking charge. "Time to make a to-do list."

CHAPTER 35

As usual, we split up the tasks. Olivia would try to track down the marriage certificate, and in the meantime, mostly because I couldn't bear to sit around doing nothing, Elle and I divided up a very long and daunting list of Lauren Joneses to look into.

After many monotonous, soul-crushing days at the lab where I spent most of my time either questioning my career or calling too many Lauren Joneses—who either didn't know Tucker or didn't answer because who picked up calls from random numbers these days?—I found my way back to the police station. For the first time, it wasn't because I was in trouble.

"You said you'd teach me self-defense?" I said when I walked up to Adrian at his desk.

He'd been absorbed in the papers before him, but I saw the change when he recognized my voice. His blue eyes went from murky to shiny as he looked up.

"Yes, Kathryn. Of course." He stood too fast and jostled the desk. After taking a moment to gather himself, he gestured to the left. "This way, please."

As we walked to the station's gym, he asked how I was doing.

"Okay. Better."

He nodded. Then, after a brief hesitation, he half asked, half stated, "No more investigating?"

We were looking into Lauren Jones mostly for ourselves, so technically we weren't investigating the murder anymore. We were just three ex-girlfriends who couldn't stop picking at the scab, right?

Even so, I couldn't tell him about that. He seemed to trust me fully now, but that didn't mean I trusted him. He was still the person capable of putting me away. And wasn't our deal over by his own declaration? So why share more than necessary?

"Just focusing on work," I told him. "Trying to put everything behind me."

Waves of relief emanated off him. "Good, good. And how is your work going?"

By the time we reached the empty gym, I'd bored him with the details of my latest experiment. Hell, even *I* was bored. But it was still better than talking about any of the elephants in the room.

"Okay," Adrian said as he unbuttoned his sleeves and rolled them up. I tried not to stare. "Let's start with the basics of self-defense. The goal is to make enough space to get away. And whenever you have the chance, run."

I wasn't sure if he was criticizing me for not listening to him at the café, but his face remained neutral so I let him continue without interrupting.

"The places to aim for are the eyes, nose, chest, and groin." He pointed to the places on himself as he talked, and I forced myself to focus on the self-defense instead of how chiseled he was from nose to jaw to chest to...never mind.

"You might have already known that, though," he said, and I wasn't sure what he was talking about. "Especially that last one."

Was he flirting with me? Because if so, this was a weird way of doing it.

"You told your friend Olivia to aim for Raymond's groin."

Right. Of course. That.

But all I could think about now was how he'd used Olivia's first name. After the café, had she become my friend Olivia instead of my lawyer Ms. McCarthy? Was everything too precarious, too close, on the verge of collapsing?

It's over, I tried to remind myself. *You're all okay.*

I managed to concentrate on Adrian's words for the next few minutes. But once we started sparring, I lost control. Instead of enjoying his strong arms wrapped around me, I couldn't stop thinking about the nonbarista. With my fight-or-flight responses taking over, all I wanted was to throw my attacker across the room.

"It's okay, we're just practicing." Adrian's deep, molasses-and-honey voice reached through the panic and centered me. As he kept talking, his words both relaxed my muscles and instructed me how to move.

Once I let his voice guide me, it almost felt like a dance. Moving in sync, following steps.

After thirty minutes, I felt like I could do this. Adrian knew how to explain things so I understood them at a fundamental level, and the physics was making sense now—like how to use my body mass and momentum in my favor. It was just science.

"You're doing great," he said, and he smiled—an actual smile, which revealed a previously unseen dimple on the left side. "Do you think you're ready to try sparring a little more freely?"

I felt safe with him. I knew he wouldn't hurt me. Yet the idea still scared me. But if not with him, then with who?

I swallowed. "Okay."

He started slow, using similar setups as before. I wasn't sure exactly what was coming, which forced me to recall quicker, and with every go, the muscle memory ingrained further.

But then he kept speeding up, faster and faster, and with each successive move, I wasn't sure I could keep up. I knew this was part of the training, but I didn't like how it made me feel.

"Wait," I said, and in my sudden panic, I tried to scurry backward, only to trip on a crinkle in the mat, which sent me flying backward. Since Adrian had been advancing, my legs tangled with his, sending him down on top of me.

He caught himself at the last second, his torso hovering over mine as his biceps flexed and his shirt strained across his chest.

The heat from his body surrounded me. Or maybe that was my blood pumping too fast. He didn't move. I didn't move.

"Sorry," he said, and it was so low it was almost a growl. "I...wanted to make sure you'd be okay if... Sorry. I should've taken it slower."

The guilt was still eating away at him. I reached a hand up to caress his cheek.

"I'm okay," I said, because it seemed like he needed to hear it. "I'm right here."

His eyes searched mine. Seeing that I meant it, that I didn't harbor any ill will, relief replaced the guilt. Then he took in the rest of my face, from my eyes to my nose to my lips. And then they lingered there.

I started to lean my face up toward his. I suddenly wanted nothing more than to taste him, touch him, connect with him.

But as soon as he started to lean down, all the warning bells in my head went off.

What was I doing?

I flailed my limbs, climbing out from under him. He immediately pushed himself away, somehow coming to his feet gracefully.

"Sorry," he said at the same time I did.

"No, no, it was me," I said, but he didn't seem to agree.

"No, I am deeply sorry, Ms. Hu." He emphasized each syllable of *Ms. Hu* as if cementing them back in place of *Kathryn*. "I promise this will never happen again." He held a hand out, which I numbly grabbed and shook.

"Thanks for the self-defense lesson."

"Of course. Please be safe." He cleared his throat. "If you'll excuse me."

He turned and left.

I stared after him, too many emotions fighting inside.

I'd lost my head for a moment, that was all. I was here for self-defense lessons, nothing more. Maybe some light flirting to remind myself I was alive, a woman, to feel something slightly pleasurable for the first time in weeks. But I didn't want anything *real*. And I'd stopped it in time, before anything happened, so everything was fine.

Besides, it could never work between Adrian—Detective Birch—and me. There were too many lies and half-truths. Not to mention, he could still arrest me at any moment.

Nothing good could have come from this.

So why was my gut roiling as I made my way out of the station?

Dish Served Hot Podcast Transcript—
Episode 93

[Podcast theme song plays, sung by creator, host, and star Mandy Thorne]

MANDY THORNE: Okay okay okay. Even *my* mind is blown, and I've had days to digest this. Can I just say that I'm so good I might be considering a permanent career change to journalist or detective? We might have to switch every future season to true crime so I can keep helping people. You know, solve one murder per season.

So obviously I've been reporting the facts as I've discovered them. And of course they're correct and as verifiable as we can manage. But for the first time, we have REAL and TANGIBLE proof of what I've been saying. That's how good I am! Thanks to how popular this show has become, we have been getting real, hard evidence from real-life witnesses. So thanks, Thornies, for blowing this up, for coming forward, for being the best detectives and journalists yourselves.

Today on the show? Your first definitive proof that Queen Victoria and Queen Elizabeth murdered their shared ex-boyfriend. And here to give us all the dirty details, please welcome Kiki, who was SITTING RIGHT NEXT TO THE GIRLS when they first started plotting.

[music]

MANDY: Hi, Kiki. Thank you for coming forward. Of course your name and voice are hidden for your safety. We wouldn't want any murderers to come after you, now.

KIKI: Thanks, Mandy. I wanted to go to the police, but I've been scared, so I'm hoping this is the next best thing.

MANDY: Tell us what you know. Don't spare any details.

KIKI: So a few weeks ago, I was meeting some friends at a bubble tea place. I was early so I was just on my phone— I promise I wasn't trying to eavesdrop—

MANDY: Suuure, Kiki. But we love you for it.

KIKI: You know, I doubt anyone in that café could've ignored these girls. Firstly, the tall one was drop-dead gorgeous, maybe even a model. I tried searching online to see if she was famous, but I haven't found her yet. I'd know her if I saw her again, though. Just stunning.

MANDY: And the other one?

KIKI: Definitely not a model. Very forgettable, even. I probably wouldn't remember her if I saw her. She just…looked like so many other people I know that, um, look like her. Especially where we were.

MANDY: So what was going on?

KIKI: It was exactly the situation you described. They had just found out they were dating the same guy. And get this—he proposed to BOTH of them!

MANDY: No! You're kidding!

KIKI: They were sliding the ring back and forth on the table! I half wanted to swoop in and grab it myself! And the whole time I just kept wondering who this guy was that couldn't choose between the two of them. I mean, was he blind? [laughs]

MANDY: So what did you overhear?

KIKI: This is the kicker. You won't believe this.

MANDY: Hit me.

KIKI: I heard the model say these exact words: *He needs to pay for what he did. He's dead.*

[Mandy gasps]

MANDY: If that's not the nail in the coffin, I don't know what is.

CHAPTER 36

"Isn't it scary how easy it is to get information?" Olivia asked Elle and me at her townhome over delivery sushi.

"Only on some people," I pointed out.

"Maybe I should stop posting so much on social media," Olivia mused. "Anyway, most marriage certificates are public record and you can request them. The hardest part was figuring out where they got married, but I started with the surrounding counties, then eventually moved on to Clark County—Vegas—and voilà."

She pushed the marriage certificate toward us with one hand as she popped a salmon nigiri into her mouth with the other.

How could this be public record when there was so much sensitive information on it? My eyes didn't know where to look first. Having had more time with it, Olivia started to distill it down for us.

"Lauren Watson is the maiden name."

"He really was married," Elle said, shaking her head. "That bastard."

I hadn't allowed myself to fully believe it either until this moment. With a renewed sense of determination, I yanked the marriage certificate closer.

"Occupation: student, for both of them," Elle said, her eyes darting back and forth as she skimmed. "Why is *occupation* on there? So weird."

Meanwhile, I looked at the date of marriage and quickly did the math. "Tucker was only eighteen when he got married."

Elle pointed at Lauren Watson's birth date. "They both were."

"You think she knew about us?" Olivia asked.

None of us answered. We didn't want to know.

"Poor Lauren," Elle said.

"Poor Lauren," Olivia agreed. "I can't believe he proposed to me when he was *married*. What in god's name was wrong with him?"

I sighed. "Is there anything else he can still surprise us with?"

I should have known better than to ask that question.

Kathryn's Tenth Law of Luck: Don't ask questions you don't want the answer to.

CHAPTER 37

Three days later, after cross-referencing Lauren Watson with Lauren Jones, I got a hit. Both names had been linked to the same address at different points in time. That couldn't be a coincidence, right?

Having learned from my, shall we say, *incident* with Ray, I texted Olivia and Elle so they knew where I was going. I didn't expect to find much—surely Ray would've already checked this location—but it was still worth a visit, just to see.

After driving for twenty minutes, I arrived at a middle-class suburb. The neighborhood was residential with similarly designed New England homes each painted a different bright color with contrasting shutters. My target was a beautiful robin's-egg blue.

Dreamy, *whimsical*, and *magical* were the adjectives that popped into my brain as I looked at the storybook home. It was fairly large, too, maybe a three-bedroom, three-bath?

I wasn't sure if I should snoop or just ring the doorbell. Did Lauren Jones/Watson know about me? Was there a chance she'd punch me in the face as soon as she saw me? Maybe I'd let her.

I did the most cowardly thing possible. I rang the doorbell, then ran off the porch and waited ten feet away. If she answered, that would give me enough time to assess her reaction and run if needed.

Nothing. Not even a flutter of curtains in any of the windows.

I tried again, this time staying close and peering through the little windows framing the door.

No one appeared to be home.

The inside looked lived-in yet abandoned, as evidenced by the large volume of mail shoved beneath the front door, likely because the mailbox was full.

A blurry face appeared behind me in the window's reflection. Before I could even scream, something contacted my shoulder.

Instinctively, I grabbed whatever it was and twisted, shocking myself and the offender.

"It's me! It's me!" I heard as I whirled around.

Adrian—Detective Birch—had dropped to his knees and was looking at me with pained eyes, his hand still twisted in my grasp.

I let go immediately. "I'm sorry!"

"I'm not. Good technique, fast reflexes." He smiled as he rubbed his wrist.

Relief rushed through me—I wasn't in danger *and* I'd successfully defended myself.

"What're you doing here?" we asked each other at the same time.

He waited, meaning I had to go first. He'd never crack.

The truth felt inevitable. Though I had to explain why I didn't tell him sooner. "Ray mentioned something about Tucker's wife. I didn't believe him at the time—I almost didn't even remember him saying it with everything that happened that day..." *Too much, dial it back.* "But I looked into it and came across this address."

Detective Birch's scarred eyebrow rose.

"I'm not investigating," I said quickly. "I just...needed to know."

"Ah." He seemed to understand.

"What're you doing here?" I asked again, hoping to get an answer this time.

But all he said was "Taking a look."

"Did you just learn about Lauren, too? From Ray?"

Helium, neon, argon, xenon; Detective Birch had no reaction. Just stood there expelling carbon dioxide—another inert gas. Not even a blink when I mentioned Lauren's name.

"Did you already know?"

His lack of an answer was my answer.

"Why didn't you tell me?"

"It's an ongoing investigation. I can't share everything with you."

Of course that was how it worked. Why did I expect anything else? Though this only convinced me further to not trust him. How could I when it was such a one-way, power-tilted relationship?

"So you knew about Tucker's wife," I said, still trying to wrap my head around it. Then I glanced back at the storybook house. And all at once, it hit me. "Oh my god. This is it. *Their* house. Tucker's house that he shared with his wife." How did I not realize it sooner?

Finally, Detective Birch gave me something—a pitying tilt of the mouth I didn't want.

"So the condo—" I started. Detective Birch nodded. "Was his second residence," I finished.

For his affairs and fraud. His desperate need for money was not only because of the debt but also to keep up his disgusting cheating lifestyle.

Kathryn's Eleventh Law of Luck: It can always get worse. From beyond the grave, Tucker was still surprising me, over and over, even after I already thought the absolute worst of him.

I glanced back at the recently abandoned house. "Is she—Lauren—okay?"

Detective Birch considered me for a moment, and then, almost as if he was just remembering that he trusted me, he said, "I'm not sure. That's why I'm here. I spoke to her several times after Tucker's death, but she barely said anything. I figured she was grieving and needed some time and space, but when I reached out to her recently to check in, she didn't answer my calls—"

"Do you think Ray found her?"

"No, though I can't tell what's real with him. He's claiming a lot of things, like how this is all a misunderstanding, and he and Tucker were actually friends."

I was standing with my back to the door, Detective Birch facing me, when, out of the corner of my eye, I spotted Olivia.

Crap. I forgot I'd texted her and Elle. Seeing the detective, Olivia froze, unsure what to do.

No good could come from him seeing her. I needed to distract him so she could leave.

I asked him the burning question on my mind. "Did Lauren know about me?"

Detective Birch hesitated, then said, "Yes. She was informed of Tucker's involvement with you. She said she didn't want to meet you, and we respected that."

Shit. I'd asked the question, but I hadn't been expecting that answer. That must have been heartbreaking for her to find out. I didn't expect her to join the Ex-Girlfriend Murder Club—she was his *wife*—but I also wished she hadn't gone through that alone.

There were too many questions in my head: *Did she know that I didn't know about her? Did she know about any other relationships he may have had but also definitely didn't?*

I couldn't find any words because there were too many fighting for attention in my head.

Olivia had turned and was leaving. Almost there.

Oblivious to what was going on behind him, Detective Birch cleared his throat. "Kathr—Ms. Hu, there's something I need to ask you."

"Hmm?" I was distracted by Elle's car pulling up.

"We found some DNA at the condo."

Oh no. Everything was unraveling in the worst way possible.

"Okay," I said slowly, trying to keep my face and voice neutral as Olivia tried to wave an uncomprehending Elle away.

"We identified yours, which was expected, but we found DNA from someone else. A woman, one we haven't been able to ID yet. Do you have any idea who this might be?"

"Lauren?" I said, proud of coming up with that great answer on the fly (baseball origin, when the ball is still in the air).

"No, not her. Someone else."

"Then I have no idea," I said, which was technically the truth. Because I didn't know which of the other two he was talking about. The two who were *right behind him* at the moment. Luckily, Olivia had gotten Elle to notice the detective, and she was back in her car.

But when the car door shut, the detective turned. Luckily, Elle ducked down so she wasn't visible. But while Elle was safe, Olivia was not.

She waved, then walked over and stood next to me such that the detective would have to face away from Elle's car to look at both of us.

At least he knew Olivia, and it wasn't completely weird for her to show up here.

Or not. "You always bring your friend slash lawyer to visit the house of your ex-boyfriend's wife?" Detective Birch asked. "Hello, Ms. McCarthy—or is it Olivia? Which role are you playing today?"

The suspicion in his voice was clear, and it sent a flare of anger through me. I was trying to find a retort—*Leave her alone! If you trust me, you trust her*—when Olivia stepped closer and put an arm around my shoulders.

With narrowed eyes, she said to the detective, "You don't think she needs support doing something like this? You should be making sure she's okay, not putting the case above her. *Again*." She turned to me and, to drive the point home, asked, "You okay, Kat?"

I nodded. "I think I'd like to get out of here, though."

Olivia glanced subtly behind the detective to make sure Elle was already gone, then walked me toward my car.

"I'm sorry, Ms. Hu." Detective Birch seemed to have learned his lesson, but then he couldn't help himself, calling after me, "And please let me know if you think of any possibilities for what I asked you about."

"I thought you wanted me to stop investigating," I snapped.

That flustered him. "Of course. Please don't. I just meant, if you think of anything on your own, without looking into it."

For the first time, I didn't bother responding. I hoped the medicine tasted bitter.

CHAPTER 38

"That was a close one," I said later on our three-way call.

We had to do better. We hadn't been using burners and being careful just to mess it up now.

"No more unnecessary meetups," Elle agreed. "Though maybe we also shouldn't be wandering off on our own for investigations?"

"How about we discuss it beforehand to assess the risk together?" Olivia suggested.

"Fine," I said, mostly because I wanted to move on to what I'd learned today. "That was Tucker's home. That he shared with Lauren."

"Of course," Olivia said, echoing my reaction.

"So we pranked his, what, second home for hookups?" Elle asked.

"Afraid so."

"I can't believe we were there today," Olivia said. "Where he had his whole other life. His primary life."

"Did you see anything?" Elle asked.

"Like what?"

"I don't know—something useful?"

"I wish there'd been a giant banner that read *So-and-so is the murderer!*" Olivia quipped.

"I barely got to look before Adr—the detective showed up." Not wanting them to comment on my slip of the tongue, I barreled on. "It seemed abandoned, though. Or at least like it hasn't been lived in for a few weeks."

"I wonder where she went," Elle pondered.

"Do you think she knew about…?" Olivia trailed off.

"She knows about me." I paused before adding, "Don't know if she wants to do anything about that."

Elle sucked in a breath. "Are you…worried?"

"I don't know. Maybe? Or maybe I'm just still freaked out after the whole Ray thing."

"I get it," Olivia said. "I'm on edge, too."

"Maybe I'm overreacting." Though I didn't feel like I was.

"Have you noticed anything strange or off recently?" Olivia asked me.

"No—" I started to say, but then an image flashed in my mind. The woman who had been talking to Detective Birch.

"What is it?" Elle asked.

"There was a woman. At the precinct. Who glared at me."

"You think that could've been her?" Olivia asked.

"Could have been. The detective did say he talked to Lauren a few times—that could've been one of the times. I can't think of another reason why a stranger would've been glaring at me there."

"Do you remember what she looked like?" Elle asked.

"Yes."

"Good. Then you'll recognize her if you cross paths again."

"Be on alert," Olivia agreed.

"Do you know how she found out about you?" Elle asked.

"The detective told her."

"No, Mc-no-longer-Hottie!" Elle cried. "Why would he do that?"

"The good news is she likely doesn't know about you two

since he doesn't, and we have to keep it that way." I hesitated, then revealed, "They found DNA."

Their resulting panic confirmed that this shit was unraveling, and unraveling fast.

"I should have just told him the whole truth from the beginning," I lamented. "I told him about the pranks and he didn't arrest me. I should have just also told him about you two, and then there wouldn't be so many lies. Because that's the worst part of this, right? That I lied?"

Olivia and Elle began talking in a jumble.

"Everything's going to be fine."

"You didn't do anything wrong."

"We won't let anything happen to you."

Their words reminded me why I'd lied in the first place: to protect them. And who was to say that even if Detective Birch learned about my lies, he wouldn't choose to still trust me?

Except I already knew: I was on the thinnest possible ice. And I had to tread much more carefully than I had been.

Dish Served Hot Podcast Transcript— Episode 94

[Podcast theme song plays, sung by creator, host, and star Mandy Thorne]

MANDY THORNE: Detective Mandy Thorne here, reporting for duty! And I'm telling you, this story is heating up in ways I hadn't dared *dream* when I started this true crime journey. Y'all, I couldn't have planned this any better.

I have another guest today who has crossed paths with the murderers, survived, and is bravely telling his tale.

[music]

MANDY: Thanks for joining us. Shall we call you Bob?

BOB: Sure thing. Always wanted an exotic name.

MANDY: So Bob called me after listening to the last episode— thanks for being a Thornie, Bob! And he had the best, most juiciest information for me. Please tell the Thornies what you told me.

BOB: I own a bar, which means I hear a lot. People either don't see you as a person and say everything on their mind right in front of you like you don't exist, or they need an ear and tell you directly. And I have a lot of downtime—business hasn't been so good recently, dang economy and all—so I listen to podcasts, and, Mandy, I sure am a fan of yours! And when I heard your episode about these girls dating the same guy, my old man ears perked right up!

MANDY: And thank gods they did! Why did that story sound so familiar?

BOB: I heard it! From girls at my bar. *The* girls. And get this! They were even listening to your podcast!

MANDY: What? Get out! I mean, of course they were, it's very popular, but also, how full circle!

BOB: Yessiree, full circle alright!

MANDY: So what happened?

BOB: Well, Mandy, I'll tell ya. They were drinking—too much in my opinion, and that's coming from me—while listening to the podcast and laughing and...

MANDY: And *what*, Bob?

BOB: They were planning. Plain as day, loud as drunks, openly discussing how they would get revenge on their shared boyfriend. Not just revenge, but *murder*.

MANDY: Let me get this straight. You heard them planning the actual murder?

BOB: Yessiree. Makes sense, don't it? After all, murder is the ultimate revenge.

MANDY: Are you absolutely sure?

BOB: Of course I'm sure! My ears are old but functional. I heard them, plain as day, saying "[*bleep bleep*] must die."

MANDY: Bob, you are lucky to have escaped their notice.

BOB: You're telling me! It's the first time I've ever been so relieved that the customers didn't see me as a person! Otherwise, I may not have made it out of there alive!

MANDY: Well, we're sure glad you did! Did you hear any details about the murder?

BOB: Nah. They knew better than to yell out the details. They're criminals! BUT! There's something I know that *no one* else knows. No one except for them.

MANDY: What? Tell us!

BOB: There's a *third* girl.

MANDY: There is?!

BOB: Yup. Poor guy picked the wrong three women to cheat on. I'm guessing the third one was what pushed them over the edge.

MANDY: There you have it! The first two found each other, wanted revenge—and that's what Kiki overheard at the boba café—and when they found out about the third one, it was too much. They banded together and murdered him. Now, I'm not sure if all three of them are *together* together like Queen Victoria and Queen Elizabeth are, but I'm going to find out.

BOB: How come only two of them came on your show?

MANDY: That's a good question, Bob. [pause] Oh my gods! I bet they used me, in multiple ways. I was their alibi! The third girl went and did the deed while the other two were on the show, pretending to not want revenge. The perfect plan! My gods.

BOB: My gods, indeed.

MANDY: Bob, thank you for risking your life to come forward with this story today. Thornies, if anything happens to Bob or me, you'll know who did it.

[music]

MANDY: Bob gave us plenty of twists with his interview, and I'm going to end on a twist of my own: the police have contacted me. They finally realize what a bang-up job we've been doing, and they've enlisted our help! We are officially the best of the true crime podcasts. Be proud, Thornies. We're doing good work out here. We're number one!

Stay tuned. I am going to hunt down some murderers! *Three* of them!

CHAPTER 39

A few days ago, before Tucker's house, before the sparring session, I would have been thrilled to hear from Detective Birch—still Adrian at that time. But today, I had a bad feeling. He asked both Olivia and me to come down, which was a first. Normally it was up to me if I wanted my lawyer to join.

We were ushered straight into the interrogation room when we arrived—another ominous sign.

"Ms. Hu, Ms. McCarthy," the detective greeted us.

We nodded in tandem.

"I'm sure you know why I asked you to come in."

"We don't," Olivia said impatiently. "And my client has to get back to work, so if you could please get to the point?"

"Ms. McCarthy, you're not here in your lawyer capacity—though I guess you are always a lawyer. But I have questions to ask the *both* of you."

Olivia's face didn't falter. I tried to match her neutrality, but my insides were melting.

"I listened to the podcast," he said.

Olivia didn't miss a beat. "What podcast?"

"The one Ms. Hu had playing while she was cleaning the victim's condo—*Dish Served Hot*? I'm sure you've heard of it."

Shit shit shit. Olivia glanced at me but somehow managed not to reveal any emotion. But I knew she was wondering how

I let that happen, and why I didn't tell her—neither of which I had answers to.

"I started listening after that day, and it made sense once you admitted, Ms. Hu, to pranking your ex-boyfriend, but imagine my surprise when I caught up to the more recent episodes."

"Mandy is speaking gibberish," Olivia said, waving her hand as if she were trying to disperse a fart, which was what Mandy was, a human fart. "You know none of that is true. Was a thumb missing from the body?"

Please don't bring up the sleeping-with-the-cop thing.

"Interesting, Ms. McCarthy, that you've been following the podcast, too?"

Olivia shrugged. "It's very popular. Everyone at work is talking about it."

"Well, while there wasn't a thumb missing, we haven't been able to locate Tucker's laptop or tablet yet. So we reached out to Mandy Thorne, who was more than happy to help. We contacted her recent guests and took their statements. And the woman from the boba café described you"—he pointed to Olivia—"perfectly."

And she probably told him I was Asian and she couldn't pick me out of a lineup, but he left that part out.

"We also talked to the bar owner from York Beach, and while he couldn't remember what you looked like"—thank god he'd been drinking—"he seemed sure of his story."

Detective Birch looked at Olivia, then me. "There were only two guests on that podcast. Queen Victoria and Queen Elizabeth. Yet the bar owner claims there are three of you."

"Kat and I were not on that podcast," Olivia insisted, which was technically true. "And I don't want to tell you how to do your job, Detective, but Mandy's podcast is a bunch of lies, clickbait, and movie plots mashed together. Why are you taking anything from that embarrassment of a show as evidence? If you believe what she's saying, then you already have your killer: find the neighbor of that woman who doesn't know how a pig roast or dog-sitting works."

"Ms. Thorne also provided Queen Victoria's email address that was used to set up the interview. We were able to trace it back to an IP address. One that belongs to you." He turned to Olivia. Her face betrayed nothing. I willed my pits to stop sweating. My insides were falling apart, but I had to hold the outside together no matter the cost.

Detective Birch continued. "So we started to investigate further. We knew you were Ms. Hu's lawyer, but imagine my surprise when phone records showed you and Tucker Jones having frequent phone calls. And *then* we noticed that your communication with Ms. Hu began shortly before Tucker's death."

No. No no no. How could the evidence look this terrible for two innocent people? If I didn't know any better, I would think we were guilty, too.

Detective Birch looked at me. "Ms. Hu, I know that wasn't you on the podcast."

I didn't know what to say to that. I refused to believe he knew me that well.

The detective's voice increased in volume as he said, "So who was it? Who's the third person involved in this?"

"I don't know what you're talking about," I said.

It was his word against ours. And he didn't have definitive proof. Mandy didn't know anything either, though I wouldn't have put it beneath her to just lie and say whatever she wanted for shits and giggles like she'd been doing all along. We should have sent *her* Elle's shits-and-giggles brownies. There was something poetic in that, pranking the Queen of Revenge.

"This isn't going well for you." As if we needed him to tell us that. "I suggest you start telling the truth."

Neither of us responded.

He leaned forward. "Did you two and another woman find out that Tucker was cheating, then band together to murder him?"

"Of course not!" I yelled as Olivia said calmly, "We're not answering any more questions without a lawyer present."

"A lawyer *is* present," Detective Birch said.

"I'm not going to represent myself."

"So you think you need representation?" he asked.

I tried to think of something that could help us. "What about Ray?" That had been our plan all along—to defend ourselves by finding the real killer.

But I knew I was grasping at straws (origin: Thomas More's *Dialogue of Comfort Against Tribulation* about a drowning man clutching at straws, or river reeds). Even I didn't think Ray had done it, and he'd tried to hurt me. It just didn't make sense— why would he send a message with such a calculated, intricate murder? Unfortunately, I didn't know who else to accuse.

"We're still pursuing that lead, but I can't ignore all this." Detective Birch gestured to us and the papers in front of him. "My boss has been giving me heat about this case."

Lead. Case. I knew he felt more emotion than he was letting on, but his words still stung.

"What does that mean?" I asked.

Sadness dragged the corners of his eyes down. "It means I don't have a choice. All the evidence is pointing at the two of you. Especially after I get some of Ms. McCarthy's DNA, which I'm guessing will match the DNA we found at the scene." Olivia opened her mouth to speak, but he quickly added, "I have a warrant."

This whole time, something had been building and building inside me, trying to escape in the form of heat or sweat or tears, but I'd managed to bottle it up. I'd been holding it together. I just had to do it a little longer, just another few minutes until Olivia could call one of her colleagues to come down here and save us.

Closing my eyes, I tried to take my mind off the situation around me, tried to escape this body and reappear in Fiji, the Caribbean, anywhere else—but I couldn't conjure up an image of a place I'd never been.

When my eyes popped back open, I saw Detective Birch's hand lifting off the desk and starting toward his waist.

My body recoiled like a spring. I knew that motion of his. I'd been here before. Why had I been in this interrogation room multiple times with him trying to handcuff me for murder?

"Fucking hell!" I yelled just as Birch's hand reached into his pocket and produced a piece of paper. Probably the warrant he'd been talking about, whoops. But it was too late. The spring had released and everything I'd been feeling for the past few weeks was coming up. Violently.

"This is such bullshit! I haven't done anything wrong! I'm so tired of the universe being so goddamn relentless. I didn't murder anyone let alone the man I once loved." Oh no, here came the tears. "I was grieving. I was trying to wrap my head around everything that happened but I couldn't because I was also fighting for my freedom. How is it possible for so much terrible shit to happen to one person in such a short amount of time? And maybe I'm selfish for thinking that when Tucker's the one who died, but I didn't steal anyone's money or cheat. And I sure as hell didn't kill anyone! Fuck! Fuck Tucker, fuck Mandy, fuck the underwear that started it all!" I was going off the rails now, but there was nothing to do but embrace it.

"And you!" I pointed an accusatory finger at Detective Birch, startling him. "What happened to never ignoring your gut? You really think I could have done this? The person you almost kissed and have been trusting for weeks?" He glanced up at the camera in the corner but I kept going. "You know me so well you're convinced I wasn't on the podcast, yet you somehow still think I did it?" Had I just admitted to not being on the podcast? My brain was too fired up to think clearly. Oh well, it was too late now—what's done is done.

"Kat." Detective Birch had never called me that before. His voice remained calm as he said, "I never said I thought you did it. I just said I couldn't ignore the evidence any longer. If you please just tell me the truth—"

"I am." *Except for Elle.* I knew it didn't help to keep lying when he knew that I was, but now was not the time to drag her down with us. He'd shown us that today. I should have worked harder to protect Olivia, but I could at least learn from that mistake.

He sighed, disappointed. "Kat—Ms. Hu, I want to help you."

Well, you're doing a shit job of showing that, I wanted to say but refrained.

"You know me," I said instead, hoping I could reach just a little deeper, communicate to him somehow that everything I was doing was to protect a friend, that I was just being loyal like he once claimed to admire. My intentions were noble, not monstrous—why was it so hard to convince him of that?

"You care about her," Olivia said to Detective Birch. She'd been silent and stoic the entire time I was going off, but when she spoke now, her voice was full of its usual confidence. "And you care about finding the truth. You know we didn't do it. Putting us away won't help you. It will hurt you, not just because you'll be putting away two innocent people, one of whom you care about, but because you'll be losing an important resource. Don't you want to find out what happened? For true justice to be served?"

Those words felt cheesy like we were suddenly on a TV show, but now was not the time to back down.

"We didn't do it," I stated, channeling all my frustration and confidence into that sentence. He claimed to know when I was lying, so when he turned to me and our eyes met, I said it again. "We didn't do it."

"One week," he said.

"What?" Olivia asked.

"I can hold my boss off for one week. If you come forward with definitive proof of your innocence by then, that would be best. Otherwise, I suggest you get your ducks in a row."

Olivia stood. "You're going to feel like a fool when we prove it. And even more so when you realize you might have just blown it with one of the best people I know."

Her words meant more to me than Detective Birch or his look of regret. So I said what came to mind even though it was cheesy as hell. "Coming from one of the best people I know, that means a lot."

We turned and left the interrogation room as a united front. I didn't look back even as Detective Birch yelled out, "Please be careful!"

Kathryn's Twelfth Law of Luck: As long as you have someone you love on your side, you can do anything, even feel hope when you're at rock bottom.

CHAPTER 40

Olivia giving her DNA sample felt like the final nail in the coffin, but it also spurred us on.

"We can do this," I said outside the precinct.

She nodded. "Of course. Never a doubt."

But there was one thing we had to do first—something we didn't want to but had to, for her protection. It was so unanimous that the discussion only lasted two minutes, ending with Olivia saying, "Do you want to make the call or me?"

"Together."

• • • •

We didn't divulge anything over the phone, just agreed to meet at Olivia's. Elle arrived only a few minutes after us, meaning we didn't have much time to prepare. But there wasn't a good way to get ready for something like this.

"Elle, we can't see you anymore."

"Are you breaking up with me?" she joked. But the mirth disappeared from her eyes when she saw how serious we were. "What's going on?"

We filled her in, emphasizing how Detective Birch knew there was someone else but couldn't prove it yet. And if the three of us were ever tied together, we'd be dragging her down with us.

As we talked, Elle's breathing grew shallow.

"We have to part ways," Olivia finished. "To protect you. We'll destroy the burners, no more contact. This is the last time we'll meet up."

Elle swallowed hard. Then she started shaking her head over and over as she said, "No. You need me. I can help."

I gave the argument I'd come up with on the drive over. "You'll help us most by keeping safe. If we go down for this, we need you on the outside fighting for us. Figuring out a way to prove our innocence." It was the truth—the best kind of argument, as I'd learned from Olivia.

"You won't go down for it," Elle said. "We're going to figure this out. *Together*—the brains, the heart, and the guts."

Olivia and I shook our heads.

Elle's voice grew more frantic. "Okay, wait. What if I defend you? I can tell the detective about the pranks, confirm your story, we'll tell them how we found the body and panicked, that we took the laptop before we knew he was dead—"

"You'll only be implicating yourself, not saving us," Olivia argued.

I nodded. "It's all risk, no reward."

"No. I refuse." Elle stood her ground figuratively and literally. "We stick together."

We were all just trying to protect each other, but it was ironically leading us to disagree.

"But we're the Ex-Girlfriend Murder Club," Elle pleaded, which showed just how desperate she was. I'd never heard her call us that before.

"You don't have much of a choice here," Olivia said, her words firm but tone soft. "It's two against one, and we're not going to take you down with us."

Elle shook her head. "We can't… I don't want…"

"I know," Olivia said. "We feel the same way."

The air grew heavy with emotion. The three of us huddled

together in a tiny circle. I wasn't sure who reached out first, but within seconds, we were holding hands, squeezing each other's palms as if we could press our feelings into the others so they would know how we felt. But we were already feeling the same things.

Olivia spoke first. "For the past two years, I've been trying to be Liv through and through, but I've been doing it wrong. I thought I needed to achieve all these societal milestones—see the world and have a big career and family and house—but you girls opened my eyes. Some of my favorite moments *ever* have been with you two, sitting right here, eating pizza or learning how to reverse sear a steak, laughing over everything and nothing."

I felt hand squeezes on both sides and returned them. They had tears in their eyes, which I could barely see because my own vision was blurred.

"You two taught me how to trust again," Elle said. She always acted so strong, so unflappable and confident, but the woman before us was the one who'd recently taken down those walls and told us about her childhood, her loneliness, her reasons for not letting romantic partners get close. "And you taught me I deserve more, and that not everyone out there is like Tucker. Or Chad."

Olivia and Elle both turned to me.

"Is it my turn? Do I have to? You two are okay."

They laughed and my insides warmed.

"You both taught me to trust again, too. And…" I hadn't acknowledged this out loud or even to myself, but I'd been feeling it all along. "Maybe you also taught me how to be myself more. I mean, I've always been myself, I think, but before the Ex-Girlfriend Murder Club, I was scared to share that with others. Ashamed, even. Tucker was the first to like the weird parts of me, but then he turned out to be Tucker.

But if the two of you can also like those parts, maybe I should be a little more confident in who I am."

"You never have anything to be embarrassed of," Elle said.

Olivia just smiled, and I knew she was thinking about what we'd said to each other right before we left the police station.

They aren't the only ones who like you for you, an unwelcome voice said in my head. But that was too confusing and also didn't matter right now. This was about the two of them, the three of us.

I squeezed their hands. "I never thought something so beautiful could come out of something so ugly. We didn't let the circumstances taint our friendship, and then it became the only thing that held me together."

The tears were falling for all of us now.

"I just wish it wasn't ending like this," Elle said.

"It's not," Olivia asserted. "It's not over till it's over."

Elle nodded. "I'm going to keep searching on my end." Suddenly, her eyes lit up, then met Olivia's. "And maybe also..."

Olivia gave Elle a wistful smile. "I guess it's finally time for you to use your writing skills."

Elle saluted, accepting her duty. "Even if I can't take little Miss Mandy down, at the very least, I'll tell your side of the story. If Mandy can have a voice, you two need one, too. I won't stop fighting, especially if you get arrested."

We put our foreheads together. What a contrast from that first day when we put our hands in and wished Tucker dead. It started with him, but it was ending with us—better versions of us, thanks to each other.

I was about to say something I rarely ever said—that I loved them—but before I could, Elle said, "Does this mean you're not going to climb McTree, Kat?"

I laughed. It was the perfect goodbye.

GARBAGE DISH SERVED HOT

By Lassy McBush

Mandy Thorne has turned her previously light and entertaining show into a pile of hot slaughterhouse garbage. Then she sent a flaming arrow straight into it. Should any of us be surprised? Unfortunately not. You don't expect serious investigative journalism from someone famous for lying about the shit she took inside the love hut she shared with twenty other contestants while being filmed 24/7. And for those of you who haven't watched *Love Hut*—which I'm guessing is most of you because otherwise, you'd be outside banging on a tree with a stick instead of reading this article—Mandy Thorne was caught brown-assed by her hut mates *and* the camera, and still tried to deny it. She also told five different men on the show that she would be their ride or die, a record for the show, which really says something.

I've been doing my own investigative work, and I've learned—truly learned, with sources and evidence, not like how Mandy learns things (with a box of crayons)—that there's a surprising reason why Mandy began *Dish Served Hot*, her only successful venture thus far other than Only-Fans. When Mandy's ex-boyfriend, DJ Quiktrix, found out she was cheating, he got quite the revenge on her. He asked her to get tattoos together. A cheesy heart with each other's names inside. He not only convinced her to get it in a giant font on her back but also to go first so that when she showed him the final product and said, "It's finished!" he said, "So are we." This is why Mandy has no other tattoos except for a giant rose on her back that is notorious for resembling a vagina. But what the public didn't know until now is that it was the only design that would cover the enormous DJ QUIKTRIX that preceded it.

The reasons for this article are threefold: 1) to convince *Dish Served Hot* listeners to view the recent episodes with a more critical eye and to think about the harm podcasts like this can cause, 2) to write an honest critique of a podcast I once surprisingly loved, and 3) for some shits and giggles, because life sucks and we all need a laugh. Wasn't that the original point of *Dish Served Hot*? But this season, we've lost that. No one is laughing except for Mandy Thorne.

First, her detective work is more Jacques Clouseau from *Pink Panther* than Sherlock Holmes. She has been making up facts, and not even that well—mystery authors are cringing across the globe. Yet I have it on good authority that she's causing problems for innocent people. Creating false narratives, bad as they may be, has consequences. But I wouldn't expect the five-boyfriend hut-shitter to understand, especially not after she was shocked that her "brilliant *Love Hut* strategy" backfired.

The reason we fell in love with *Dish Served Hot* was because it was silly, funny, and appeased our desire for justice. A wonderful formula she happened to stumble upon. And she fit the part to host this—a silly, petty, funny (by accident) host who egged her guests on and wanted to know the tea. But this same person is not the right host for a serious true crime show. The reason this latest season has gained so much popularity is because it's a car wreck we can't look away from. We know it's not true, yet we can't look away, and it's entertaining for the same reason *Love Hut* is. But reality shows don't talk about true crimes, and there's a good reason for that. What Mandy is doing is irresponsible.

All this has left me with one question: Why has Mandy done this? For money? Because she doesn't know any better? It certainly can't be to make a point about how much people can get away with on these true crime podcasts. Maybe I would have believed that if she hadn't been kicked out of the hut for insisting that animals wouldn't care about having products tested on them if they knew how frizzy her hair was.

So I end with an ask: let's hold Mandy accountable. If she's going to continue talking about this so-called murder case, she has to do a better job. But since we all know she can't, let's insist she go back to the silly, petty, light-hearted show she was born to do. And, Mandy, if you're reading this, you hit the lottery with *Dish Served Hot*. Don't let this show be the first thing you actually flush down the toilet.

Dish Served Hot Podcast Transcript—
Episode 95

[Podcast theme song plays, sung by creator, host, and star Mandy Thorne]

MANDY THORNE: Who does Lassy McBush think she is? That skeezy little unfunny bitch!

Okay, first of all, I SWEAR I DID NOT SHIT IN THE HUT! I didn't! It was a camera trick! They can make you look like you're doing anything nowadays! And of course the other contestants said I did it—it was a competition! And I was the biggest threat!

And as for why we made the switch this season, it's not *any* of the ridiculous things she said! So why did we become a true crime podcast?

Because.

Because, my Thornies.

[somber sigh]

Here's the truth of it.

I feel bad for what my brilliant, wildly popular podcast has done. Even though we have only featured funny, petty, nonviolent pranks prior to this season, I can't control how other people react. I obviously did not know when I started *Dish Served Hot* that it would lead to the most unforgivable revenge. Murder. You heard Bob—the murderers were listening to *my* podcast when they were plotting! So I feel the need to do my part to help bring them to justice. I do not condone violence and I do not condone what they've done.

I am doing this out of the goodness of my heart. I have not been lying. I have not been making up facts. Unlike Lassy and all her slander—and don't you worry, my team is on it and we're going to sue once we figure out who she is—I am simply trying to bring injustices to light, which has always been the mission of *Dish Served Hot*.

[another sigh]

Okay! So let's all collectively put this horrible huckster out of our minds because she doesn't know what she's talking about and she's just trying to ride my coattails to gain a second of fame. And stay tuned, because our next episode will not only be back on track to solve this case, but [drumroll] it's going to be our sold-out, intensely buzzed about, highly anticipated live show! Detective Mandy is still on the case, don't you worry. And, Lassy McBush, fuck you. You better hope I never find out who you are, because I am the Queen of Revenge, and I can't wait to *actually* take a shit in your house—my first time doing that indoors, swear to gods.

CHAPTER 41

Olivia and I had to get down and dirty, put our noses to the grindstone, and there was no time for dilly-dallying, not even to look up the origins of those sayings. Our freedom was at stake.

At least we no longer had to worry about burner phones or being careful when we met up. Though it was only a reminder that we were down a piece. Missing our guts. But what a silver lining it was to see Elle's article—or Lassy McBush's, no surprise there on the pen name. It went viral within a mere three hours of posting, a powerful combination of Elle's writing talent and *Dish Served Hot*'s popularity.

"I'm proud of her," Olivia said to me the next time we met up. "Elle's writing is getting the attention it deserves."

"Maybe this will help her career," I said excitedly, and then I remembered. "Except she can't tell anyone she's Lassy McBush."

"Well, it'll be a huge confidence boost at the very least."

I nodded. "Okay. What's our next step?"

"We reach out to everyone again?" Olivia suggested.

The clock was ticking and there were too many suspects. There had to be another route. "What if we go back to the source?"

Olivia began nodding slowly. "That makes sense."

"But how do we find out more about Tucker, stuff we don't

already know?" We'd already looked through his laptop—how much more personal could we get?

"There *is* one place we haven't looked yet…"

As soon as those words came out, I knew exactly what she was thinking. "No. Liv, no."

"You said it was abandoned, right?"

"No. We cannot commit another crime."

"Kat, we're at rock bottom. It's Hail Mary time."

"Yes, we're already at rock bottom. So let's not give the detective even more reason to arrest us."

"The road to hell is greener on the other side. Come on, Kat."

How dare she use a malaphor to sway me. But what she was suggesting felt like a line we shouldn't cross. The previous crimes were different—we took the laptop by accident and we left the scene of the crime because we were (rightly) scared we were in danger. But if we broke into Tucker's house, we'd be consciously doing it, deciding ahead of time to commit the crime. Breaking and entering in the first degree.

The teasing quality of Olivia's voice disappeared, leaving behind pure rawness. "I don't know what else to do."

Against my better judgment, I relented. "Okay. Hail Mary, Jesus, and Joseph."

• • • •

It was eerie being back at the house where Tucker had maybe carried his bride over the threshold, where he probably told his wife about his day over dinner (when he was home), where they would perhaps fight over who would do the dishes.

I couldn't imagine it. It was almost as if that Tucker was a completely different person from the one I knew, which, he kind of was.

"The house is just in Lauren's name," Olivia said as we exited the car. "That's weird, right?"

"Is that why he didn't just sell it and use the money to pay back Ray? Do you think she bought it with her money?"

Olivia shrugged. "Or maybe Tucker the jackass put everything in her name on purpose."

"To hide it from the people after him?"

Olivia's eyes darkened. "Or to put her neck on the line instead of his."

Shit. "Do you think she'll come back if she finds out that Ray is in custody now?" I asked. "Or...maybe she's already back?" That was a possibility that hadn't dawned on me until this moment, and I wished I'd considered it sooner. Maybe we shouldn't be here.

Olivia disagreed. "If she's here, that's even better. She might be able to help us."

If she doesn't physically kick us out first. But I kept that thought to myself.

"Ready?" Olivia asked.

"As much as I'll ever be," I said as I moved off to the side, just in case. After all, Lauren only knew about me.

Olivia rang the doorbell, and when no one answered, we made our way to the back door. As Double-Oh-livia went to work with her lockpicks, I looked around for a fake rock or spare key just in case.

No luck. Maybe Tucker was extra cautious because of the people after him, and for good reason.

"I'm in," Olivia whispered as she stood and returned the tools to her jacket pocket.

I missed Elle. If she were here, she would have told Olivia how badass she was and how she wanted to be her when she grew up.

I followed Olivia inside. Immediately, a home alarm began blaring.

Why hadn't we thought about that before going in?

Just as I was about to tell her to run for it, she said, "I got it," and dashed off in search of the keypad. I caught up just as she was punching in the last digit.

"All his passwords are on his laptop," she reminded me.

"Right. Thanks, Double-Oh-livia," I said, and she beamed. "I think I just assumed he wouldn't have an alarm since he didn't have one at the condo."

"Maybe he thought the condo was safer?"

"Or maybe he was keeping sensitive stuff here. Maybe it's good we came." My hope was rising, and just in time—I would need it to power me through the long search ahead.

"Divide and conquer," Olivia said. She began scouring the foyer as I turned and headed upstairs.

• • • •

Two hours later, we were almost done. Olivia had finished her level first and joined me in the bedroom. There wasn't much to go through because the important items had been cleaned out. No papers sitting out, no important documents or files in the drawers, not even a single used tissue in the wastebaskets. It looked like it had been done in a hurry, though, with lamps turned over, clothing draped over askew furniture, and Tucker's beloved mystery books strewn about.

"We could tear the end chapters out," I joked, remembering Olivia's suggestion at the very beginning of all this.

But she was distracted by the mess. "Do you think someone broke in here? Or maybe searched it ahead of us?"

"Maybe. It could have been Ray or someone who worked for him. Or it could have been Tucker or Lauren or both trying to make a fast getaway."

Olivia shook her head. "Tucker wouldn't leave without his underwear."

She was right. Balls In briefs were scattered among Tucker's suits and shirts, as well as Lauren's pastel cardigans, tasteful sweaters, and yoga clothes.

"Maybe the cops?" Olivia suggested.

"Whoever it was, there isn't much left for us to comb through. Did you check the mail?" I asked.

"Yeah. Just junk mail and bills—a lot of them, but nothing out of the ordinary."

"Shoot."

We both sighed.

"One more quick scan," I suggested.

Olivia nodded. "Together this time."

As we made our way through the house again, we pointed out little things we noticed—a tilted abstract painting here, a lump in the armchair there—but nothing revealed any hidden passageways or stashed evidence.

I was now seeing the downstairs for the first time, but it was the same odd combination of messy and bare as the upstairs.

When we entered Tucker's home office, I asked, "Did you find any hidden safes?"

"No, but we might as well look again."

Olivia and I checked the cabinets together. After a minute, she nudged my elbow with hers. "Easier when the room's not covered in poop, am I right?"

I chuckled, then took an extra-large gulp of nonstinky air just because I could.

Coming up empty, Olivia moved on to the closet as I began rummaging through the desk. As Olivia had already told me, the only papers in the drawers were completely blank. I thumbed through anyway, just in case. I even examined each page at different angles for imprints that might have been left behind from writing on the sheet above.

"CSI shows make this look so easy," I joked. "Where's the one hair we're missing, and when will the camera zoom in on it?"

"While they're at it, can they show us the secret panel to reveal the hidden safe in the wall?"

I looked through the errant paper clips, pens, and thumb-tacks on top of the desk. Who even used thumbtacks anymore? There wasn't even a corkboard in here.

"Wait," I said, my eyes fixing on an object of interest. Olivia was next to me in a flash.

"Look." I grabbed a pen out of the pile in front of me. The one that didn't quite belong amid the long lawyer, dentist, and doctor names on the others.

"'Mass Life,'" she read out loud.

"Life insurance. Do you think…" My brain was working overtime.

"I think we can look that up," Olivia said, grabbing her phone. Her thumbs began flying.

"How?"

"I know his social security number," she said without paus-ing. "From his laptop."

"Right." I was both glad and worried that Olivia knew so much about Tucker. Glad that it was helping us, and worried it would only sink us—and especially her—further. I made a mental note to tell Olivia to delete everything before our ticking clock with Detective Birch was up.

Her eyes suddenly bugged out of her head.

"What? What is it?" I couldn't handle the suspense.

"Four million dollars," she squeaked. "His life insurance was four million dollars." She finally looked up from her screen and her eyes bored into mine. "Paid out to his wife."

Jackpot. In so many ways.

CHAPTER 42

Lauren Jones/Watson had a double motive: she knew her husband was cheating *and* she had a large check coming her way if he died.

"What I don't understand is why there's no trace of the policy here," Olivia said once we were back at her place with Tucker's laptop open in front of us. We'd just finished searching his email and hard drive. "There's no correspondence about it, no copy... He would have had to at least sign the paperwork at some point."

"Or...what if he didn't? What if he didn't even know about it and—"

"She forged his signature, of course," Olivia finished for me. "That's exactly what she would've done if she's guilty of, you know. Can't alert him beforehand and have him on guard."

That seemed to make the most sense. And it was the ultimate revenge. If she'd known, Mandy Thorne would have been way more interested in Queen Lauren than the Ex-Girlfriend Murder Club that committed pranks Tucker couldn't even smell.

Olivia drummed her fingers. "If we could somehow get our hands on the policy signature and compare—"

"Or maybe we don't even need that. Can't we just tell Detective Birch what we've found? Surely this has to be enough to exonerate us."

Olivia nodded. "Great. Let's go talk to him. And don't be above using some of your feminine wiles if it'll help."

"You sound like Elle."

She smiled sadly. "Someone has to."

"You make the innuendos and I'll be the guts and force us to do stuff."

She chuckled. "Deal."

• • • •

"Taking out life insurance isn't enough to prove murder," Detective Birch said.

This was not going as well as we expected. He'd even made us go to the interrogation room, which I was hoping to avoid, but he'd told us it was to diminish the heat from the rest of the precinct. So while it was in our best interest, it was also a reminder of how the sand was almost out in the hourglass.

"But for *four million dollars*?" I had no choice but to keep pushing. This was the best piece of evidence we had, even if he claimed it wasn't evidence. "Check the contract—specifically, the signature. It was likely forged. And check the date the policy was taken out."

"Those are all theories," he said, his face solemn. "Even if she took it out the day before, it's suspicious, but it's not evidence of murder, not by itself."

"But that plus the forged signature?" I pressed.

"*If* it's forged. I can look into that, of course." There was a brief pause. "How do you two know about Tucker Jones's life insurance policy?"

No, this was not supposed to turn into an interrogation of us. At the same time, it was shrewd of him to ask.

"My client won't be taking any questions at this time," Olivia asserted.

Detective Birch raised a scarred eyebrow. "Are you here as a civilian and possible murder suspect or Ms. Hu's lawyer?"

"Both?"

I'd never heard Olivia so unsure of herself.

But she regained her confidence as she said, "Actually, we don't want to speak further until our lawyer gets here." She grabbed her phone and made a quick call, asking the person on the other end to come to the station.

As we waited, Detective Birch kept trying to catch my eye. When I continued to avoid his gaze, he finally spoke. "Kat, are you okay?"

"Make up your mind if you care or not."

He sighed. "Of course I care. If I didn't, I would have already arrested you. How can everything that happened before not mean anything?"

"If you cared, you wouldn't be imposing a deadline giving me almost no time to do *your* job. Don't you see, Detective? All the evidence points to you not caring."

"Kat—"

"Don't call me that."

"Ms. Hu, I've been fighting for you this whole time. As hard as I possibly could. It's just gotten to a point where my hands are tied. I'm going to look into the life insurance policy—I already have been—but it's not producing what I need, and the evidence we do have points to the two of you."

I finally glanced over at him and noticed the sunken hollowness of his eyes. Maybe he had been pulling long hours, doing whatever he could to help me. Or maybe he was using me for information before and now was just doing the best thing for his job—producing a convincing arrest to appease his boss.

After all, I'd been wrong about potential romantic interests before. And I might be the problem, it's me.

When Olivia's colleague—our new lawyer—arrived, she pulled us out of there immediately.

I didn't want to, but I looked back at Detective Birch on my way out.

I'm sorry, he mouthed to me.

I didn't react.

Too little, too late.

DISH SERVED HOT GOT SERVED

By Lassy McBush

Does anyone else remember that movie? They don't make dance movies anymore.

I think it's clear from Mandy's response that we have hit the not-very-sharp nail on the proverbial frizzy-haired head. And because Lassy McBush is not like Mandy Thorne, we will not take any more unnecessary hits. We will only take necessary hits, like informing you that I dug up old footage of Mandy pretending not to know the difference between chicken and salmon for an unaired reality show called *Blondes Have More Funnies.* At least I assume Mandy was pretending since she's already an expert at it, having a Southern accent (sometimes) but being from Idaho. Either way, it doesn't bode well for the same person currently claiming to be a better detective than the professionals.

And for those *Dish Served Hot* fans who love the new direction of the podcast and are reading this article, that there in the last paragraph was actual journalism with true facts. I know it's difficult for you to tell the difference, just like how chicken and salmon sometimes look the same.

Mandy, remember that time a celebrity came under fire and they got out of it by doubling down, losing their shit, and calling themselves a winner? Great job.

And scene.

Dish Served Hot **Podcast Transcript—Episode 96**

[Podcast theme song plays, sung by creator, host, and star Mandy Thorne]

MANDY THORNE: Thornies, this long-awaited episode is finally here! We have an entire studio full of excited Thornies because…today is our LIVE SHOW!!! And whoo, is this going to be a doozy of an episode. Because we also have a special guest! Welcome, everyone, and welcome, Tim!

[audience cheers]

TIM: Hello!

MANDY: Tim, we are so glad to have you on the show. Especially because you said you know *both* Elizabeth and Victoria—we're stripping their Queen titles, of course. Should've done it sooner.

TIM: I do, I do. Also, Mandy, what do you think of Lassy McBush?

MANDY: [flustered] Tim, you're here to talk about Elizabeth and Victoria. And he has the *juiciest* tea to spill! Please, go ahead.

TIM: Is it true that you made up facts about a real ongoing murder investigation for ratings?

MANDY: Tim, could we please—

TIM: I've also confirmed with my sources that you—

[muffled noises]

[Mandy cursing in the background]

[feed ends abruptly]

CHAPTER 43

Time was running out. There were only a few days left before Detective Birch would arrest us. Olivia's firm was looking into the life insurance, but it was moving like molasses. Lauren Jones/Watson seemed to be our best bet, but we didn't have concrete proof of her involvement or a way to track her down.

I went back to some of the other pieces we'd found. The USB list, the invoices, and...the ledger that had been in Tucker's safe. Looking at it again now, something clicked.

CA 35 and *LSU 150*. "Tucker owed Cousin Aurora thirty-five thousand dollars and Ray—or Loan Shark Underwood—a hundred fifty thousand," I told Olivia over the phone, excited.

We reexamined the other ledger entries with renewed vigor. But it only lasted an hour.

"It's impossible without knowing their exact relation to Tucker," Olivia argued. We'd located everyone from the USB list—including *US* for *Uncle Sebastian*—but we hadn't identified any new suspects. "And Tucker already gave us the people he suspected most. The ledger's a dead end. Just like everything else."

She hung up without saying goodbye.

Throughout this whole ordeal, Olivia had maintained a manner of calm and control beneath the surface, her lawyer training kicking in to make her assess the situation and determine the best way forward. But lately, she was unraveling. Maybe it was because the Ex-Girlfriend Murder Club—our family— was broken up, and we needed Elle to balance us out.

Or maybe we were fucked and she was right to give up.

Not knowing how to help her or myself, I needed to take my mind off the impending doom. Off how we didn't even have a next step.

I wanted desperately to reach out to Elle, but I wouldn't do that to her. I couldn't save Olivia, but I could save Elle.

I thought about calling Melissa, but again, it was the middle of the night in London, and it felt like too much to explain. Just the thought of telling her about Tucker cheating let alone the rest of it exhausted me to my wet bones (here I was channeling all three of us—Olivia's malaphors plus Elle's writer skills to alter the saying plus my scientific knowledge about bones).

I wanted to talk to someone, anyone, even if it was the worst idea ever. Wasn't that all I did anyway, the bad ideas?

"Wei? Yushan, is you?"

"Hi, Ma."

"You get my last package?"

"Thank you for the George Foreman grill. Um, why did you send it?"

"No man to grill for you. This is next best so you can do yourself."

I wanted to tell her I just learned how to reverse sear steak, but that memory made me sad now.

"Thanks, Ma," I said, because it was easier.

"How are you?" she asked, which sadly threw me off guard. *The worst I've ever been. Please help me.* "I'm having a hard time."

"With what?"

"Um, so I have this friend. And this friend is, uh, in a lot of trouble at work. People think she did some bad stuff, but she didn't. And she's trying to figure out who actually did it, but she hit a dead end. So she's really stressed."

"What bad stuff?"

"I mean, it's bad. Really bad. They think she killed someone." My mother screamed. "Someone's plant! They think she killed their plant!"

"Aiyah, still terrible!"

"Uh, yeah. It's been hard on her. I'm trying to help, but the situation seems hopeless." I didn't expect anything from that. It was the worst story of all time. "Anyway, sorry, it's not important—"

"I help your friend," my mom said, and the determination in her voice felt like a squeeze to my heart. "You tell her she can find the bad egg in one step. Like magic. All she must do is meet the parents. If the parents good, the child is good. So whoever is doing this terrible thing—I mean, why hurt the plant? Is innocent!—the parents also bad."

Not this again. She was one step away from bringing up Zhuang Ayi's son. Wasn't this also egocentric of her to say? Maybe I should tell her that I was wanted for murder, see if she changed her views after that.

"So you think she should find a way to meet the parents of all her coworkers," I said dryly.

As usual, my mom didn't pick up on my sarcasm. "Yes. Then she know. For sure. No question."

I rolled my eyes. But then, it hit me.

She was brilliant. A genius. All I had to do was look at her words in a different light.

"Thanks, Ma. You're right. You're absolutely right."

"Of course I am. Yushan, you kind to worry for your friend. But focus on you, okay? I worry about you."

She'd said those words to me plenty of times before, but this time... Well, maybe I should have been looking at them—

looking at *her*—in a different light, too. Maybe I should have been thinking about how this woman who used the same rag to first clean the dishes, then the sink, then the floors, then the toilet cared *so much* that she was willing to pay for an expensive monthly Life Alert subscription for me. One that had ended up, surprisingly, saving my life. It was ridiculous and outrageous and laughable, but it was also her way of showing love.

And all I'd been doing in return was getting annoyed, barely putting in effort, and now fabricating stories. Didn't that make me part of the problem, like everything else in my life?

"Um, actually, I'm the friend," I admitted.

"You as a friend? You a good friend, Yushan, the best. Number one. Trying to help your mess of a friend."

Okay, maybe there were other problems here, too, but my original statement still stood. "Is Ba there?"

"Hang on." *Click.* "Your baba also on now."

"Wei, Yushan, that you?"

I took a breath. "Ma, Ba, I don't say it enough, but thank you. For pushing me, for doing your best, for caring. Just… thanks."

There was a brief pause before my father said, "You make us proud. We know you work hard."

"Dermatology, business—we just want you to be okay."

I swiped my hand under my suddenly wet nose. "I know."

"We worry," my mother said. "You not seem happy with what you do."

"You noticed?" That surprised me.

"Of course," my mother replied just as my father said, "You sound so sad when you talk about your job."

Maybe I hadn't been alone this whole time. I just hadn't opened my eyes or heart enough to realize it.

"Thank you for noticing," I said, the words not feeling like enough, but I couldn't seem to find any others. "I'm working on it." *If I'm not going to jail.* "I still want to do chemistry, but maybe something different in another lab."

"Oh." The disappointment in my father's voice was undeniable.

Same for my mother as she said, "Perfect world is you find something that make you happy *and* make you lots of money, eh?"

Instead of feeling frustrated, a chuckle bubbled up and out of my throat. Just like when I'd laughed about my mom's stance on tampons with Elle and Olivia.

Then I forced myself to say the next three words while I still could. "I love you."

"Mm-hmm," my father said.

"Same," my mother said.

If I managed to stay out of jail, I vowed to try harder with them. Maybe I could find some recipes for us to try together over video chat, or a brand-new interest to bring us closer. After all, there was still so much good that could come from our relationship, our conversations. As was just proven by my oblivious but also somehow genius mother.

After I hung up, I called Olivia immediately.

• • • •

"Her family?" Olivia said to me over the phone.

"Yes. Since we can't find her, we should try to locate her family." It was the next best thing: talk to the people who knew Lauren Jones/Watson best. And maybe they could help us track her down, as long as we didn't let on that we were looking for her for possible murder.

"How do we do that?"

"We know her name and address. Anything else?"

Olivia snapped her fingers. "The marriage certificate! It had her parents' names on it. Julie and Bernard Watson."

"Thanks, Brains," I said.

"Right back at you."

"Actually, it was my mom's brains."

"Like mother, like daughter."

I wanted to laugh. First, because that statement couldn't be more wrong, and also because that had been my mother's exact point.

"Okay," Olivia said, the vigor returning to her voice now that we had something to do. "Let's get on it."

"Great." I refrained from telling her the only downside: that I was terrified of meeting Lauren's family, of them maybe knowing that I was the mistress, and especially of finding Lauren the possible murderer, who definitely knew I was the mistress.

But that was a problem for Tomorrow Kat, right?

CHAPTER 44

Tomorrow Kat had different problems. Olivia and I were glad to have a next step. Borderline ecstatic. The problem? Finding Lauren's parents was like trying to find a needle in a haystack. (*Don Quixote* origin. No fun backstory, unfortunately. Just a saying for something hard.)

Having the parents' names helped, but we didn't know where they were from. And without a narrowed-down location, the haystack was, well, the entire country. We suspected Lauren and Tucker grew up near each other since they got married at eighteen, but Tucker was laughing at us from his grave because, shocker, he lied about being from Topeka. We tried contacting Tucker's family again, but they unsurprisingly refused our calls.

I then reached out to Lacey, which was not only unhelpful for us but unhelpful for her.

"A *wife*?" she'd screeched to me over the phone. "You have to be mistaken. There's no way."

We hadn't even gotten to where he was from because she'd only wanted to talk about that.

While Olivia and I still had hope, every step we took seemed to be followed by ten steps back. Like we were trying to get out of quicksand, and all with a dwindling clock over our heads.

But then, with the clock almost out, Olivia came through with the Hail Mary we'd been desperate for. Thanks to her racking her pseudo-photographic memory, she remembered that Tucker's emails included high school reunion invitations. And it turned out, his high school was only an hour away in Hadley, Massachusetts.

The fact that Tucker had grown up near here blew my mind. I truly knew nothing about him.

After searching for Julie and Bernard Watson in Hadley, we found several possible results for Julie but just one for Bernard, who used to teach math at the local community college. Through that, we tracked down an email address. Unfortunately, we weren't sure if Bernard was still checking it, and while we did send him several emails from different accounts, we couldn't sit around twiddling our thumbs waiting for a response.

"What now?" I asked Olivia over video chat, trying to keep the panic out of my voice.

"Leave it to me."

And with that, Double-Oh-livia, Esquire, went to work.

When she texted me an address hours later, I refrained from asking any questions, including whether she had to break any laws to get it. Instead, I hurried my ass into her car when she pulled up, and we set off for Hadley, Massachusetts, in such a rush we didn't even have snacks.

All of our eggs were in one basket. And it was not lost on me that the origin of this saying was (again) from *Don Quixote*, in the context of how foolish it would be to do such a thing.

The car ride was mostly spent trying to come up with our opener. Because if we couldn't even get our foot in the door, all was for naught.

"How about we pretend to sell them something?" Olivia asked.

"That's the way to make sure we don't get in."

"Okay, then what's your grand idea?"

We were both on edge. Desperate.

"Why don't we take a step back. A deep breath. Maybe belt out one Taylor Swift song," I suggested.

She obliged on all three.

By the end of the hour, we had a plan for how to get in and what to ask. It wasn't the best, but it would have to do.

All the eggs, one basket.

We just had to hold it together a little longer.

• • • •

"My Lauren's in trouble?" The shock on Mrs. Watson's face told us what we needed to know: she hadn't talked to her daughter lately.

We told her about Tucker's passing next, and she gestured us inside frantically.

I felt bad, but at the same time, we hadn't lied. And we had information she wanted, so maybe we weren't horrible people?

Mrs. Watson ushered us to the kitchen table. The news was big enough that there wasn't room for normal niceties— offering a beverage or, lucky for us, asking more about who we were. We had briefly mentioned when she opened the door that we were acquaintances of Tucker, and that seemed to be enough for her.

"What happened?" she asked, her eyes filled with worry.

Olivia jumped into a summary of Tucker's death and how we suspected foul play but didn't know more since it was an ongoing investigation.

"And what about Lauren?"

"We're worried about her," Olivia said. "Nobody has heard from her in a while, and we fear that whoever was after Tucker may be after her." Partially true, though we kept our suspicions about Lauren to ourselves.

Mrs. Watson grabbed a napkin and dabbed her eyes. "Lauren

might be in danger from whatever monsters *killed* Tucker?" She inhaled shakily.

Olivia took Mrs. Watson's right hand in hers. I did the same with her left.

"Mrs. Watson," Olivia said kindly.

"Julie, please."

"Julie, I don't know when you last talked to Lauren, but in case you haven't heard from her—maybe because she's in hiding— we're here to warn you. I'm not sure if those people will try to look for Lauren here, in which case you and Mr. Watson could be in danger. And if she comes here seeking refuge, it might be best if you alert law enforcement. For protection."

Mrs. Watson pulled her hands free to dab her eyes again. "I haven't talked to my Lauren in so long. We…had a falling-out. Actually, it was because of Tucker. I guess I'm not surprised there are people after him. But I should have tried to protect Lauren more. I shouldn't have…"

She paused to catch her breath. Olivia handed her a new napkin. I was waiting for Julie to tell us about Tucker stealing money from them, but she surprised me by saying, "We didn't want them to get married. They were so young. He was the first person Lauren was ever with. We told her there was no rush. We wanted her to go to college, or travel, or anything else. And it wasn't just her age. It was Tucker. He was charming and handsome, and I understood why she was so smitten, but he worried me. I couldn't put my finger on it, but he just rubbed me the wrong way. I never had anything concrete, though, nothing I could point to—I wish I did. Then maybe it would have been easier."

She sighed. "I rethink all of this at least ten times a day. Bernard hated Tucker even more than me. Called him a no-good-son-of-a-crooked-uncle. Said he reminded him of a snake wearing a movie star's skin. 'Like looking at the sun,' he would say to me. I tried talking to Lauren, even begging her, but Bernard took a different approach. He gave her an ultimatum. Said she had to choose: him or us. So you know how that turned out."

I wanted to give Mrs. Watson a hug. Make her a cup of tea in her own home. I even wanted to give Lauren a hug. To have chosen Tucker, to have given up your family for him, only for all this to happen? She knew about the cheating, perhaps even knew about the debt and fraud. Did that cause her to snap? Was it too much? All of this plus the insurance money screamed motive.

Mrs. Watson wrapped her arms around herself. "We shouldn't have cut her off. We should have been there for her. But Bernard was sure—if we made our dislikes clear enough, she would find her way back. But she didn't! She was alone, no family, and completely dependent on him. Last I heard, she wasn't working. She must have felt trapped, especially without us supporting her."

She was beating herself up and I didn't know how to stop it. And every word she said only filled in more of the picture. If Lauren had been dependent on Tucker, the life insurance plan could have been her way out of everything—giving her financial freedom, freedom from her marriage, freedom from an adulterous liar.

Mrs. Watson began rocking back and forth. "This is all my fault. All my fault."

"No," Olivia said sternly. "It's not."

She put a comforting hand on Mrs. Watson, who only rocked faster and closed her eyes. I put myself in her shoes and tried the only tactic I knew would help me: distraction.

"Mrs. Watson—Julie—do you have any pictures you can show us?" Maybe remembering when Lauren was happy would help.

That finally brought her out of her trance. "Yes. I do." She stood abruptly and retrieved an album from the other room.

"This is from their wedding." The cloud returned for a moment. "We didn't go, of course, but Lauren still sent us this, maybe to show us how happy she was." She opened the cover and touched the first page. The creased spine didn't creak—Julie must look at this often, which only made everything sadder. "So beautiful. And she did look so happy here."

She sat down, and Olivia and I scooted closer so we could look with her.

I jumped back in shock. Olivia did the same, and our enormous, widened eyes met over the album.

"You okay?" Julie asked.

"It's just...jarring to see Tucker again, alive and well," I said, which wasn't untrue, but that had nothing to do with the bomb that had gone off in my head.

The photos featured people we recognized from previous recon—friends and family of Tucker whom he'd stolen from. But that wasn't the surprising part.

This album was proof. These photos told us everything we needed to know.

And the truth was overwhelming. Almost unbearable.

Olivia and I stood at the same time.

"Julie, thank you for your hospitality today," Olivia said.

"I'm so sorry about everything you went through," I added. "We hope the best for Lauren."

"I'm sorry we have to leave, but we both live in the city, and we need to get back."

After a few more pleasantries, we left.

Once we were back inside Olivia's car, we both screamed.

We knew exactly what had happened. We didn't even need to exchange a single word.

It was the wife. Lauren Jones/Watson murdered Tucker. We were 110 percent sure of it.

SAVE THE QUEENS

By Lassy McBush

I have been conducting my own investigations and I believe that Queen Elizabeth and Queen Victoria are innocent. Not only have they been unfairly treated, but I believe they have been framed. At the very least, the suspect list is a mile long, and it seems like our Queens were simply in the wrong place at the wrong time. While I do not yet have definitive proof of this, I implore all you Lassies out there to contact the Boston PD and ask them to look further into this before making any hasty arrests.

Some of you may accuse me of pulling the same stunt as I accused Mandy of doing, but this is different. First, we are fighting for more evidence, for a just system, which is especially important now in the wake of what Mandy has done. She has been fighting for their arrest without evidence, and we are fighting for the opposite.

If there is enough public sympathy, we may be able to have an impact. I believe in the power of our voices and what can happen when we band together. So let's own that power and make something happen. For Queen Elizabeth and Queen Victoria, who have suffered enough. They represent all Lassies, so this is not just for them, but for all of us as well.

Dish Served Hot **Podcast Transcript—**
Episode 97

[Podcast theme song plays, sung by creator, host, and star
Mandy Thorne]

MANDY THORNE: Okay, we're trying the live episode again
today! Apologies for the technical issues last time, but I think
we've fixed it. I also apologize for our horrible guest who turned
out to be a reporter in disguise. There were so many details to
figure out for the live recording and some things fell through the
cracks, as I'm sure you can imagine. But that won't
be an issue today. So, moving on.

Thornies, I want to start this episode by telling y'all to stop
reading Lassy McBush's articles. They're all lies, and they're
undermining the great work we're doing here. And if you want to
send me messages about that liar's words, I will ban you from this
podcast! I'll do it!

But also, thank you to those of you who have stuck around.
And welcome, new listeners. I promise you won't be
disappointed. I will no longer be responding to anything Lassy
says, so please, sit back, relax, and enjoy the episode we have
for you today.

Also, we are *not* asking for an arrest without sufficient evidence.
We are doing the police's work for them! What we're doing is
noble, more noble than what that little shit's doing—

Anyhoo, please welcome today's guest, who is going to tell you
about how they got into an argument with one of the murderers
at the grocery store over the last *cleaver knife*! Ooh-la-la! Can
you imagine? Our guest might have *had her fingers on the murder
weapon*! Let's hope the killers wiped it before they murdered, or
this could lead to a very sticky situation!

Welcome, Katie! Thank you for coming on the show today!

[audience cheers]

KATIE: Hi, Mandy! Hi, everyone! Oh, this is just so exciting. Mandy, I want to tell you that I am such a fan, and I also know who Lassy McBush is personally, and, Thornies, you can't trust her. She's spouting lies.

MANDY: You heard her, folks. Lassy McBush is not to be trusted.

KATIE: Nope, not at all. Not one bit. Just a lying, liar, sack of lying human garbage.

MANDY: Wow. Powerful words. Thanks, Katie. And you not only know Lassy, but you believe you had a spooky and terrifying encounter with one of the murderers?

KATIE: Oh yes, my heart is pumping just thinking about it! I like to eat vegetables, and so I needed a cleaver knife—my old one was just too old, you see—

MANDY: So you went to the grocery store.

KATIE: Yes, yes. And there was only one cleaver left! Imagine that! When I reached for it—

MANDY: Was it huge? Sharp? Did it look like a murder weapon?

KATIE: Oh yes. The most murder-weapon-looking knife I've ever seen. Not that I wanted it for that reason. I just wanted a cleaver knife—for my vegetables, as you'll recall—and that was all that was available.

MANDY: So then...

KATIE: Right. Then this horrible woman reached for the massive murdery knife at the same time as me. And all hell broke loose!

MANDY: What happened?

KATIE: She screamed at me! And hit me!

[Mandy gasps]

MANDY: Are you alright? That's terrifying! Did you see what else this person was buying?

KATIE: Yes! A, um, hammer? Yes, a hammer. And...

MANDY: Didn't you say you saw a shovel as well?

KATIE: Right. A shovel. A gigantic one.

MANDY: Whew, Katie, I have to say, you are so brave for coming forward. Because we were able to obtain footage from the store, and we now have the identity of the person we believe to be Elizabeth.

KATIE: Um, really?

MANDY: We'll be handing that person's identity over to the police—

KATIE: Um, I'm not feeling so well.

MANDY: Just one more question—

KATIE: No, no. I'm sorry. I can't. I can't do this. Not even for the money. Everyone, it's not true. Mandy asked me to—

[feed ends abruptly]

CHAPTER 45

"I thought we weren't going to meet anymore," Elle said as soon as she arrived at the park equidistant from our places. "Not that I'm complaining. I've missed you lasses."

We exchanged hugs.

"Great articles, by the way, Lassy," Olivia said. "Thanks for having our asses."

Elle smiled. "Always."

"We wanted to tell you what we found out," I said. We started this together and that was how we were going to end it.

"Though this will be the last time we meet," Olivia interjected.

Elle nodded sadly, then waited.

"The wife did it," I said. "We think it was because she found out about the affairs and came up with quite the brilliant plan."

"Now, if I were the wife," Olivia said, "she has a few options. She could cut and run to Cuba and never look back, or she could turn herself in, after which the authorities would be more lenient. The latter option would also make life easier for Kat and me since we're the prime suspects and all. If she does turn herself in, she should make sure she has a good lawyer on her side, and that lawyer should ask for leniency and a reduced sentence *before* she admits to anything. And she could also try to make deals for statements against Ray, for proof about the fraud Tucker committed, any other illegal activity she might know of."

"Okay," Elle said, confused. "I guess that all makes sense? Do you want me to write about this in my next article since Lauren's probably following them?"

I shrugged. "It's up to you."

"We figured all this out," Olivia said, "when we went to see Lauren's mom. Who's okay but is pretty broken up. Blames herself for not being there and regrets how she handled things."

"Why are you telling me all this?"

"Because I've changed. We've changed," I said. "I thought I'd never trust another person after what Tucker did. But then I met you two. And you taught me that just because there are some untrustworthy people out there, it doesn't mean that everyone is, and if I'm going to live, I have to at least try. I'll never know other people's true motivations. But I'm choosing to believe that my gut isn't wrong about everyone."

"Are you talking about the detective?" Elle asked.

I shook my head.

"Then you've lost me."

"That's okay." I pulled her into a hug. "It'll make sense soon enough."

When I let go, Olivia embraced her as well. "Take care, okay?"

We turned and left a very confused Elle standing there. When we were several feet away, I turned back. "You know, I always thought it was funny how Tucker had nicknames for the two of us but not you."

Olivia also turned. "It's nice to know what Elle stands for now."

We saw when Elle finally understood, her expression changing from confused to utterly shocked.

Olivia put her arm around me, and together, without a backward glance, we left.

CHAPTER 46

"I think that went okay," I said to Olivia once we reached our cars.

"As well as it could have."

She suddenly swept me into a hug so tight I couldn't breathe for a second. "I know we're not saying goodbye, but it feels like the end of an era, you know?"

"I know." She started to pull away, but I squeezed her closer. I would have never done that a few weeks ago. "You were the best thing to come out of this for me."

"Me too."

Finally, we broke apart and shared a sad look tinged with hope.

"Thanks for being there for me," I said, thinking of so many things, including our phone call from the lab. "If we don't go away tomorrow, I think I want to shift my research agenda. I'm interested in learning more about forensic chemistry and toxicology. I'm not bad at it"—I thought back to the day in the interrogation room when Detective Birch showed me the red bucket—"and it kind of makes sense for me. I want to help people, especially those who might be wrongly accused, and I want to figure out what happened. Figure out—"

"The full story," Olivia said, understanding filling her face. "That's perfect for you—the one who always wants to know the origin and how things got from point A to point B."

We shared a smile.

"On a similar note," she said, "I'm going to devote more time and resources to helping the wrongfully convicted, the ones who've been given the shit end of the stick."

"Who were in the wrong place at the wrong time?" I suggested.

"Or maybe even framed."

I sighed, the world suddenly feeling heavy.

Olivia squeezed my shoulder. "You were right about everything you said back there. About your gut being right, about being able to trust other people."

"I know. That's why we did what we did." It hadn't been easy, but I'd finally forgiven myself for not seeing what Tucker chose to hide, and I decided I didn't want that experience to completely change how I saw and treated others.

Olivia nodded. Then, after a pause, she added, "Maybe you can trust your gut with someone else, too." I started to open my mouth, but she barreled on. "I know the one time you let a guy in, you got burned, and in the worst way possible. And maybe this has made you swing too far to the other side, not wanting to let another one in. But it's okay to put yourself out there, you know. And you have been, but it's okay to keep going."

I wanted to shake my head and argue with her, but I was also so tired.

Olivia kept pushing. "Tucker saw you, yes, and he liked what he saw, but he also put you on a pedestal. He was never on your level. You need someone who likes you but also treats you like a human being and isn't afraid to tell you what he thinks. Who has a moral compass as straight as yours, so straight that he would still do his job, sort of, while also giving the woman he cares about more outs than she's earned." She smiled. "I think you've got a good one there."

After a beat, I said, "You know, those words don't mean anything coming from you. The two of us, especially together, have the worst judgment in the world."

She laughed, mostly because she knew her words had already gotten through to me.

Right after we parted, I drove straight to the police station. Where I walked up to Adrian's desk and kissed him.

His initial shock disappeared quickly, and then he closed his eyes and kissed me back.

It wasn't fireworks and hot sauce like with Tucker; it was fireplaces and hot tea with honey and boba. It was comfortable, safe, and beautiful, like we'd been doing this for years.

Adrian's hands wrapped around my waist as I slipped mine into the hair at the base of his neck. It was as soft as I'd imagined. He pulled my torso and waist closer, pressing my body against his as we deepened the kiss. His tongue found mine, igniting sparks deep within me, sparks I had previously thought had burned out.

"Ahem," someone grunted from behind me.

I turned to find myself face-to-face with the woman who had glared at me in the precinct all those days ago. I knew she wasn't the wife now, but I still didn't know who she was. Except I did know. Because her presence caused Adrian to back away from me and she was also wearing a uniform this time. And now I understood why she had been glaring that day.

"Captain," Adrian said.

"Are you kissing the prime suspect in one of your cases?" she asked.

"If my instincts are right," I said, "not for long." And because

I was me, I added, "Meaning me being the prime suspect. The kissing, I hope, will continue."

She was not amused. But Adrian smiled. So wide I could see his dimple.

Kathryn's Thirteenth and Final Law of Luck: There are no laws; you make your own luck.

Through the Looking Glass

Three Days Later

From the point of view of Elle—or "L," short for
Lauren

This turned out even more deliciously than I could have
imagined. Not that I tried the final product—I had to
mix the pot and laxatives in from the start, crushed up and
blended. But I made a side batch for myself, sans drugs,
that I nibble on now as I walk to the post office. One
big ol' box of homemade brownies "from your number
one fan" to a recently disgraced and discredited Mandy
Thorne—courtesy of me, thank you very much, I'll take
my bow. And while I'm at it, I'll take my bow for these
brownies because they're the fucking bomb. It's amazing
what you can learn on YouTube, isn't it? The best ooey-
gooey brownie recipe, how to reverse sear a steak, and
even how to murder. And how to do it in such a way that
you don't even have to be there when it happens.

Which I didn't want. To be there, that is. The murder
part I did want. That was the plan. But I didn't want to
be there partly because it made it easier to get away with,
and also because this was still Tucker, the person I'd de-
voted my life to, and supposedly vice versa. In fact, when
I saw the body for the first time, the immediate reaction
was regret. My heart had broken all over again.

But my heart had been broken too many times, and that was just one more to add to the list I started the night I used a sleeping Tucker's thumbprint to unlock his iPad so I could check his calendar and plan a surprise anniversary dinner—a last-ditch attempt to revive our stagnant but still loving, I stupidly thought at the time, relationship. But his iPad was connected to his phone, and the screen was filled with texts from another woman.

Then there was not just one but *two* mistresses. And he'd fallen in love with one of them. Kathryn Hu. Kathryn was different, even from Olivia, definitely from me. The man I had exchanged vows with, who I became estranged from my family for—how could he have done this to me? Though I guess this was also the same man who insisted there was no reasoning with my parents so I should leave, who promised to take care of me so I didn't need to and *shouldn't* work, who would yell and throw things and make me feel small when we disagreed.

How did I not see it before that night? How he'd been controlling me and my life. He'd ensured my world would be so small I'd forget any other possibility. He'd taken the trust of a lost, lonely girl and converted it into his stranglehold over me.

Was it conscious? On purpose? Or was he so insecure and narcissistic that he needed to be the center of my universe?

I wanted a divorce. But he'd made sure I was dependent on him in every way. I had to know I'd be okay after I left. But when I logged in to Tucker's bank account through his iPad…well, the heartbreak turned to rage.

What I found was as upsetting as the affairs. Embezzling, loan sharks, screwing over his friends and family. He hadn't just thrown me away like garbage; he completely fucked up both our futures *and* put us in danger. The loan shark was out for blood, and Tucker didn't even think I deserved a warning. And *everything* was in my name. Everything.

Though that ended up being helpful in the end.

After the post office, I return to the motel I've been staying at this past week and pack my bags. Just like the brownies, I couldn't have predicted all this turning out quite so perfectly even with my meticulous planning. And it was the cleverest of plans, thought out down to the smallest detail.

Everything was orchestrated by me, the one determining the plot as Olivia unknowingly said right after we met. The universe hadn't been against Kat like she believed—it was me! No one has that much bad luck. She was the perfect scapegoat. And it was almost too easy. With access to Tucker's phone (thanks again, iPad), I texted Kat so she'd interrupt Olivia's proposal, which I knew about from his texts and receipts. Then I told Tucker I saw the York Beach Airbnb info on his calendar and acted so over the moon about his "surprise getaway trip for me" that he had no choice but to bring me there. For the pranks, I of course decided to cover the condo in dog poop so Olivia and Kat would think I didn't know about Tucker's anosmia. *And* it gave me the excuse to wear gloves, thus preventing any spread of fingerprints. Tucker's fake Tinder profile, the complaints to the police about the smells from his condo that caused Detective Birch to show up while Kat was cleaning—all me. I was also Mandy's anonymous source, though I wasn't alone there. I hadn't planned on the story growing so big that actual witnesses like Kiki and Bob would come forward. Once Bob outed a secret I needed under wraps—that there was a third girl involved—I had to discredit Mandy. Luckily, that was not only easy but fun, more fun than pretending to be Elle.

Though maybe I really am more Elle than Lauren. Maybe I've always been her, just deep down where no one else could see it. Elle is everything Lauren always wanted to be—confident, fun, a pistol. The only difference is I don't have the sexual experience. All the times the girls thought I was hooking up, I was actually plotting, planning, or texting Tucker so the evidence would show that we were on good terms when he died. But thanks to reading and now writing romance novels, I think I played the part well. There was one time I thought the girls might be on to me—after I offered to seduce Tucker's boss, they seemed to think something was off—but I saved it by telling them about "Chad."

I finish packing, then trot downstairs to the waiting taxi. I tell the cabdriver my destination with all of Elle's—now my—confidence, then relax into the seat.

Oh how victorious I am! Tucker thought he was the master manipulator? Well, I showed him who was *actually* master of his universe. And all from my cheap little craigslist rental that became my new home once I had to become Elle and leave Lauren behind.

It was perfect. Perfectly plotted, perfectly executed. Did I expect any less from myself? No. And my future is perfectly plotted as well. My plane ticket to the Maldives under my new identity is waiting in my purse, my villa picked out, and my cash from Tucker's life insurance already in an untraceable account. And what better non-extradition country could I end up in? A much better choice than Cuba, which is too close for comfort.

I'm the ultimate brains. The puppeteer. The storyteller.

But...

There's something even I didn't plan for.

Olivia and Kat.

Olivia and Kat, who I thought I was going to hate. Who I did hate before I met them, hence why I tried to frame them for murder. But then, against all odds, they were on my side. The fucking Ex-Girlfriend Murder Club. Without meaning to, I shared parts of my life I hadn't shared with anyone—about my family, about Tucker (or Chad, same diff). And then, god knows why, they sacrificed themselves to save me. *Multiple* times. They put me above themselves, again and again. No one has ever done that for me before.

No one.

And the most unexpected? When they figured out the truth, when they knew what I did, they still gave me a choice. Even though it's their necks on the line.

Is it really a choice, though?

The taxi pulls up to the police station. Olivia, looking like a boss in her pantsuit, is waiting outside. I wave. She gives me a somber smile. An oxymoron. Which is exactly what I feel like right now.

I walk into the police station, my head held high.

It's not only lasses before asses, but lass before your own ass.

★ ★ ★ ★ ★

ACKNOWLEDGMENTS

What a joy it is to write the acknowledgments for my sixth book! Thank you for picking up *The Ex-Girlfriend Murder Club*. I'm so grateful to all my readers for making my dream job a reality. Working on this novel was some of the most fun I've had thus far in my career, and I hope that was evident as you read.

Kathleen Rushall, my rock—thank you for loving this story and for your endless passion, support, and wisdom. I feel I can do anything with you on my side.

Leah Mol—thank you for your enthusiasm for this story from day one, for being so on top of everything, and for your sharp editorial eye that brought the book to another level. Your love for these characters means so much to me. And I'm beyond thrilled to get to continue working with you on more Ex-Girlfriend Murder Club shenanigans!

Quinn Banting—thank you for bringing *The Ex-Girlfriend Murder Club* to life so brilliantly and capturing the tone of the story perfectly. The cover is better than I could have dreamed!

Thank you to all the wonderful people at MIRA and Harlequin who helped bring this book into the world: Cathy Joyce, Amanda Roberts, Elena Gritzan, Sophie James, Ambur Hostyn, Randy Chan, and the larger marketing, publicity, and sales teams.

Thank you, Kim Yau, for your hard work and enthusiasm. It's been such a joy getting to work with you on so many projects through the years. Thank you for understanding my characters so well and helping me navigate the film and TV side.

Taryn Fagerness—thank you for your enthusiasm and for all the time you've put into all my projects! Thank you especially for your excitement over this one.

A huge thank-you to my early readers. Raul Campillo and Nadia Farjood, for your legal expertise and such fun, enthusiastic conversations about Olivia, the detective, and the interrogation room. Lexi Klimchak, for helping me hone the big beats and milestones—your smart questions were invaluable. Javier Burgos, for your encouragement from the beginning and for providing wonderful notes on a first draft. Benjana Guraziu, for your great insight and for sparking some friendly competition with another early reader, haha. Melissa Richart, for your enthusiasm, for your careful reading and in-depth comments, and for introducing me to Emma! Emma Straley, thank you for your helpful feedback and raising questions I hadn't thought of. Alicia Zhou, thank you for answering my questions about beta-mercaptoethanol (and sorry you had to work with it so much)!

All the thanks to the wonderful booksellers and librarians who have supported my books, and the readers and influencers who have read, posted, and reviewed. Special thanks to Audrey Mueller, Nicole Miller, Kathleen March, Audrey Huang, Rachel Strolle, Sarah Hollenbeck, Suzy T, Paul Swydan, Anderson's Bookshop, Barbara's Bookstore, Women & Children First, the Book Stall, the Book Cellar, Porter Square Books, Belmont Books, the Silver Unicorn, Call and Response Books, and 57th Street Books.

Thank you to my fellow authors who continue to inspire and support me. Special thanks to Jilly Gagnon, Mia P.

Manansala, Laurie Elizabeth Flynn, Lori Rader-Day, Kayla Olson, Susan Blumberg-Kason, Samira Ahmed, Lizzie Cooke, Kat Cho, Rena Barron, Ronni Davis, Anna Waggener, Ann Liang, Julian Winters, and Rachel Lynn Solomon.

Mom and Dad, I love you. And of course Kat's parents are not at all in any way, shape, or form based on anyone that I know.

Anthony—every word I write is because of you and for you. This book will always hold a special place in my heart because of your love for it. Thank you for always supporting and believing in me, for making every second we're together fun, and for your endless, unwavering love. Thank you for a life better than I could dream.